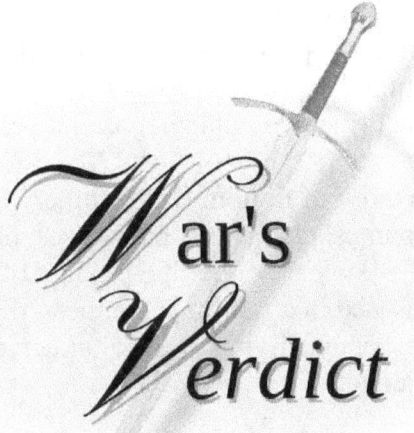

War's Verdict

*For every person who says you can't... laugh while you prove
to them why you can.*

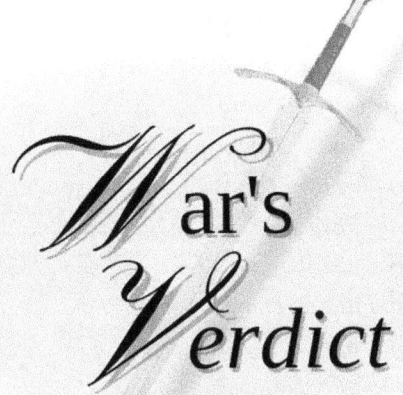

War's Verdict

Arrival of the Four Horsemen Series

Marcelle Valentine

Contents

Chapter One: Eternity

For by your words, you will be acquitted, and by your words, you will be condemned.
Matthew 12:27.

~ Death Fall 2025 ~

*I*N ALL MY long existence, I never thought to be among the ones who would be held within these cells. My choices were simple: always obey his commands, follow the path he bestowed upon me, and question nothing he asked of me. But all this changed when a chance meeting with one incredible soul veered my life in another direction.

A soul filled with compassion but resolute in their convictions. A mortal who risked their own safety for someone they had never met. And as this soul tended to wounds inflicted by others, she mended the well of disdain growing within me.

With one look from curious eyes.

Through one soft plea spoken.

With one tender stroke from a gentle hand.

From one beautiful woman named…

"*Avalon*," I whisper her name to the empty space, and this single word carries both pleasure and pain.

My exquisite little Apple. A caring soul who showed kindness to a being who had only experienced their pain and hostility. A young soul who knew all too well the dark hearts many of her kind concealed from the world. But with one selfless act to save the life of another, she restored in me everything they had taken.

And they have removed her first from my touch and now from my view.

For I have no way of knowing the outcome of their pending battle. They could have failed and fallen at the hands of the men they hunted. They could have succeeded and recovered what my brother held in such high esteem. The woman who showed him what my Apple showed me. But because of Michael's insistence on placing me in my new lodgings the instant my sentence was passed, I have been unable to check their progress.

An issue I plan to rectify the instant I can pierce the veil shrouding their world from my view.

"I must admit, seeing you shackled and chained brings me such solace and a certain amount of satisfaction."

"What do you want, Michael?" I ask, lifting my eyes to the cell door he's filling. I could have resisted as they delivered me to my eternal punishment for defying his rule. My creator gave free will to all his children, yet it seems he did not intend for a being like me to exercise this gift.

"I merely wanted to inquire how you are finding your...." his eyes search the barren stone cell, vacant of everything except the chains tethering me to this wall and the shackle clamped around my neck, ensuring I cannot use my might to break them. "Deluxe accommodations?"

"This place does not differ from any other."

"Minus the pesky interruptions of your brother, who has failed in his task much as you did, or the foolish mortals you seem so fond of."

"My sentence will not last forever, and when it ends, remember you will have no doors to hide behind—"

"I plan to ensure your stay will remove all these hate-filled thoughts plaguing you."

"and I do not forget," I finish the sentiment he cut off before it was fully voiced.

"Is this a threat, Reaper?"

"A proclamation, Warrior." Michael advances into the room to grab the chains before jerking. His pretense is to test their strength; however, knowing him as I do, this was done to prove a point. One which confirms my chains will not be released anytime in the near future. His hand moves up from the manacles to the collar to test its strength. A glib smirk creeps across his face when he discovers how snug the collar is around my throat, which informs me this little trinket was by his order alone. He wanted me removed, but instead, our creator saw fit to lock me away. This is Michael's retribution for what he

11

views as an affront. A grievous mistake made by our father.

His eyes never leave mine, just as I refuse to drop my gaze from his. The first sign something went wrong is the searing fire filling my chest, followed by unbearable pain. The growl I release as the agony overwhelms me has a grin sliding over Michael's smug face.

I know what this means. Another seal has been broken, and now fear fills the space the pain once claimed. Fear knowing if the seal was opened, something went horribly wrong.

"Well, it seems at least the lamb understands what we expect of her since she has awoken another rider."

"Release me," I snarl, frantic with the need to know what fate befell her and Pestilence because I know he fears for the safety of his chosen and his son above all else. If another rider is called to their world, he may have to choose a side, and he knows our brother does not tolerate defiance within his ranks. War is many things. Forgiving is not one of them.

"I think not. But perhaps your sentence will end sooner than either of us thought."

"You will regret your actions if it does."

"Oh, but Death, you cannot believe I would permit you to return to her."

"You will have no say in the matter, Michael."

"I will when I ensure your memories of her are erased long before she holds the last seal in her fragile little hands. You will reap her soul as you reap all the others, and as she kneels before you, begging and pleading, you will see only another mortal on their knees and nothing more."

"You better pray it works, because when you fail... it will be your soul I reap," I growl, yanking on the chains. The stone walls they are anchored to cracks before releasing a cloud of fine dust to float through the air. The bindings he was so confident would hold me for the duration of my sentence will not last the eternity he had planned. As my wings erupt behind me, Michael stumbles out of the room, never once turning his back to the death he knows he will soon face.

"If you know what is best, Warrior... you will run," I advise. The calm, resolute demeanor with which I deliver the warning has him whirling to escape the cell as I slam my hands forward. Resulting in another thin crack within the stone wall meant to hold me.

Chapter Two: The Red Rider... Bringer of Battle and Strife

When He opened the second seal, I heard the second living creature saying, "Come and see." Another horse, fiery red, went out. And it was granted to the one who sat on it to take peace from the earth, and that people should kill one another; and there was given to him a great sword. Revelation 6:3-4.

~ War Fall 2025 ~

I AM AWAKE after millennia of waiting to clutch my sword and swing it in battle. The time has come. The seal is broken, and the reign of the horsemen is upon them. While I slept, they granted me glimpses of Pestilence's time among them. The disease he released, the black death he brought, and the lamb he grew close to. But even this was at our brother's behest.

With my sword returned, I test the feel of it in my hand, and it is as I remember. When I take my first swing, the honed steel cuts through the air with a low whistle, confirming the edge is still as sharp today as the day they made her for me. And with each swing I take, the stiffness one only knows after centuries of sleep releases its hold on my vessel.

"Welcome back, Rider."

"You are not who I was expecting."

"Thanatos?"

"This would be the accurate assumption."

"Come, I will take you to him."

"Is there a reason he is not here to welcome me, Raphael?"

"I believe it would be best for you to speak with him yourself." He is one of the few of his kind worthy of my respect. This is why I do not question him about my brother further and opt to follow him as he leads me through passages. Raphael is the most levelheaded of the archangels and someone I respect. Unlike his brother, who believes all the other beings of this realm should declare fealty to him. Something my brothers and I have made clear we won't ascribe to, which does not place us high on his list of allies.

"Tell me, Raphael, is Michael still an insufferable prick?"

"If you are asking if he is still unyielding, I can assure you this has not changed."

"Would you prefer if I called him a determined prick?" With this, Raphael throws his head back and laughs. It's the sound one can only produce when genuinely amused. As a member of our creator's inner council, I appreciate he has never taken himself too serious, unlike his brethren.

"I only wish you to speak the truth in your heart," he said turning to place his hand on my shoulder. The smile on his face fades, replaced by a look of sympathy that is hard to put into words. "And I hope you can hear the truth in mine when I tell you how truly sorry I am to be the one to reveal this to you. Honestly, how sorry I am it has happened at all."

"What are you talking about, and why have you brought me to the prison?" He nods to the cell next to where I stand. It boasts a door made from the finest of ebony. A wood already chosen for its strength, but with the addition of the titanium bar it receives a significant boost in its hardiness. The runes embedded within its surface are the last component and the one most detrimental to our kind since they remove all our gifts. After a brief hesitation, I look through the tiny barred window, and what I find has my blood boiling.

"Why in the seven realms of hell is my brother held within here?"

"For restoring a life. A life Pestilence begged for."

"My brothers do not grant life. They take it."

"Yet this soul was one who your brother was not prepared to lose and one he now calls son."

"Why?" This makes little sense; our time has begun. The prophecy fulfilled. The hour to remove the souls of their world... not restore them, is here. And while I have always known Thanatos possessed the ability to do this, never in his long existence has he meddled in what fate had decreed. Why would he do it now, and why would Pestilence give a piece of himself to tie one to him?

"Raphael, we have been friends for more lifetimes than most, but if you do not explain why my brother toils in this cell, I'm afraid this is where it will end."

"Shall we say Michael and Thanatos had a difference of opinion on how to handle this situation."

"Is Michael responsible for my brother's confinement in this godforsaken desolate place?"

"Among others. Not everyone believed the mortals deserved the chance your brother pushed for."

"Thanatos sought their pardon?" The one aspect of our long sleep I have always despised is that we are only ever given brief glances into their world, even after the lamb calls our brothers there.

"Not only did he seek it, but he also pled for it, and when our father denied him, he turned from his path, which is why I must insist the door remain sealed," Michael says while he lumbers toward me.

"This is not entirely true, Mic—"

"We all see where your loyalties lie, brother," Michael sneers, taking a menacing step closer to one of his brethren. I don't know what he planned to do, but I've had enough of his over-inflated opinion of himself.

"Open this devil's be damned door, or I will remove it," I growl, which gets one archangel moving in the direction of the prison containing Death.

"Raphael!" Michael's warning is low and menacing. "I said no."

Stepping past my friend to confront the one I blame for Thanatos's current situation, I give my response. One they will heed if they know what is best for them. "It was not a request. Open. The. Fucking. Door!"

The sound of the lock clicking out of place confirms one of these archangels has a modicum of intelligence.

17

Stepping closer to the cell, I turn to give the angel glaring at me a warning. "Remove all thoughts of locking me in this cell."

When Raphael places himself between the door and his brethren, I know he will not permit Michael to act in a manner I am confident his baser desire is demanding, allowing me to stroll inside.

"Imagine my surprise to wake and discover my favorite straight-laced brother has allowed himself to be taken prisoner by our father's guards." Upon hearing my voice, Thanatos lifts his head. His face twists in what I can only equate to a mixture of fury and agony.

"War."

"Thanatos."

"So it is true the second seal has been broken."

"It would seem so. Right now, I am more curious about the events which put you here."

"Long story."

"It's okay. I have time."

"No, you do not. It is long past the time for you to begin the task they created you for," Michael snarls from outside the cell.

"One would think after all these millennia, he wouldn't still be an insufferable prick." My focus may be directed at Thanatos, though my comment is meant for the angel interjecting himself in my private conversation.

"And I see your long sleep has not taught you better manners," Michael snaps.

"An insufferable prick who has yet to learn his place," Thanatos confirms.

"As you were saying before the gnat interrupted."

"Short story. I found them worthy of redemption and told our father this much."

"But he did not believe you?"

"Quite the contrary. He did."

"Then why are we awake?"

"Raum tricked the lamb into breaking Pestilence's seal."

"Pestilence? Tricking would denote it was unintentional, so why am I awake?"

"I don't know what happened. The lamb was traveling with our brother. They were attempting to retrieve a companion of the lambs from the ones who took her."

"If he was working with the lamb, does this mean his opinion had also been swayed?"

"It had."

"And you have no knowledge of what transpired to wake me?"

"I was… detained."

"I see," I tell him as my eyes follow the countless cracks traversing along the wall serving as his prison. "And it is still your belief they are worthy of our forgiveness?"

"It is."

"War! It is past time for your arrival. You will also require a briefing on the progress or lack thereof by your—"

"Do not say another word, archangel. I am aware of what you seek from me. I am also keenly aware you are why I find my brother held here, so if you wish to see another day, I suggest you return to your post. Because I am not as forgiving as my brother Pestilence."

"You walk a fine line here, Rider."

"And as we are both warriors, I am happy to prove my worth. Are you?" I ask him before I pull my sword from the baldric strapped across my back.

"Just try to do what your brothers failed miserably at carrying out."

"Let me tell you one thing, Michael. Neither one of my brothers has failed in their mission."

"Pestilence—"

"Found them worthy of forgiveness." Michael's stare turns icy. His lip curls on one side, and his eyes narrow to little more than slits.

"Death has—"

"Not been called forth yet."

"Our father sent him there once already."

"To judge not extinguish, and my brother fulfilled that mission." Michael takes a step towards me. I cannot say if his intent was to intimidate me. It does not. Stepping forward until mere inches separates me from the being who has pushed me past the point of leniency, I deliver my response. "And if you wish to continue disparaging my brothers, it is the steel of my blade you will taste."

"You do not have to defend me, brother. As for you, Michael, it is high time you scurry off to find our creator unless you wish to test our tolerance." Michael's face contorts with rage, but he makes the wise decision to return to his post.

"I enjoyed watching him squirm; it has been far too long since we have reminded him who he is." I laugh while my hand finds my brother's shoulder, giving him a reassuring squeeze.

"War—"

"You don't have to ask, brother. Luckily for you, I despise the warrior our father has chosen. As such, I give you my word. I will stay my hand for a time, but if the humans of this world attack or fail to prove the faith you have bestowed upon them…."

"I understand you will follow what our path commands. Nevertheless, I must thank you for this," Thanatos replies.

As I step out of the cell my brother has chosen to remain in, I provide only one order to the prick I have never liked before making a request of my friend.

"Stay away from my brother." Michael's glare is all the answers he plans to provide. "See what you can do about this shit." Raphael's singular nod is all the confirmation I need to know he will at least try.

"Michael, if you require a reminder of my might, you can find me preparing my horse for my arrival. Feel free to stop by."

"What do you plan to do?" Raphael inquires.

"It seems I have a lamb to find."

"This is not your task, Rider," Michael yells. With a laugh, I spin on my heels to retrieve my companion since my mission has now changed.

Chapter Three: A Rider to Aid

There are far greater powers at play here, and humanity's existence hangs in the balance....

*B*ELLUM.

It's the singular word written across the parchment.

And I'll bet my ass it means War. Because why wouldn't I bring the one rider who wants an all-out battle with us to our world? Here's the thing: based on the book I had no use for until all this shit happened, these riders each arrive in a specific order. So it would not have mattered what seal I broke; it would have revealed the same word. Damn it, why the hell couldn't Death have been the second rider? Nope, because if I remember the bible correctly, he will be the last. Just my damn rotten luck.

Raum throws his head back as he lets loose a hideous laugh that is disturbing. Well, calling what is coming out of him a laugh is ridiculous because it's closer to the howling growl you believe is coming from under your bed as a child.

When his head slams back in place, there's a split second when I see the mistake I just made in his eyes. Before the first scream tumbles through my trembling lips, he drives the blade into Pestilence's chest. His figure glimmers for a fleeting second before it diminishes. The issue is he still has Pestilence held tight in his grasp.

This fucker plans to drag Pestilence back to hell with him if I don't do something to stop him. Red-hot rage floods my system, creating a volatile concoction but giving me the strength I require for what must be done. Three things happen after this: a shrill laugh rips through the night. My body hurls headlong at a demon who is determined to make us both suffer, and a rider's tortured cries shatter the nearby windows as the blade pierces his heart.

I reach them just as Pestilence's form fades. My hands pass through him, and the horror of knowing what he will soon face fills his eyes. It's the worst goddamn thing I have ever had to see. It is the confirmation he failed and the understanding he is not the only one whose life has been reduced to a hellish nightmare. Because it is in looking at his eyes that I see the terror he feels when he realizes Greer and Wren will have to face this nightmare without him.

23

Not knowing what else to do, I grab his bow, nock an arrow, and release it at the demon who has orchestrated every horrible act I've carried out of late.

The world stands still as I watch the arrow sail through the air where he had stood not seconds before, and for the briefest time, I believe I have failed him, but when Raum howls from pain, I know it found its mark. This was his first mistake and the only chance I would get because the instant the sound roars from him, his shape fully materializes, which means the rider is back as well. Launching myself at Pestilence, I grab him while biting down on the arm confining him.

Raum screams as he yanks away from the assault. With Pestilence free, I pull his bow back up and release a second arrow. Raum transforms into a raven as the missile rips through his wing. He flies away with one last rage-filled shriek as a third arrow misses him by inches.

With the last of my adrenaline spent, I collapse onto the ground next to my friend. My breathing is coming in short ragged gasps as my body trembles from the events that have transpired over the last hour.

"You need to move, Avalon." I'm not sure if the command was one I thought, one I heard, or one I imagined; either way, I need to heed it.

"Pest—Pestilence," I stammer, and this is the first time I realize how bad this shit just got because he isn't moving. At all. Not one finger twitches at the sound of my voice. The fear I may have still failed him rips away the relief I felt only moments before. I struggle to keep my composure as I roll him over. One thing plagues my thoughts: I need to act, and I need to do it now.

The blade Raum drove into him is still there, as are the arrows that allowed the asshole to gain the upper hand to begin with. The arrows I remove, but the knife is a different story. What if it's some super-fucking-natural blade, and it does not come out or, worse yet, does but prevents him from healing?

Shit! What am I supposed to do now? What-do-I-do, what-do-I-do. What the fuck do I do?

Is he breathing? Is his heart still beating? Would CPR even work on a being like him? Since there is no one around who can tell me and he isn't in any shape to guide me, I have to make this decision on my own. Sucking in one last deep breath, I hold it as I choose. Here's hoping I don't make everything fucking worse.

When I first yank it, I fear my initial thought may have been correct because it doesn't move. I reposition my hand while leaning over him to gain more leverage, and when I pull this time, it slips out easier than I thought it would. But this is when the blood begins streaming from the open wound left behind.

"Shit!" With no other option, I yank my shirt over my head to apply pressure to the injury, hoping to stop the steady river of blood.

"Please, Pestilence. Please wake up."

"He will return, lamb. If you wish to save the Rider, you must move." Again with this mystical, formless, faceless fucking voice. A voice I know doesn't belong to Thanatos. Honestly, I'm not even sure if Thanatos still watches over us because I have not heard a peep from him in months. He doesn't come to me in my dreams any longer. He doesn't invade my thoughts. Hell, unless I mention him first, Pestilence no longer even brings him up.

"Now, Avalon."

"Okay-okay," I yell as I look around for someplace I can take him because I sure as shit can't carry him, but with much of the buildings destroyed during the worse of the fighting, I know they offer nothing in the form of protection. So with no place to hide and nothing to assist me with moving him, I grab him under his arms and begin the slow, arduous process of dragging him in the direction I know we will find Storm.

Could I leave him here and run to retrieve his horse? Yes. Would it be faster? It would. Will I? Absolutely fucking not. Why? Because I refuse to leave him here defenseless and at the whim of a demon hell-bent on torturing him if he arrives before I can return.

I make it just outside the city limits when I collapse, unable to go any further. This is when the first sound of a pissed-off demon shatters the silence with his furious scream. There's no way we can outrun him. I've got nothing left to give. This is when I know I have really and truly failed him. But I still refuse to leave his side because if this bastard wants to take him, he'll have to take me too. And a dead lamb can't break any more seals. Something I know Raum is hell-bent on seeing through to the end because no more seals mean no more riders.

"I'm sorry, Pessy," I softly whisper as I pull his body up to rest against my own. This is when, like a white knight charging into battle, Storm gallops into view.

"Thankyou-thankyou-thankyou," I mumble until another thought takes form. How am I going to get this behemoth man on top of him?

"As you did with Thanatos," my helpful new friend whispers. With my plan in place, I leap up to wave Storm over to where I'm hiding. Afraid that if I make any noise, the action will only bring death crashing down on us because the mocking calls of Raum are back, and they're moving closer.

26

When Storm slides to a stop in front of us, his front hoove slams at a frantic pace on the ground in front of me. He must sense the danger coming at us too. Here's hoping he will understand what I need and follow my lead, much like Ghost did when his Rider required aid.

"I need you to lie down," I whisper as I raise my hands and repeatedly lower them toward the ground. Much to my surprise, although after being around these unique creatures for this long, I don't know why they still amaze me, he follows my directive and lowers himself to the ground so I can load what I'm sure Storm feels is his most precious cargo.

Once completed, I slide on behind him to hold Pessy in place. With a click of my tongue, he stands as easily as if he had no one on top of him. Even though I want to rush off into the night, we still need to retrieve another person.

"Take me to Greer, but we need to be quiet," I whisper into his ear, and as requested, he turns and silently treks to where we will find her. The problem is that I may have used too much caution because Raum screams from the road behind me the second she leaves her hiding spot among the brush and walks into view. A sound confirming only one thing… I am out of time.

I know if I stop to let her on, he will be on us before she gets one leg slung over Storm's side. With Pestilence still incapacitated while he heals, at least I pray that's all it is, leaves me with no other option but to spur my heels into Storm's side as he races toward Greer. Her eyes widen as she sees what is chasing us and thank god she understands what I intend to do.

"God, please let this work. Otherwise, Storm will be racing away, minus the two of us." With my prayer in place, I lean over as far as possible with my hand outstretched. My desperate plea seems to have worked for once because I catch her wrist in my grasp, allowing me to pull her as Storm gallops by. The effort brings her halfway on top of the racing horse but dislodges me in the process, and I almost tumble off the other side. Twisting the reins tighter around my hand, I somehow manage to right myself just as Greer swings her leg over his side.

"Run, Storm!" With my command given, he picks up his pace, leaving one pissed-off demon screaming on the path behind us while Greer gives a strangled sob after finding Pestilence in such a dire condition.

*****

We ride through the night because my irrational but warranted fear is that Raum will find us. And even though I have heard several groans from Pestilence, he is still incapable of protecting himself, let alone Greer and me. Then there's Greer, who is not in the best head space right now. Not to mention recovering from the damage Jay inflicted.

We might have made it back sooner if not for Greer telling me to get off the road every time we heard others approaching us. Which I questioned at first until she told me about the group Jay was taking her to. Let's just say if we crossed paths with them, it would not end in our favor. So it seems caution is the word of the day.

But when the winds kick up, and the skies turn gray, I'm done hiding because we're out of time, and if I have any hope of them surviving this, my only option is to get them back to camp before we come face to face with the next Rider. I can't imagine he would be in a forgiving mood if he discovered his brother knocking on… well, for lack of a better word, Death's door.

The storm is upon us when we arrive at the camp. Turning the skies dark and making it appear closer to dusk than mid-day.

"Avalon, what the hell happened?" Xander shouts over the whipping winds.

"We ran into issues. Pestilence will need to rest until he recovers and is at full strength, and Greer needs medical attention, but no men."

"I'm not leaving him," she advises as she slips off Storm. If not for Xander standing there to catch her, she would be on her ass looking up at us right now.

"Greer, can you handle Xander being in there with you?"

"If it means he will help Pestilence, I can handle anything." I motion for several of the men in camp to help carry him inside before beckoning Xander to follow me.

"Where's Renny," Greer yells as Suki runs out to see how she can help.

"He's in the kitchen with the other kids. We thought it was safer for them in there." She nods while following the four men responsible for carrying her Rider into my cabin, with Suk running to check on the kids.

"What the hell happened, Avalon?"

"Jay was taking Greer to the military camp, the asshole Cole told us about. When we got there, we were outnumbered by a lot, but Pestilence held them off while I got Greer out."

"Is she… Okay?"

"He raped her, Xander."

"Fucking bastard! Tell me he's dead."

"Yeah. It's how Pestilence ended up that way. He left cover when Jay tried to run." I yell as I shield my head from the flying debris. I opt to leave out the demon who tried to carry him back to hell, figuring there's only so much tragic news people can handle before falling apart, and right now, I need Xander's head in the game.

"Okay, well, let's get in there and tend to them."

"Wait. I can't stay."

"What the hell are you talking about? You're not leaving."

"I have to, Xander."

"No goddamn way am I letting you go out in this or with those assholes out there."

"I have to go."

"Why the hell would you do this?" He yells as he reaches to grasp my arm. I know he did this, believing it would keep me from leaving... it won't.

"This storm is because of me."

"Avalon, I understand there's something special about you, and I don't profess that it's something I will ever comprehend, but this doesn't mean you can convince me you're capable of conjuring a damn hurricane."

I take a deep breath, attempting to steady my nerves before giving him my confession. "I broke another seal. This is the start of the Rider's arrival."

"Why would you do that, Avalon?"

"It was the only way I could save them, Xander. You have to believe me. I would never have done it if there was any other way."

His face softens as his hand slides up my arm before coming to a rest on my shoulder, and with this act of compassion, he reassures me he doesn't blame me. It's the one thing I need right now, but it doesn't change a thing.

"I have to go before the Rider comes looking for me. It's the only way I can assure you all are safe, especially since Pestilence is in no condition to defend this camp or stop one of his brothers if they show up here deciding we've lived long enough."

"We'll figure something out, Avalon."

"No, I'm not putting the people who live in this camp at risk of meeting another rider, so I'm leaving. I need you to look after them and protect Pestilence until he can act as their guardian again."

"She's never going to understand this. You know that… right?"

"I know. Tell her I love her." He nods as I grab my pack from Storm's saddlebag. "Don't leave him out here in this shit, okay?"

"I won't." I turn to leave but stop to ask him for one last favor. "Promise me you'll take care of them, Xander."

"Always." I give him a small smile as I lift my hand to say goodbye before turning to put as much distance between me and this camp as possible.

*****

The first thing that registers is how much worse this storm is than the one marking Pestilence's arrival. The second thing is how slow my progress is due to constantly having to avoid flying debris. Several times I have had to duck behind something to escape being hit. I've been out in this shit for almost twenty minutes, and I'm lucky if I made it a couple of miles from camp.

Not to mention in the back of my head, I have a growing fear the next rider will find my happy ass. Or worse than the rider… what if a pissed-off demon is the one to stumble across my path? With the howling winds surging through the trees, I would never hear him in time if he rode up behind yours truly.

With this plaguing my every thought, I take a chance to glance over my shoulder, hoping to put an end to this irrational fear, and shock rolls through my entire body when I discover I'm not as alone as I was praying for. But it's not a raven-shifting demon I find following me. It's the sweet face of the little boy who stole my heart.

It seems Renny followed his Aunt Avalon out of camp. Something I could have easily missed for quite a while if not for him tripping over a branch that blocked the road. I guess my unfounded fear of a certain demon prick did something. It forced me to check over my shoulder, and this was the only reason I discovered him following me since this damn rider's storm muffled his faint cries.

He was struggling to stand up as I rushed back over to scoop him into my arms. "Renny, what are you doing out here?"

"Peek," he cries as I wipe the dirt from his hands.

"Little man, were you playing Hide-n-go-seek with me?"

"Peek," he whimpers again as he scrubs his hand under his nose while I wipe away his tears.

"It's not safe for you to be with Aunt Avalon right now."

"Lon," he says as he touches my cheek. The contact shocks me because Wren never does this except with Greer, Storm, and sometimes Pestilence.

"Renny, I would love for you to be with me, but you can't, honey. Come on, little man, let's get you back to your momma before she goes crazy with worry." I turn back toward camp only to find a sight that sends a chill racing through me. A tornado the size of a goddamn building has touched down.

And the damn thing is heading straight toward us.

Chapter Four: Out Of The Storm And Into The Fire

W/ITH THE TWISTER almost on top of us, I have no other option but to run. The problem is, it's catching up with us faster than I can go. As the last of my hope fades, I round a corner to find the only thing that may offer us protection. A barn.

As the winds increase, I race to what I hope will be our salvation and make it inside when the first tree is ripped from the ground and slams against the door I just entered. I shove against the door, which refuses to move. I hope I don't regret coming in here since the damn thing has blocked any hope of escape if I discover this place isn't the sanctuary I am praying for.

Rushing to the furthest interior wall this place offers, I tuck Wren under me as I do my best to protect him from the crumbling frame.

"Hold on, Renny," I scream since the freight train has arrived, and the first part of the roof is ripping away, giving me my first glimpse of the hell that has caught up with us.

Piece by piece, board by board, this fucking place is crumbling. If this storm doesn't pass by soon, there won't be a barn left to protect Wren and me. Not to mention I have to throw my body on Wren's because of the updraft the damn beast has caused. Wren slams his hands over his ears, hoping to drown out the noise from the damn twister. His screams are only outdone by the roars of the tornado. The instant my body becomes weightless, I know it won't be long before we are both ripped from the structure. Since this isn't fucking Kansas, and I don't have a little dog named Toto, I don't imagine we'll be safely transported to the magical munchkin-filled lands of Oz. Where the worst thing I will face is an ugly ass witch with horrible taste in socks.

As my legs lift inch by gradual inch toward the gaping hole in the roof, I slam my hand around the board in front of me, impaling my hand on a nail I didn't see. As horrible as the pain is, I can't let go for fear of being sucked up into the product of another of my epic fuck ups. I lose my grip when the force increases, and the shift rips the nail that is visible from the back of my hand up closer to my fingers. If it happens again, I won't have to worry about being impaled on it any longer because it will tear my fucking hand in two, and now Wren isn't the only one screaming.

The storm's noise isn't the only sound I hear as the barn groans from the force of the winds. It's fucking shredding around us. With one last crack followed by an explosion, the roof is gone, and the walls come tumbling down on top of Renny and me.

*****

The next thing I become aware of is the winds and rain are gone. I have Wren cradled against my chest, and I cannot move. Pinned down by a barn that wasn't built to withstand what I can only guess was a category-three or four tornado.

The sounds of dripping water and boards creaking from the few walls still standing are the next thing I register, and lastly is how still Wren is next to me. My head is pounding, and I realize a thick liquid is running down my face, which has to be blood from what I can only assume is a pretty nasty head wound. But hey, on the plus side, the board with the nail is gone, and my hand doesn't resemble a damn lobster claw. There's a hole the size of a dime in my palm, but I can live with that.

"Wren," I say, having to clear my throat of the dust I've been breathing for god only knows how long. "Renny, wake up."

I try to lift myself off him, but the walls that collapsed on us are preventing me from doing anything other than shifting enough to pull his legs out from under me and put my arm under his head as I try to hear if he's still breathing. The instant I feel him exhale is the sweetest damn moment of my life.

Okay, time to think, Avalon. How the hell am I supposed to lift a barn off of us? Pull the little man out of the wreckage and not pass out again in the damn process. Every plausible scenario plays out for me, and they all circle back to one. It's fuckin impossible. At least on my own. We need help, preferably before the four-legged predators find us.

As the day passes to evening, it appears my fears of being discovered by an animal were not unfounded, because I can hear something moving around the destroyed barn. And nothing about the movements screams human. As luck would have it, this is also when Wren decides this would be the perfect time to wake up enough to cry out when he attempts to move his tiny body.

"Shhh, shhh-shhh. It's okay, Wren. Aunt Avalon has you. Don't cry, little man." Thankfully, this is enough to calm him, letting his eyes slip closed again. This is a blessing in itself because it's only then I hear the first sound coming from the beast, and I almost break down.

"Storm?" I ask with the last bit of hope I have left of getting us both out of this alive. Obviously, he can't respond with a 'hell yes,' and a 'we've been looking for you all damn day,' but he does stomp the ground before releasing a confirmatory snort.

"Thank God. You need to get your rider. We can't get out. Bring Pestilence back, Storm. Hurry."

By some miracle, these horses listen to me, and I know he is doing as I asked when I hear him racing away to retrieve his rider. We only need to hold on until he gets back.

I didn't realize I had dozed off until the sound of boards and pieces of the building being pulled away woke me. He came, and with any luck, he will have us unburied and out of here before the first star appears.

"Help is here, little man. Not much longer now. I need you to hold on, Renny." I whisper as I stroke his hair, but it seems darkness prefers my company as the slow pull of oblivion draws me under.

Something falling on my face wakes me again. This is when I realize I can see the sky, which means we are almost out of this mess. I am getting ready to thank Pestilence until a face appears, and I realize it is not him.

"The lamb, I presume."

"Let me guess, the second rider?" I inquire, already knowing the answer before I'm done asking the question.

"Were you expecting another?"

"No, it seems my dance card is already full," I snap, making him throw his head back and laugh as he disappears from view. Is he going to leave us here stuck under the rest of the debris? He clicks his tongue a few times before the last remnants of the defunct barn are pulled off us.

Since I have no damn idea what this rider's plans are, I am not eager to accept the hand he is offering. I would refuse if not for the stress and strain I've put my body through over the last couple of days, but this isn't an option because I'm exhausted. At least it's not an option if I want to get my ass off the ground while keeping Wren clenched in my protective arms. Pulling my little man close to my chest as I reach my hand—you know, the one without a fucking hole in it—up to accept his offer.

The second I'm upright, I take a defensive step away from him, only to have him take a decisive one in our direction.

"Step away from the lamb, brother."

"Et tu, frater meus?"

"Afraid so, brother."

"Well, it seems we have a conundrum, agnellu. Two riders seek you. Only one will walk away with you. Which will it be?"

"I can assure you it won't be you."

"You say this with so much conviction. I almost hate to prove how wrong you are." I make the mistake of looking over my shoulder as I move further away from him. It is done to confirm there is nothing I could trip over as I hasten my retreat, which is a wise decision since I am now sidestepping one of the beams that used to hold up the roof. With the rest of my path to Pestilence clear, I bring my eyes back to him only to discover he stands directly in front of me. The little shrieking gasp I give is all he needs to seal his declaration as he snatches Wren out of my grasp.

"Let him go, brother. In fact, I will take both of them. Right now!" Pestilence growls as he moves closer to us. War clicks his tongue before a slight grin appears on his face. Pestilence's reaction to his brother tells me this negotiation will not be as smooth as Pessy had hoped. I suspect it has something to do with him coming to retrieve us before he recuperated fully from the damage Raum did. The problem is, War can sense it as well.

"Ùn siate avidità, fratellu pocu. Tuttavia, sò dispostu à dà unu di elli.." (You are greedy, little brother. However, I am willing to give one of them.) War says. Surely, I misunderstood the tone in which he delivered his message since it almost sounded playful.

"War, you are testing my patience," Pestilence snarls.

"Okay… fine, the boy can go. She comes with me."

"No!" War laughs at Pestilence's response as he moves his focus to me.

"I believe in choices, agnellu. Choice one: you come with me. Choice two: I take the little one. See, I can be fair, fratello."

"I said, No... and I meant it."

"One, and I mean it."

"Pestilence, I don't see any other option here," I quietly say when he slowly begins backing away with Wren still held in his arms.

"Avalon, don't."

I know what I am preparing to do will piss Pestilence off, but I will not allow his brother to take Renny. "I choose one."

"You heard her brother? She comes with me." War's grin broadens as he walks past, with any hope it's to return Wren to his brother. Even if Pestilence was at full strength, I'm not sure he could overtake the giant man lumbering in his direction. He is at least four inches taller than Pestilence and outweighs him by fifty pounds of raw muscle.

"Will Renny be okay," Since the storm, he hasn't been awake much, making me fear it injured him more than I initially thought.

"This is an answer I cannot give you... but I know there is one who can." War's eyes shift back over to the other rider. "Tell us, brother, will the little one be okay?" Pestilence snatches Wren from War, whose laugh only causes a growl of frustration from Pessy.

"Allow me to assure you he will be fine, agnellu," War informs me as he mounts his horse, which I didn't even register was standing here until right now. Although, how I could miss him is something I will never be able to explain. What irritates me is if War already knew Wren would be okay, then why the hell did he say he couldn't give me the answer? Was this him just being an asshole?

"Shall we?" War asks as he rides up next to me, offering me his hand, which is a damn good thing since I don't think I could get up there if I tried. He pulls me up with about as much effort as lifting a feather. He surprises me when he doesn't put me behind him since this would be the normal thing to do. But oh no, not this damn rider. He makes a production of placing me in front.

"This is not over yet, War," Pestilence says with a snarl as he swings his leg over Storm.

"Well, as I am riding away, I would respectfully have to disagree, little brother."

*****

We ride in silence. I'm not sure where we are going, but then again, neither does he. Throughout my travels with Death and Pestilence, I was never afraid. Not of the ones we came across or the men I traveled with. But this mammoth man behind me… well, is quite a different story because, let's face it, he makes me more than just a little uncomfortable.

Not to mention, I know Raum is out there somewhere, and I don't imagine I'm high on his favorite 'mortals I won't be killing' list. Especially after I shot his ass not once, but twice, before stealing away his prize. A rider he planned to torture. Too damn bad for him. Because I consider Pestilence a friend, so there was no damn way in hell I would ever permit some asshole to drag my friend off to hell.

War ends my thoughts of the asshole demon when he pulls his horse to a stop. He whips his leg around me before dropping to the ground, and I swear the damn world just quaked from the impact.

Without a word, he reaches up and pulls me off his horse, which is as different as the other rider's horses. As I've mentioned, War's horse is the size of a damn barn and as wide as one. His coat is a rusty red with a coal-black mane, and much like his rider, when he slams his paw against the ground, it responds with a shake.

"We'll make camp here. You may begin." I look at him, wondering what the hell he means. All the while, he leans against a rock the size of a Buick. His muscled arms crossed over his chiseled chest as if waiting for something. I know he's not used to having anyone question his demands, especially some mortal woman. He's going to be pissed when he figures out I'm not so good at listening to these riders. As he remains seated against the rock staring at me, I decide the prudent choice here is to clarify what the hell he wants.

"Begin what?"

"Setting up my camp. Did you miss the part where I said we would make camp here?"

"No, did you miss the part where you said '*we*?' Because I sure as shit didn't."

"Then permit me to rephrase; *you*... can make camp here." Yeah, I'll get right on that a-hole. Right around the time I call Thor's hammer down to clock you in your mammoth head for thinking I'm going to do all the work while you park your ass there like some damn oversized king sitting on his rock thrown. Damn chauvinistic pig.

"No," I pointedly respond, mimicking his posture by putting my arms over my chest. Here's the problem: his horse doesn't take kindly to a mortal talking to his rider like this. The way he informs me of his extreme displeasure is for him to stomp on the ground right behind where I'm standing, forcing me to scamper out of his range. After recovering, I return my attention to the rider, grinning about the abrupt turn of events. I don't know if this reaction is because I came away from this interaction in one piece or because his horse almost smooshed me. Either way, it's damn irritating.

"No?"

"It's what I said. What part of the word are you having problems with, the N or the O?"

"The defiant part."

"Hmm, well, I suppose if you didn't want someone who would defy you, then you should have taken a...." I pause, trying to figure out the perfect word to use here. Right from the start, I want to make it clear to him that I don't bow down to anyone, including these damn riders.

"Mouse?"

"Yeah, thanks. Like some meek damn mouse."

"I would never expect you to be a *'meek damn mouse,'* but a compliant lamb is not out of the realm of what I expect."

"Alas, rider, I think you will be sadly disappointed," I say as I amble over to his horse, the one who sidesteps the closer I get.

"Resta calmu mio fidu amicu. Trattate l'agnellu cum'è u vostru cavalieri." After he says whatever the hell he said, his horse calms down, allowing me to approach him. Damn, to think the only thing I wanted to do was retrieve my bag. With my meager possessions in hand, I turn on my heels and march away from this infuriating rider and his pain-in-the-ass mammoth horse.

"Where are you going, Bella Agnellu?"

"Don't know what that means," I tell him over my shoulder.

"Perhaps I will tell you if you're a good little lamb."

"Doesn't matter," I bellow back as I wave at him over my shoulder.

"You still have yet to tell me where you are going."

"Well, I don't know about you, rider, but I plan on sleeping in that house over there. You know, the one already put together." And I can't believe rather than hearing the stern, 'No!' I would have received from Death or the exasperated, 'Why must you be so difficult?' Pestilence would have muttered; this rider throws his head back and releases a howl of laughter that makes me jump. What the hell? This was not the reaction I expected.

As I walk across the expansive porch, I don't miss the heavy footfalls of War behind me. "I thought you were all about setting up a camp?"

"Where you go, I go, *Bella Agnellu*," he says the last part in a teasing tone.

"Still don't know what the hell that means."

"I am aware," he chuckles as he pushes past to enter the house before I can. He stops just inside the doorway, scanning the interior. I can't say what he hoped this deserted house would hold. Not sure I care. I do know one thing: while he is looking for it, I plan on taking my tired ass to the nearest couch to sit down. When I attempt to move around him, his arm snakes around my waist faster than I can pass to pull me back to him.

"No," he murmurs with his mouth pressed against my ear only after giving me a disapproving tongue click.

"No?"

"It is what I said. What part of this are *you* having problems with? The N or the O?"

44

"The asshole part." His grin is not what I expected. "Hilarious, right?"

"Very."

I try to push past him again, only to have him block the attempt. "Um, Rider, you do understand this is kind of the whole reason I came over here. You know, to enter the house you're blocking." When his infuriating grin remains, I continue pushing. "So I could clean up and get some damn sleep. Which requires you getting out of my way so I can accomplish my *task*."

"I appreciate the word you chose there, lamb." Yeah, I figured he would like the task bit. "But my answer remains no."

"Why the hell not?"

"Because, Bella Agnellu, you never enter an area before I have cleared it. Now stay here like a good little mouse." Even though this directive from War pisses me off, having him pat me on the head is so much worse.

"Seriously?"

"Do I look as if I'm joking?" Is he for real? I almost ask until I see his stern "don't push me on this issue" stance. Rather than fighting him about it, I roll my eyes, release an aggravated sigh, and jerk my head as I present the house to him with a flourish of my hands. My actions were a way to communicate my frustration and urge him to get his ass moving. With any luck, he understands subtle—or, in this case, not-so-subtle—hints.

He strolls back into the room he left me in a couple of minutes later with an apple in his hand. My mistake is believing he is bringing it back for me since I know the riders don't require food to sustain life. Not like this hungry mortal does. I am preparing to thank him when he takes a bite of the fruit.

"Seriously?"

"You like this word, don't you?"

"Only when dealing with assholes."

"Are you calling me an asshole, Bella Agnellu?" he says with an irritating smirk. I am beginning to realize this is something he gives any time he finds something amusing. And one thing is apparent, since joining his company, I'm a fucking comedic genius.

"Merely calling it the way I see it. Tell me there is another apple in there."

"There is another apple in there," he mimics my tone perfectly. Sighing my frustration, I push myself off the wall and storm into the kitchen.

It's one of those open, airy rooms with tons of windows, cupboards, and every damn gadget you could ever want. It's the type of kitchen any home chef would have envied before the world fell to shit since it has everything they could ever wish to have for preparing their beautiful gourmet meals. Except for one thing....

"So where's the apple at?"

"In my hand."

"You said there was more."

"No, I simply repeated what you told me to say."

I can't help the dramatic eye roll I give him because now it's clear he just duped my sorry, aching, bruised ass, but it doesn't stop me from asking anyway. "So... no more apples then?"

"Sorry, this is the last one."

"Wonderful," I mumble, heading back into the living room to grab my bag to rifle through, hoping to find anything that might pacify my rumbling stomach. And, of course, with my new shadow close behind.

"Do you wish to bite my apple? Here, allow me to first remove the juice created as I experienced such a delicacy," he says as his tongue runs over the fruit before raising it toward my mouth.

"I'm good."

"Hmm, that remains to be seen." My head whips up to assess him. Surely, he didn't mean what most mortal men would have intended with this statement. Before I can decide, he pushes the apple closer to me. "Are you certain you do not wish to have some?" He leans over, bringing his mouth by my ear to continue his thought with his lips skimming against it. "It's tender, juicy, and delicious. A real treat for the senses." Okay, that seals it. This is, without a doubt, within the realm of flirting.

"Hard pass," I confirm, pushing past him so I can drop my bag before plopping down on the couch. Only to hear him once again laughing as I did it. Glad I can amuse him. He flips the apple in the air before pulling out a knife and slicing it in half, handing me the part he didn't eat from. If I wasn't so hungry, I would have told him where he could shove it, but the growling hunger pangs win out as I accept the apple he is offering. And as hard as it is to do this, I mutter a quick thanks.

"So what did you say outside to your horse so he would let me get my bag?"

"Inquisitive little mouse, aren't you?"

"Never mind," I sigh and roll my eyes before turning to look out the bay window the couch is situated against.

"I advised him to remain calm and treat you as he would his rider."

"Really?"

"Yes, Bella Agnellu." The low groan I give him causes him to rethink what he calls me. Although it's no damn better, and to be quite honest, it's more irritating since I can understand this one and positively do not like it. "Yes, mouse?"

"I think I like the Bella shit better." Resulting in another laugh, and I'm beginning to think he does this to rile me up.

With my stomach finally silenced, my thoughts switch to the still-pounding head wound I suffered during his arrival. A low hiss rushes past my clenched teeth the instant my fingers graze over the gash still crusted by the blood I had no way of stopping earlier. When he sees my reaction, he stands from where he had been crouching by the fireplace as I go to the kitchen, looking for anything I can clean it with.

As I rummage through drawers and cupboards, I feel his presence lingering inside the doorway. One thing is for sure, this rider is nothing like his brothers. He's almost arrogant in his actions and words. As any self-absorbed, believes they are god's gift to humanity, confident with a means to back it up, gorgeous asshole can be. Hell, he may even give the former pretty boy assholes of the world a run for their money. An attribute I can assure you neither Death nor Pestilence possess, or at least they don't flaunt it as he does. Both these men have an understated confidence, a quality this brother could learn from.

"Hot damn," I yell, discovering a towel in the last drawer this kitchen had. It's like a little victory, something I haven't experienced much of lately. Aside from thwarting a damn demon... but let's be honest, that victory wasn't mine alone; I had help. Lots of it. But this doesn't stop me from my little victory dance as I pull my water bottle out of my backpack and only stop when I spin and find him smirking at me.

"What?"

"If a simple piece of cloth can elicit such a response, I wonder what something more important would grant me."

"Grant you?"

"As I was the only one here to witness the show, then yes, Bella Agnellu, grant *me*."

"What the hell does that even mean?"

"What?" he asks as he tilts his head, which is irritating as hell because he knows exactly what I'm asking about. I contemplate not answering him, but something tells me it will delight him regardless of which path I pick.

"Bella Agnes, or whatever the hell you keep calling me."

"It's Bella Agnellu, and as I have already informed you, if you wish to know, you must be—"

"Yeah-yeah, I know a good girl. Got it," I snap, dumping some of my water over the towel before bringing it to my head. The instant it makes contact, the pain damn near drops me to my knees. Couple this with the world swimming around me, and I know fainting is not outside the realm of impossibility because not only is it possible, it damn well happens.

And as the tunnel swallows my vision, I hear the unmistakable chuckle of a rider as he quietly declares, "If you wished me to carry you, you only needed to ask."

Why does this keep happening to me?

Fuck. My. Life.

Chapter Five: Best Rest

*W*ITH THE LOSS of all things clock-like, I have no way of knowing what time it's getting to be or how long I've been sleeping, but the light filtering through my closed eyelids confirms it has to be at least mid-day. Here's where I stand on this issue, for the first time in a long time… I don't care because exhaustion doesn't begin to explain my current state. Besides, my muscles are still aching, so my only plan includes staying in this incredible, comfortable bed because I haven't been this happy since sharing one with Thanatos. Another silver lining is that I bandaged my hand before I passed out. I don't remember doing it, but I must have since I can't imagine the asshat rider doing anything so… human or nice.

Speaking of the asshat, I wonder where the hell War got to. Something tells me he's not one to exercise patience while waiting around until I'm fully rested, ready, and raring to go.

"Good afternoon, lamb." I contemplate pretending I'm still sleeping until I feel something sliding over my back. My eyes snap open as a new horror takes root. The nice soft bed isn't a bed at all; it's War. I'm fucking sleeping on top of War. Jesus Christ, how the hell did this happen? As I try to pull away from the mammoth man, his arms tighten, holding me in place, ensuring I'm not going anywhere.

"War?"

"Yes, Bella Agnellu."

"Care to explain why I'm sleeping on top of you?"

"Because you would not let me go last night."

"I wouldn't…. What now?"

"Release me. After you passed out, I cleaned and dressed your wounds before carrying you up here. When I attempted to lie you down, you refused to release my shirt."

"You couldn't… I don't know, maybe pull it out of my damn hands or something?" I snap and scurry out of his arms to the other side of the bed.

"I suppose this would have been possible if…."

"If what?" I shout, sitting up, which sends the world swirling around me. With a groan, I make the wise choice to lie back down.

"If I wanted to. Which I didn't."

"Why?"

He doesn't answer my question, opting to ask one of his own. "Tell me what happened to my brother and what put these bruises on you."

"The bruises would be from a *Fucking Barn* falling on me. One that only fell to mark your arrival."

"No, this is where the cuts came from. The bruises are several days old. In fact, they appear to have occurred prior to my release. So try again."

"Some of them may be from when Pestilence and I had to fight the assholes holding Greer against her will. Which is also when Pestilence was injured."

"What is a Greer?"

"Greer is not a what she's a who, and who she is would be a woman who has been traveling with us."

"My brother risked everything for someone who only traveled with you?"

"Um, how do I explain this? Okay… for lack of a better word, she's your brother's girlfriend."

"Girl friend? This is a term I am unfamiliar with, lamb."

"It means they're together." He shrugs his shoulders, suggesting he still doesn't have a clue what I'm insinuating, but honestly, I don't have the strength to have this conversation with him right now. "Ask your brother. Maybe he can explain it to you. Regardless, the bottom line is that a band of assholes has joined their evil forces together to dispatch you riders. Or at least this is what they are hoping to do. My guess is you all may have something to say about it."

"Dispatching?"

"Killing." Of course, this word he doesn't seem to have any issues understanding if the low growl coming from him is any clue.

"They wish to remove us from this plane?"

"This plane and just about any other."

"Come, Bella Agnellu," he demands as he vacates the bed and storms across the room.

"If you're not going to tell me what the name means, would you please stop calling me it?" This part is more mumbled for my benefit than his. *"It's more annoying than being called a little lamb, for Christ's sake.* And where are we going?"

"No, I will not, and we will travel to my brother."

"Whoa, hold on there, horseman. I'm not comfortable with you strolling into a camp that houses every person I consider family."

"Your family has nothing to worry about from me unless they are among the ones who wish to dispatch us." When I shake my head to confirm they are not, he continues. "Then they have no cause for concern; however, these mortals who oppose us are another story. Besides, I am merely doing as you advised."

"I never told you to go to my old camp."

"Are you certain of this?"

"Yep, pretty damn sure I would remember saying something like 'hey, let's go visit the one place in this world holding every person I love and consider family,' because that shit never crossed these lips."

As War leans over, the creaks and cracks of the bed's protest fill the room. His weight on the mattress causes me to roll straight into his muscled arms. His warm breath tickling along the bare skin of my neck. Okay, I guess he has more to say about my challenging comment. "Because I clearly recall you telling me to ask my brother who this Greer is to him."

Well, shit, he got me there.

*****

Within fifteen minutes, we are out the door, on his horse, heading to the last damn place I ever thought I would willingly take this rider. Here's hoping I don't regret this shit.

With what is fast becoming his custom, he has me perched in front of him with his arms wrapped around me to control his horse's reins. I'm so lost in thought, playing out all the potential scenarios that could happen when we arrive back at the camp I ran from, hoping to prevent this specific thing from occurring; I almost miss him saying something. In fact, I would have if not for the vibration of his deep voice against my back.

"Huh?" I mumble.

"I sense my brother's essence upon you."

"I've been with Pestilence for a year. So yeah, I figure some of his rider mojo shit probably rubbed off on me. Damn, that didn't sound good. I didn't mean it like that."

"Good to know. But I was not speaking of Pestilence. It is Thanatos I am detecting. You are the one who traveled with him for a time."

"Yes, I was in his horde."

"But you did not only travel with him in his horde. There was a time you journeyed with only him." He leans forward, looking down at me and the breast nearly exposed from the shirt torn at the collar.

"Hey! What the hell do you think you're doing?"

"Contemplating."

"Contemplating what?"

"Why my brother would keep you with him for so long."

"He didn't like losing members of his horde."

"Ah... Well, I would say, based on my observation of certain attributes you possess, it may have less to do with a horde and more to do with your form."

"Hey-hey-hey, how about you keep your observations on the road and not on my... my...."

"Form?"

"Yes!"

"Then I will make no such promise."

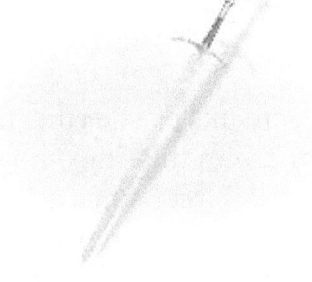

~Pestilence~

I let her down by permitting my brother to take her without so much as a cross word, let alone fight, but Avalon's pleading eyes told me to let her go. She knew I was in no condition to take on my brother. So she opted to protect Wren and me rather than hoping for me to step in. For the little lamb shielding the people she considers family is more important to her than facing the unknown of going with my brother.

I know War will not hurt her, but this doesn't mean I will leave her within his ranks. The simple truth is, how could I not bring her home when she shielded my son to the detriment of her own body, which was left bloody and bruised because of War's arrival.

My brother's plan will include growing an army as he decimates everything he comes across. This does not foster a safe environment for anyone among his ranks, specifically a certain someone who will stick her neck in the noose for anyone she deems worthy.

Even though the only thing I want is to remain with Greer to ensure she is okay and comfort her if she is not, I will have to leave to reclaim the lamb. But first, I need to return Wren back home. My son is still sleeping peacefully in my arms. The trauma of what happened has taken a toll on him. One I will assure he recovers from before I depart to find them.

"Wren," Greer screams as she runs from Suki's cabin.

Upon discovering him missing, she was determined to search for him herself. Greer's heartbreaking cries that no one can understand her anguish because he is her son, not theirs, filled the camp. But this is not true, and these words break me since I comprehend the terror my chosen feels all too well. The issue is I have yet to tell her Wren is no longer only her son. He is our son. However, knowing the trauma she experienced and her fear that she had lost her son did not lend to this being the proper time to inform her of this.

"Is he…." She cries as I depart from my horse.

"He's fine. His body requires rest from his experience."

"But he's okay?"

"Renny has a nasty bump on his head that should heal with time. Aside from this, he is well." Her eyes search my face, beseeching my words not to be a lie spoken to spare her the heartbreak she was preparing for, and the sight is devastating. Reaching up, I settle my hand on the back of her neck as my thumb caresses her cheek. I give her what she needs. "I promise, love. Wren is fine."

56

With her fears laid to rest, she wraps her arms around me, embracing us as if she is worried if she lets go, we will just float away like some cruel dream shown only to torment her. I drop my hand to her back to pull her closer while she quietly cries against me. She does this for her son, for what she experienced, and for me, as her following words confirm.

"I was so afraid. Afraid I had lost you only to lose my Renny as well. Please don't ever leave us again. Please, Pestilence. I need you to promise me you will be with us always. Please, I need to hear you say the words."

And this is where my eyes slip closed because this is a promise I cannot grant her, but a heartache that can wait until tomorrow.

*****

The determination of my chosen is clear as she stands with her hands on her hips, tapping her foot with enough force to let me know how unhappy she is about this situation. As promised, I gave her last night, holding her and my son while they slept. Something they both required to let their bodies and minds heal from the traumatic events they have suffered.

I did not ask her what had happened... I didn't have to. Because I felt his taint upon her, and if it takes me until time ends, I will make it my mission to reverse what this man did to her. I only wish I had not killed him in the manner he met his end. A quick death was not something he was deserving of.

"So take us with you!"

"No."

"I'm with Greer here because if you think I'm going to sit my happy ass here waiting for you to bring my best friend back, you're crazier than the loon who took her."

"My brother is anything but insane." I meant for my words to offer comfort, yet the look they all give me tells me they matter not. The instant I confess I did not find Wren alone that he had, in fact, been protected by the lamb, the little one demanded to know why I had not brought her back with me. She went so far as to instruct I should have thrown her ass on the back of Storm and tied her there if she refused to come home.

It's not long before she refocuses her anger on another when Xander speaks on my behalf, advising her the lamb would have refused to return. Unfortunately for her chosen mate, it, would have been in his best interest to remain silent.

"Explain this to me again because I'm struggling to understand why A would have broken another seal. Let alone how you knew about it, honeybuns, but didn't tell me," Suki snarls as her stance now rivals my chosen one.

"We have discussed this ad nauseam, little one."

"Tough shit! Now ad nauseam, some more fucking details, tendril boy, and tell me how she ended up with another seal, broke it, rescued a rider before saving our Renny only to be carted off by your damn brother, and don't leave anything out."

"I believe you have covered the events already."

"Then cover them again because I want to hear… Every. Last. Fucking. One. Of. Them."

"Suki," Greer hisses as she covers Wren's ears.

"Sorry, little man, but this big ass—prin owes your Auntie Suki some ding-dang-darn answers. So get to talking and tell us again why you think you'll be the only one going after her."

"Because my brother holds her and will not be so inclined to relinquish her."

"Yeah, something I'm starting to figure out about all you dick—tators," she corrects as her eyes flick over to Wren, who finds his furious aunt amusing.

"Yes, brother, explain. Because this is something I should love to hear as well." My head whips in the direction of the approaching horse, resulting in a flood of emotions that overwhelm me. Trepidation from having him so close to the people I protect and jubilation knowing she survived her injuries. And by all appearances, she looks to be well cared for. By my brother's hand, nonetheless.

"A. You're alive. Now, how about you get your ass— sorry little man—down here and explain to me what the hell you were thinking."

"Sembra chì avete e vostre mani piene cù questu, fratellu chjucu." (It appears you have your hands full with this one, little brother.)

"Ùn avete micca idea, fratellu." (You have no idea, brother.)

"Hey-hey-hey, none of that shit," Suki snaps, pointing her finger at me and then at my brother, who mercifully finds it amusing and stays his hand rather than removing her head with a quick slash of his blade.

"Mi piace u spiritu ardente di questu." (I like the fiery spirit of this one.)

"Dì mi chistu quand'ella ti tene un cuteddu à a gola, o in u vostru casu, palle, minacciate a vostra esistenza per piglià l'ultimu pezzu di torta." (Tell me this when she is holding a knife to your throat, or in your case, balls, threatening your existence for taking the last piece of cake.) Which makes him throw his head back and roar with laughter, a sound I did not realize how much I have missed until now.

"Um, am I not talking over here 'cause I'm pretty freakin' sure I am. I mean, my lips are moving. Not to mention, beyond a doubt, sounds are coming out of my mouth. The words are spoken in English, which you two a-holes could take a lesson from. So yes-yes, Suki, you are most definitely talking," the little one mutters more to herself than the rest of us.

"Better get used to it, Suk. He does it a lot," Avalon tells her with an irritated little groan.

"Well, apparently, you're having difficulty with simple English as well since your ass is still perched up on the gargantuan beast. I mean — cover your ears, little man — that's one big ass horse. Which ordinarily, I'm all for big things, but damn, it's like a freak of effing nature."

"F, G, H...."

"That's right, little man, Auntie Suk was saying the alphabet, not naughty words Mommy will bust the soap out for."

"I don't think Greer sees the distinction, love."

"Whose side are you on, honeybuns? As for you, A, mind telling us how the hell you got up on the jumbo pony over there?"

War's horse snorts, hearing the little one call him a pony while his rider chuckles as he leans around the little lamb to await her response, resulting in her doing something I have grown quite accustomed to during our time together. She rolls her eyes as she mumbles, "With help."

A confession that must please my brother to hear as he dismounts his companion before lifting the lamb down.

His way of showing the little one how she accomplishes such a feat. I don't miss how his hands linger on her hips. This minor act makes me question if Thanatos was there to welcome his return for some reason. Because I have little doubt, our brother would make the same request of War that he made of me if they spoke. He would urge him to care for the mortal he continues concealing his feelings about. Stubborn ass. Or could this mean his reparations for restoring Wren's soul have begun? Yet another thing I shall have to inquire about when War and I have a second alone.

Once Avalon is free of my brother's grasp, Suki rushes her, diving into the little lamb, almost knocking her off her feet. In fact, if not for War's quick reaction, they both would have been on the ground staring up at the horse and rider who returned her here; instead, it is only the little one. However, she does not remain on the ground alone for long since she sweeps the lamb's legs out from under her, and this time War does not interfere.

"What the hell were you thinking, A?"

"I was thinking I screwed up again and wanted to put as much distance between you all and another one of my colossal eff ups as possible."

"I, for one, am pleased with your choice. Even more now," War tells her as he leans against his horse, smirking down at the women lying at his feet.

"What's his deal?" Suki mumbles as she pushes up to her knees, and the lamb's response causes another chuckle from my brother.

"Don't ask."

"Come, brother, for we have much to do," War says as he slowly lifts his eyes from Avalon, who is busy brushing the dirt from her hands and backside to me.

"Um… No," Greer says as she steps around me.

"Excuse me—"

"She means there is no effin toot-a-lootly way that the big P is sashaying his hiney anywhere but right here."

"I understood this even less. You may have to translate, Bella Agnellu."

Did I hear him correctly? Did he just call her Beautiful Lamb? I raise my eyebrows in his direction, hearing his moniker for the little lamb, to which his response is another grin.

This confirms he did not speak with Thanatos, which means I may need to travel to our realm to find out what fate has befallen our brother.

"I told you to stop calling me that," she hisses, but is it because she knows what he said to her and she does not want the others to hear, or she doesn't know what his words mean, and he merely says them to tease her. My guess would be the latter. Hence, the reason why her cheeks have not turned scarlet yet.

Which begs the question, when she finds out, will my brother's manhood once again be in peril of being removed by….

One pissed-off little lamb.

Chapter Six: Richard Cabeza

~Ember Late Fall 2025 ~

THE FEEL OF the ring on my finger as I absentmindedly twist it has become almost an unconscious act in the days since they ended up around my neck. A reminder of things lost. Of a life I had, one I resented at the time but would do anything to go back to now if I could.

To say I miss them would be the damn understatement of the year. Because most days, the only thing I can do is push every memory of them to the furthest recesses of my mind so I don't sit down and wait for the end. Because if I don't, these fucking memories feel like they might swallow me whole.

A smack to my ass snaps me out of the thoughts I would have preferred to remain in rather than deal with the asshole who delivered it.

"Get this sexy ass out of bed. We got shit to do," Trevor announces when he rolls onto his back.

"A simple 'time to get up' would have sufficed," I snarl, irritated he thinks he can hit me, not to mention now I have to contend with a sore ass.

"Would it have made you move any faster?" he asks before leaning over to bite the spot still stinging from the last bit of attention he showed me.

"Probably not."

"Which is why I smacked it. Now get up. I'm not fucking around. Wayne wants a debriefing on how things got so colossally fucked up yesterday."

"Maybe he should have joined us. Then he wouldn't need a recounting of the events. He would have had first-hand knowledge."

Trevor's hand snakes around me, fisting the hair he finds at the nape of my neck so he can yank me upright as he brings his face in direct line with mine. "I enjoy this little arrangement we got going here."

"Little arrangement?" I snap, knowing it will only piss him off further, but right now, I don't give a shit.

"I like fucking you. Even more when this defiant little mouth of yours is wrapped around my cock, but make no mistake, Ember, I won't put up with any woman talking to me like that. Now get the fuck out of bed, put on some damn clothes, and get your ass out to the yard before I do more than give you a love tap. Am I making myself clear?"

"Perfectly," I hiss, trying to keep my lip from twisting up, revealing my fury.

"Good answer," he says, smashing his mouth against mine, then the asshole pushing my head away like I'm bothering him. I am prepared to give him the one-finger salute as he ambles his ass toward the door, but luck seems to be on my side when my finger gets stuck in the smaller ring I wear around my neck. Otherwise, he would have caught me when he whips around to growl one last order before he left me cursing his name. "And make sure you get that sweet little ass of yours back in my bed tonight. I have plans for us."

"Fucking prick," I mumble to the empty room. There will come a day when he discovers I am not the woman to screw with.

*****

I slam the door to his unit closed when I storm out of the damn thing. Most days, I wish I would never have let this prick touch me. He's a cocky, arrogant bastard who's way too fucking full of himself, but he's also one of those alpha pricks I always seem to gravitate toward. Not to mention the second in command of this little uprising. A role he took by force along with his best friend Wayne, who's the actual person in charge of this growing group.

"How's the kitty feeling today? Well and truly abused, but utterly satisfied?" Sophie asks, wiggling her eyebrows to further drive home her point of what kitty she's talking about.

"It's the same as every other time you've asked me this question."

"Satisfied," she interjects. Satisfied is most certainly not how I would describe it.

Trevor has the capability of being a good lay, but his primary concern is getting his rocks off. Satisfying the woman he's with is nothing more than an afterthought and one he doesn't think about often enough. More than once, I've had to wait for him to fall asleep prior to taking matters into my own hands. Something he caught me doing once mid-act. Which must have been a hit to his manhood because it's the only time he screwed me the way I wanted to be fucked. After which, he informed me he better never catch me doing that shit again unless he has given me the very explicit instruction to touch myself while he watches.

"Fucked. It feels fucked," I correct as we make our way over to where the damn meeting will be held. I don't miss the glares from the group of women who believe they should be the ones sauntering out of his place. They're welcome to it because he's not the only dick in this camp. Sophie, being Sophie, waves at most of them and flicks off the others. Which means she's about as well-liked around here as I am.

"So, how pissed do you think Richard Cabeza is after the epic fuckaroo yesterday?"

"Ya know, if he ever figures out why you call him that, he's gonna lose his shit, right?"

"Well, since he's more worried about bulking his muscles than his brain, I don't think I have much to worry about there."

"Yeah, but the triple bitches." I look in the direction of the three Wayne and Trevor groupies, Candy, Mandy, and Sandy. Yep, their fucking names rhyme. Something they like to point out every chance they get. The dumbasses even try to claim it was written in the stars for them to find each other and become best friends. Proof positive it's a sign of all the good things to come. I like to remind them it was a rider named Death, which means these three coming together isn't written in the damn stars, and in fact, it signifies the end is near. In other words, it's a bad fucking omen. "Are smart enough and would have no issues telling him. So you better watch how loud you say it."

She giggles while looping her arm in mine so she can drag me toward the meeting I have no desire to take part in. In fact, if the memories of them didn't still plague me, then I would question my reason for being here at all. "Oh, Richard can go suck on a lemon."

Richard Cabeza is Soph's nickname for Wayne because she can't stand him. A sentiment I share but keep to myself. Wondering what the hell this means? Well, if you add Dick, another name for Richard, to Cabeza, the Spanish word for head, you get... Dickhead.

Five minutes later, the field is packed. Wayne, Trevor, and the rest of their thuggish gang have taken their place on the makeshift stage. They had constructed to further prove they're the big cheeses running things around here. As if anyone is contesting this shit. Wayne and Trevor alone rule with an iron fist. If you step out of line, you either end up eating through a straw, waiting for broken bones to mend, or—in some cases, depending on the egregiousness of your fuck up—you vanish altogether.

"So a group of men and women leave here with one task, to retrieve new members and deliver them to the camp, but is this what happened? No, not by a fucking long shot because not only are most of our new members food for the vultures, but it seems the ones sent to retrieve them are lying facedown in the fucking dirt too. So, does anyone have anything to say about this monumental fuck up?"

I start to open my mouth to tell him the same thing I said this morning, this being he wouldn't have to ask if his ass had been there with us, but one look from Trevor has me snapping my jaw shut.

"It was on account of one of those fucking horsemen." There's a word that's bound to piss off old Richard Cabeza.

"A fucking horseman, huh? Well..." he pauses to look over at Trevor, who in turn glances at the guy to his right before he leans forward and mumbles the man's name in our illustrious leader's ear. "Chuck, one of the few jobs you have at my camp is to put down these god-forsaken riders, not LOSE TO THEM! So is this what you're telling me happened? You LOST to one of these fucking riders?"

"We-we weren't pre-prepared for one of them to show up," he stammers. Oh, for the love of Pete, this idiot needs to shut the hell up. But apparently, he hasn't learned his lesson yet since he continues with his idiot-of-the-day commentary. "He wanted a woman who was traveling with one of the new recruits."

"A woman. I can completely understand the issue now."

"You-you can?"

"Yes. Because don't you know most wars have been waged over pussy, especially when it's great pussy. So tell me, Chuck, was it just pussy or great pussy?"

"I-I-I don't no-know. I didn't sam-sample it."

"Didn't sample it. What a fucking shame," he says with a mocking laugh as he hits Trevor's chest. An act that causes a laugh from his second while this moron keeps digging the hole deeper and deeper for himself.

"Well, what's there to be done? A being sent here to destroy us found the power of pussy, and now he wants it more than he wants to kill us. Perhaps we should all take a fucking knee and bow to the bitch who saved us all with nothing more than her sweet, wet cunt."

Chuck makes the mistake of laughing before saying, "What's a man to do?"

Every person surrounding him takes several very deliberate steps back while I adjust the bow slung over my shoulder. Wayne looks at Trevor once while he beckons Chuck to join them. Now, most people with half a brain would know this wasn't going to end well for them, but not old Chuckie Boy since he bounds his ass up on the stage like Wayne is going to offer him a spot in his inner council.

Wayne drapes his beefy arm over Chuck's slender shoulder to further perpetuate his ruse while he leans closer to him. In the same deceptive manner he used to lull Chuck into a false sense of security, his tone remains calm the entire time he informs us, "You kill the fucker, Chuckie, much like this."

I'm not sure if Chuck even realized Wayne is the one responsible for the pain I suspect he feels in his lower abdomen until he pulls the blade out and wipes it on the dying man's jacket.

"Any further questions about how we deal with these motherfucking riders?" He pauses, letting his gaze surf over the stunned faces of the men and women gathered before snapping. "Perfect, now get some rest. We'll be heading out in a few days."

When I turn to leave, a hand on my arm stops me. I know who it is prior to him saying a word. "I saw what you wanted to do, pet, and I don't fucking appreciate you doing the opposite of what I instructed."

"And what was that?"

"To keep your fucking thoughts to yourself about where Wayne should or should not have been during the extraction." Extraction? What the hell are we, Navy Seals, Green Berets, Army Rangers? I can assure you we aren't any of these things or anywhere near as honorable. A distinction my dad possessed. "We will discuss this further tonight."

"I'm sure we will."

"Don't get fucking cute, Ember," he snaps before strolling over to the triple bitches.

"Wouldn't dream of it," I murmur as my hand finds the rings around my neck.

~One Year Earlier~

The punch is something I wasn't prepared for, and because I let myself get distracted, it sends me plummeting to my ass. Even as I lay here on the ground staring up at the sky, panting, I can hear his frustrated sigh.

"Damn it, Ember! How many times do I have to tell you to keep your damn head out of the clouds? Do you think the pricks out here will give you a second chance?"

"No, Dad."

"Then how about you stop playing games and focus?"

"Yes, Dad."

"Hey, knock the damn attitude off. I'm trying to teach you how to defend yourself because I can promise you that the assholes in this world won't stop with only hitting you."

70

"Heaven forbid someone might actually want to deflower your little princess."

"I'm not talking about having a relationship with someone. I'm talking about these pricks raping you—"

"Pete!" Mom — always the pragmatic one — is trying again to reel my dad in before he goes into one of his hour-long tirades about the way the world is today. How idiots who would love to get their hands on a girl like me are roaming the roads. Which in dad terms, 'a girl like me,' translates to a virgin. The thing is, I haven't been a virgin for a long time. I lost this distinction in the back seat of Billy Horner's car long before the first horseman started his march. Something I would prefer having back since it was about as alluring as being mauled by a damn black bear. Even less when he kept telling everyone at school how he was the man until I told them all his little dick would say otherwise.

I do like sex, and from what I'm told by the guys I am with, I'm pretty good at it. Too bad I can't say the same about them. But even if the men I've been with don't satisfy me the same way I do them, it's still a release, and nowadays, any release is a welcome one. Specifically when it's of the orgasm kind. The issue is there are few opportunities for the old bump and grind when your dad never lets you out of his sight.

Had I known what we would face that night, I might have welcomed the lecture since it would have been the last lesson Dad would give.

I can still hear my mom's shrieking cries when my dad stumbled forward several steps and then collapsed to his knees. Even now, I can feel the heat from the fire surrounding me. But the worst part is the memories of my mom's desperate pleas for me to run. Because I did. I ran like a scared little girl, but not before I committed to memory the hazy form of the one responsible for everything. The one I owe every bit of my heartache to and the one I plan to kill the second I get the chance. A bastard who never knew their names or the love they shared. But one I fucking promise will pay for his mistakes. And I don't care that he's the one they call....

Pestilence.

Chapter Seven: I'm What Now?

*M*Y BROTHER'S WATCHFUL gaze informs me of two things: he fears what my arrival at this camp means, as much as he is concerned for the well-being of the little lamb. The first, he need not worry about. The second is no longer a concern he must bear.

"Brother, a word?" Pestilence quietly asks as he walks by me.

"Pestilence?" the one who put herself between him and me says. The concern lacing this one-word question makes it apparent she is closer to him than the others.

"My brother need not fear me, daughter of Eve."

"Greer."

"Greer?"

"Yeah, you know, as opposed to a daughter of Eve. My name is Greer." Ah, so this is who Avalon meant when she spoke of the one my brother risks his mission for. She is attractive and a mortal my brother would be drawn to because her demeanor is much like his. Calm, meticulous, and careful, the exact opposite of me.

We walk over to where he has established a hold for his horse. His companion is a perfect match for my brother, and I am happy to see him again. Upon my approach, the snort he grants me confirms he has also missed me.

"It's good to see you as well, old friend," I say, patting his snout affectionately.

"Thank you for returning the lamb."

"You know this is not what I'm here for."

"One could hope. So if this is not what you came for, what is?"

"I was advised there may be a gathering of mortals who oppose our mission and arrival here."

"Do you believe we would react any differently if it was they who invaded our world and threatened to reap us?"

"I suppose we would not have a choice much as they do not since this is our divine path, not theirs."

"Will you not stay your hand for a time?"

The answer I give him, I suspect, is not what he believed he would receive. "I have not killed any of them." He releases a visible sigh of relief a beat too soon. "Yet."

"Brother," he groans.

"We should return to the matter at hand. A group of individuals oppose us. Which means they present a risk to anyone around us. This includes your girl friend," I say this last part, slowly trying to recall the correct phrase used by the little lamb.

"Girl friend? I don't understand this term. What is it?" The only answer I can give him is a shrug, but I will inquire about this further when I am alone with Avalon.

"We leave today," I tell Pestilence. I pat his companion once more before turning to retrieve the lamb. At present, she is hugging the tiny human who was with her when I discovered her beneath the rubble.

"Come, Bella Agnellu, we are leaving."

"No! Wait. Avalon isn't going anywhere with you. You... you big ox," the fiery one says as she looks at my brother. I am unsure what she thought this would accomplish since he is also coming with us, and neither he nor I will leave her behind. "Why the hell are you still walking away with her?"

"The lamb comes with me."

"Do something, bow boy," she yells at Pestilence. When my brother raises one brow in confusion, she proceeds, "Shoot him with the big ass bow you got strapped on your back."

She intended my brother to be the one to intercede on the lamb's behalf. He wasn't.

"She stays," the one named Xander says as he grabs her arm.

"It would behoove you to remove your fucking hand from her," I growl, advancing on the one who felt he could deny me what I wanted.

"I'm not letting you take her."

"And who do you propose will stop me?" I ask while reaching for the sword strapped to my back.

"Stop. Stop it," Avalon yells as she puts herself between them and me.

"War, brother, please allow the lamb to remain with them."

"She comes with me, as will you. It seems our task does not include these mortals in this camp since I sense your protection upon the sons of Adam and daughters of Eve hiding here. But we do have an uprising that needs to be halted."

"Fine." He snarls.

"Fine?" Greer asks as she steps closer to Pestilence before placing her hand on his arm.

"Greer, my brother is right. We must stop them because they pose a risk to you and Wren. Something I will not allow."

"But what about…." She stops, unable to continue her thought. It is clear this daughter of Eve cares for my brother, and the way he places his hand upon her face makes it clear he also cares for her.

"Bring her brother. Bring all of them."

"Why? Why would you want them to travel with us?"

"Because I will require an army. They can be the start."

"No," the lamb yells, repositioning herself between the people in this camp and me. She is much stronger than many of her kind. An attribute I admire. "Take me; just leave them alone."

"Hell no, if you're going, then so am I, A," Suki declares as she storms toward her cabin. Her fiery temper flaring to life makes for an amusing sight.

"You have until tomorrow to gather what possessions you wish to take," I announce before taking the lamb's arm to lead her back to my horse. I place her where she belongs… right in front of me.

"Wait. Where the hell are you going?" the one called Xander snaps.

"The lamb and I have something we must attend to."

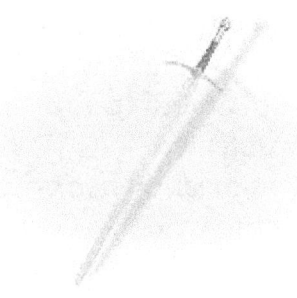

~Avalon~

It's humiliating having this, to coin a phrase from Suk, big ox manhandling me with so little effort. I would have loved to climb up on his horse without his help, but the fact is, as big as Ghost and Storm are, this beast is twice their size, making it impossible for me to climb on top of him. But have no fear because the always helpful War is there to assist and has no issues pulling me on the horse. I just wish he wouldn't put me in front.

I admit I'm torn between leaving my family behind and having them with the riders. The thing is, I know traveling with the riders presents a risk, but leaving them unprotected can be almost as dangerous. It's a shit situation no matter how you look at it, but in the end, I believe having them with these riders is the best of a shitty situation. If I had it my way, they would stay here safe and sound, with Pestilence as their guardian.

I don't understand what War and I could possibly have to do. Regardless, he wasted no time leaving camp. Only after he and Pestilence decided on the location where we would meet up tomorrow at the specified time.

Like yesterday, we rode for almost an hour in the same direction we traveled then. If he felt we needed to do something, why in the hell did we not do it last night or, for that matter, this morning? I would have preferred this to him showing up at our camp and demanding his brother leave it unprotected.

"Tell me what you meant when you use the words girl-friend when explaining who this Greer is to my brother."

"First, it's one word. Girlfriend. And I suppose it's similar to a wife only without the piece of paper."

"Wife?"

"Yeah, the person you choose to spend the rest of your life with."

"Chosen. The word girlfriend means chosen."

"I suppose so."

"Either it is, or it isn't."

His stupid response has me grumbling a slew of curse words under my breath, but if he's anything like his brother, then the best thing I can do is answer him. "If this is the word you will understand, then yes."

"You could have saved us both a lot of time by using the correct word then, Bella Agnellu."

"Stop. Calling. Me that." His response is to laugh, which leaves me seething in front of him. If this rider knows what's good for him, he'll keep his mouth shut.

We rode the rest of the trip in silence after he figured out I would not answer any more of his stupid questions. I am preparing to ask him where he's taking me when we arrive at our destination. Imagine my surprise when he stopped his horse in front of the same house we stayed at last night.

"Um, War, why are we here? I thought you said we had something we needed to attend to."

"We do. Sleep."

"We could have done that back in camp."

"Not without their watchful eyes upon us."

"What the hell do you think is going to happen?" A wicked but sexy smile slides across his face, making me wonder what he has planned.

"Because I felt you may want to return to the bed you were so comfortable in last night. I know my body is ready for another restful night of sleep. Perhaps you will wish to sleep on top of me again."

"Hard pass."

"The day is still young, Bella Agnellu." Something tells me this is going to be a long night. As I creep behind him up the steps, I'm not paying attention and run headlong into his back when he comes to an abrupt stop to hold the door open for me. The grin that my red face elicits from him tells me everything I need to know. It's going to be a very... very long fucking night.

*****

At the moment, we are occupying opposite ends of the table in the dining room. It's one of those long-ass ostentatious damn things you must yell when seated at one end so the person on the opposite side can hear you. This, in part, is why neither of us speaks. The other reason is that we had a heated argument. Well, I argued... he laughed. Which, I can assure you, only pissed me off more. Especially since he doesn't have a damn clue what he's talking about.

I stormed in here, hoping to get away from him, but of course, he felt he needed to follow. And now he's perched at one end while I seethe at the other. A playful grin covers his face as my fingers drum the table. When he surges to his feet, I believe he's finally grown tired of the silent treatment. Note to self: this can be useful when he's being pig-headed. If you want to make a rider leave you alone, ignore them. Excellent advice, Avalon, and not a moment too soon because I had had enough of his gloating.

Or at least it was my hope.

But unlike my initial belief—the one which had him leaving—he seems to have other plans as he dramatically drags the chair he was sitting on to my end of the table. I figure he does this because only the chairs at the head of the table have armrests; the rest do not, and I'm sure he knew if he didn't, I would have stormed down to the chair he had just vacated.

"Do you plan to remain silent for the rest of the evening? Because if so, I say we retire now."

"Listen rider, I understand you don't know us, but I can guarantee I'm not full of shit."

"I did not declare you were full of anything. I merely disagreed with your statement, u mo Bella Agnellu."

"And you think you know what a human needs more than I do?"

"I have had thousands of years to watch your kind."

"My kind?" I snap, letting my frustration seep out with my question.

"Retract your claws, Bella Agnellu," he laughs. "I merely meant humans. I have watched you mortals for thousands of years."

"Well, I don't give a shit because I'm telling you, if I don't eat soon, I'm going to starve."

"And as I have said, this is simply untrue. Your kind—" The pointed look I give him has the rider correcting his words. "Humans are capable of sustaining life for months without food."

"Yeah, and what's your stance on water?"

"This you require no less than four to five days, and since you ate only yesterday, you do not require nourishment today. You may desire it, but this is where it ends."

"Okay, then I want to eat something, asshole."

"Fine." He tells me as he stands and offers me his hand.

"Fine? We just sat here for over an hour, and now you're *fine* with me eating."

"Yes." I huff my frustration, which only serves to make him laugh again.

"Nevermind. I think I've had enough of your sparkling personality for one day. I'm going to bed."

"Okay," he says as he turns to follow me.

"Alone, rider!" He gives me a wicked grin, but thankfully he doesn't follow any further. To ensure he won't come in, I lock the door before falling into the bed I now refer to as my own little slice of paradise.

*****

I'm not sure how long I have been up here because I must have fallen asleep, but the nagging sense of someone looming over me has me dragging my heavy eyes open. Only to discover it's not a someone. It's a something... one pain-in-the-ass rider named War.

"How did you get in here? I know I locked the damn door."

"And you believed this would stop me?" he asks with a playful grin tipping the corners of his lips.

"It is the entire point of a lock," I mumble as I flip over, turning my back to him so I can return to the second thing I wanted to do tonight, sleep.

"Then may I suggest you use something I cannot open by merely applying some extra force." I sigh, knowing there isn't a lock in this world that would fit this damn description. But when I inhale, something heavenly fills my nostrils. My eyes snap open only to discover a plate of food fit for a king held under my nose by the hand of the rider, who told me I didn't need it. I suppose it's a good thing he has such quick reflexes since I would have knocked the plate out of his hand when I bolted upright if he didn't.

"You made me something to eat?"

"You said you were hungry. So yes. I made you something to eat. May I sleep in bed with you now?"

"NO!"

"Why not?"

"Because us 'mortals' don't go around sleeping with just anyone."

"Are you sure of this? Because I can assure you—"

"Yeah, okay, some do, but this human doesn't sleep with just any person." He opens his mouth to interrupt me. Since I have little doubt he planned to point out the obvious, this being he is anything but human, I course correct so I can prevent him from interjecting his thoughts on this matter. "Or riders. So my answer remains no."

"Then permit me to sit with you while you eat."

"What is it with you?"

"Let us say I enjoy your company. Something many of your kind—excuse me, mortals... cannot claim. Nor will they ever." He must have recognized the argument I was fully prepared to nail him concerning his word choice. So he corrected himself from saying the word I hate him using when referring to us, which means he drops the word 'kind' and replaces it with mortals. Although I'm not sure how fond I am of being referred to as nothing more than a mortal, either.

I don't know what the meat is on the plate, and if I'm being honest, I'm not sure I want to know. I can tell you one thing though, I haven't seen any chickens running around since our arrival yesterday. Regardless, it's delicious, and I devour every morsel along with the vegetables I know War procured from the backyard greenhouse. Hell, even the company is enjoyable.

War recounts several of his memories of humanity over the last hundred centuries. I was never a fan of history, but hearing it from someone who witnessed it firsthand and not some bullshit half-truth or outright lie written in history books makes me want to hear more. The thing is, with my belly full and my body all toasty warm and comfy in this bed, it doesn't take long before I drift off to sleep listening to him talk.

*****

My body jerks, and for a second, I don't remember where the hell I am, but after seeing the plate on the nightstand, it doesn't take long until everything returns in a flash. Based on the moonlight filtering through the window, I would have to guess it has to be around one or two in the morning. I release a content little sigh, knowing I still have plenty of night left to sleep. With this happy idea dancing through my head, I snuggle further into the pillow.

I am almost back to sleep when another thought occurs to me. Why the hell did I wake up? But I am not left questioning this for long because the answer comes faster than I expected when a crash from somewhere on the ground floor jolts me upright. I am preparing to holler out for War to inquire if he's okay when a hand from someone lying next to me covers my mouth to seal off all thoughts of this.

My head whips over, only to find the rider staring down at me. What the hell! How do I keep ending up in bed with him? He brings his finger to his lips in the universal keep your mouth shut motion. When he is confident I won't blurt the question he has to know I want to ask, he leans over to position his mouth against my ear to give me his straightforward directive.

"Stay here, u mo Bella Agnellu. It seems we have guests I need to attend to." The warmth of his breath and how it skims over my neck has my skin becoming one big goosebump. Another thing I wasn't prepared for tonight.

Before he can slide off the bed, the door flies open, revealing three bulky men standing in the hallway.

"Well, what do we have here?" With a pending sense of déjà vu, I am thrust back to the night Death and I sat next to a pond, only to have stupid men ask this precise question when they stumbled across us. And much like that night, I am just as confident tonight will not end well for the raiders who had the misfortune of breaking into the only house around here occupied by a rider of the damn apocalypse. A rider the men and women of this world have not yet met. But something he plans to rectify if his reply is any indication.

"Unfortunately for you, since you are not under my brother's protection, I'm the being who will teach you the folly of waking a rider when he is sleeping next to such an exquisite beauty."

"I'm a… what… now?" I mumble as he climbs off the bed, just as the men slowly filter into the room, but I only receive a laugh and a quick wink from this infuriating rider, followed by a simple answer.

"I'll be right back. We can revisit what I said upon my return, u mo Bella Agnellu."

Twenty seconds passed between the instant his feet slammed against the bedroom floor and the men who invaded the house to end up in a bloody heap. Twenty damn seconds is all it took for this massive rider to eliminate the men in the room. Two minutes to clear the house and another sixty seconds to have my ass deposited in front of him on his horse as we rode to meet up with Pestilence and the others from our camp.

I don't have the first damn clue about how I went from living with my family to being in another horde. Not to mention how I ended up traveling with not one rider but two. Or how War went from no followers to the start of his army.

Chapter Eight: The Man With A Plan

I *HATE HOW* Trevor thinks he owns me. The problem is, I knew what the hell I was getting myself into when I took him up on his offer and followed him into his room.

One night of wanting to feel anything other than the despair my life had spiraled headlong into since the night I lost my parents, and this is what I get. A prick who is only slightly better than a lousy lay. A guy who doesn't give a shit about me or anyone except maybe Wayne. Who happens to be an even bigger asshole than Trevor.

Two group leaders who don't value the insignificant peons they have deemed us to be even though we underlings are the ones who put them in their position of power. Not to mention the granddaddy of them all, the one thing that has always been the number one thing I strove for and the one thing it seems I have lost....

My damn freedom.

I have lost my right to decide how, who, and when I want to fuck someone and if I want to remain with them after said lay. Not to mention stifling my normally outspoken personality because Trevor is quick to tell me my actions are a representation of him. How this arrogant asshole comes up with this shit is beyond me, but then again, I did say he was arrogant. He seems to think the world revolves around him, his best friend Wayne, and... well, for lack of a better word, his dick. Which, may I remind you, isn't all that spectacular.

However, if you ask the triple bitches, they will tell you a vastly different story than mine since they have each taken a turn. It's a tall tale about how he rocked their world. To which I call bullshit because if he was so stellar, why wouldn't he have pulled out all the stops when fucking me yet?

I'll tell you why.

He buys into the hype those three dimwits are selling. What I don't understand is why he's chosen to hold on to me when I in no way feel the same as the giggling trio of idiots waving at him while he grins at them.

"You're staring," Sophie tells me in a singsong voice.

"Yeah, I know."

"Wanna clue me in on why? Because I happen to know you don't go all weak in the knees for a certain leader who doesn't know how to make your kitty purr."

"Really, Soph, kitty?"

"I have a New Year's Resolution—"

"It's not New Year's yet."

"So call it a head start."

"Okay, Soph, I'll bite. What head start resolution results in you referring to my vagina as a kitty?"

"The one where I try to clean up my potty mouth." I raise my eyebrows and bite down on my lips, trying my best not to laugh at her. "What? I can totally do this shit. Oh shit! Fuck! Oh, damn it. I can," she yells before she slips again.

"Because you just proved it with that last bit. I'm pretty sure you only need an ass, cock, cunt, and prick to complete the full montage of your dirty words."

"What can I say... just needed to start with something easy."

"Like my—"

"Kitty. Now you're getting it."

"Come on, my foul mouth shameless friend, we have work to do." As we walk away, the triple bitches take this second to increase the volume of their conversation, all hoping to get a rise out of me. The only reason they are willing to risk my frustration is that Trevor is still lingering not far, and if I hit them, he'll come running. Because, of course, he would see this as an affront to his standing within the group.

I still can't figure out how my actions affect him, but he sure as hell likes to tell me this shit repeatedly until one of two things happens. Either I storm out of his room, having heard enough from him, or he fucks me, trying to prove he is the one in charge.

Only once has he come close to hitting me. This was when I tried to point out the obvious: if he would only distance himself from me, then my unacceptable behavior would no longer affect him. Something he isn't so keen to do. Although I have no damn idea why.

"So Candy, the scuttlebutt is Trevor plans to make you scream his name tonight... repeatedly," Sandy says entirely too loud for the distance between them. But then again, it was more meant for me to hear as opposed to this airhead's desire to confirm the gossip she was probably present for anyway.

"He does," she confirms while swirling the sucker in her mouth. Her eyes remain glued to me the entire time. For Christ's sake, is she kidding me with this damn not-so-subtle use of the sucker? It's like high school, only with older, less intelligent students.

"I'm sure he can't wait to be with a woman who knows how to please the man she's with again. Especially since he hasn't had the pleasure of our company in the last few weeks. I can only imagine the bitch he has been fucking is a lousy lay." Okay, Mandy's snarky response was clearly directed at me. But I couldn't care less; their issue is my friend sure as shit does.

"Mandy." When Mandy looks from me to Sophie, she continues. "You three dumb bitches wouldn't know how to please a man even if he was a sex-deprived virgin." After this, she kisses her middle finger before flicking them off. This garnered the reaction Soph wanted since they stood there slack jaw, shooting daggers in our direction.

"Bye-bye now, triple bitches," Sophie says with a smug grin and arrogant finger wave before looping her arm in mine as we head to our job assignments.

*****

By the time I get to my room, I'm exhausted. It's been a long day, and the only thing I want to do is wash up and fall into my bed. I have no more than closed my eyes when someone storms through the door.

"Did you forget I said I had plans for us tonight?" Trevor, of course, it has to be this prick. Why can't he take a damn hint?

"I'm tired, Trev," I opt to use his pet name rather than Trevor or the name I would prefer to call him, asshole.

"What the hell do you have to be so damn tired about."

"I don't know, maybe the five-hour forced scavaging party you and Wayne put me down for."

"If you don't want to do shit jobs, stop being so damn disagreeable." Lifting my upper body off the bed, I narrow my eyes at him while forcing myself to remain calm.

"And I suppose you're the one who decides when I am and am not being disagreeable?"

"Now you're getting it." He says as he returns the picture of my parents to the shelf. Besides their wedding rings, it's the only other piece of memorabilia I have of them. "Come on before we're late."

"Late? What the hell could we possibly be late for?" I ask as I lie back down and try to find the same comfy spot I had before he interrupted me.

"Get your ass out of bed, Em, before I yank you out and toss you over my fucking shoulder."

"Bullshit." This was a mistake because the word no sooner tumbles past my lips before being pulled from the bed and tossed over his damn shoulder. He doesn't waste any additional time waiting for me to get ready, and he doesn't seem to mind that the only thing I have on is my panties and a thin camisole. "Trevor, I don't have any goddamn clothes on."

90

"Had you got your ass out of bed when I told you to, you could have gotten dressed, but since you wanted to test my patience, you go like you are."

I thrash, hoping to break his hold on me, which ends with his hand slapping my ass. This fucker just smacked my ass in the middle of camp with dozens of people milling around to witness the humiliating display. I am so furious the instant he drops me to my feet; my hand comes up to hit him, but I drop it just as fast when the reality of where he took me becomes clear.

Wayne's war room.

This is the one place in the camp that is off-limits unless the prick himself grants you permission to enter. And it seems Trevor and I are not the only ones in here tonight. The entire council is present and staring at my half-naked ass. Of all nights for me to strip out of my clothes, it had to be tonight.

"Trevor, mind telling me why you brought Ember to the meeting with no clothes on?"

"She wouldn't get her ass out of bed, brother. So she comes as is."

"And you didn't think a half-dressed bitch wouldn't be a damn distraction?"

"Well, since these fuckers all know she's mine," I want to argue this point with him because I don't belong to anyone, least of all Trevor. I also have some thoughts about Wayne calling me a bitch, but seeing as I'm not exactly dressed for a fight, discretion wins out. Which means I opt to keep my mouth shut rather than the argument I had all prepared to unleash on them. They better be smart enough not to let their eyes linger for long unless they want to deal with the asshole who believes he owns me.

"They better remember their place," he finishes.

"Damn, if I knew this was what we had in store for tonight's meeting, I would have been on fucking time." Fred, the newest member to join the council, moans when he struts in, which brings Trevor's full attention toward him.

"What the hell are you assholes all looking at?" Trevor snarls.

"Um, Ember's tits," Jon says with a grin as he leans around Phil to get a better look at me.

"Keep your fuckin eyes to yourself," Trevor snarls before he yanks his jacket off and tosses it in my direction. Oh, now he aspires to be some chivalrous knight in shining fucking armor. Where the hell was this version of him when he was carrying my ass out of my room and through the entire camp like this?

After I'm covered, the meeting can finally begin, and I am again left questioning what I'm doing here. Wayne unrolls something and places it on the table. His beefy finger lands on what I can now see is a map.

"This is our destination."

"Why would we go to Alabama?" I can't help myself, and I blurted the question before I stop to consider whether I'm an active participant here.

"Because it's where Fort Gaines is located." Wayne may have answered me, but the irritation that accompanied his response, along with Trevor's eyes snapping to mine, informed me I was supposed to be a silent observer tonight and nothing more.

"Why the hell are we commandeering Fort Gaines? There are much more defensible forts in Alabama," Phil asks as he points to a different location on the map. "Like—"

"The fucking place is already occupied by a bunch of men and women. Do you really want to fight another group for it? I would prefer keeping our forces intact rather than losing half of them for a pointless fucking fight. Particularly since this place doesn't have anyone we have to evict before taking over."

"It also only has three damn walls protecting it, leaving our asses wide open for anyone who wants to take advantage."

"This is why we need builders. We'll build the fourth damn wall to prevent leaving our asses out in the wind. Does this satisfy your goddamn objection, Phil, or do you want to bitch about something else?."

"How long do you think we have before these riders are breathing down our neck?"

"How fucking long do you think you have left if you talk to me like that again? Fort Gaines is our destination. If you don't fuckin like it, shove off," Wayne barks as he stands to full height. Apparently, I'm not the only one who didn't get the memo that this isn't a collaboration. They discuss a few minor details, but the conversation ends when a knock interrupts us.

"I see the entertainment portion of the evening is about to begin," Jon says as he straightens his collar and smooths back his hair. Entertainment? What the hell kind of entertainment are they talking about?

"On that note, I will take my leave. Gentlemen... and Ember. I'll see you in the morning," Phil announces as he picks up his jacket. "Ember, as always, it has been a pleasure."

"See you tomorrow, Phil," I reply, placing my hand over his. His smile is off, and I'm unsure how to read it or what it means.

"Me too," Henry says, following Phil to the door. I am not left wondering long what kind of entertainment they have planned, and I can assure you I don't plan on partaking in it either. Candy, Mandy, Sandy, and the dumb girl who follows them around like a lost puppy, Samantha, enter.

Candy sets her sights on Trevor, who is leaning against the table, and something about how these four women stroll in tells me this is a regular occurrence at these meetings of our elite leaders. Is this why he brought me here to witness this shit? Did he think it would bother me? Because I can assure him it doesn't.

The bitch who leads the other bobbleheads continues to pretend I'm not standing here when she saunters over to him and presses her lips to his. I don't know if he thought this would bother me. I can promise him it doesn't matter in the least. In fact, with any luck, he'll fall head over heels in love with the twit, and I can return to being nothing more than a member of this group.

"I'm taking a page out of Phil and Henry's book," I announce as I turn to leave. "Until tomorrow."

"Come on, Em. I thought maybe we could—"

"Don't fucking finish that sentence, Jon," Trevor snarls as he pushes Candy to her knees in front of him. His furious glare is settled on Jon, waiting to see if he'll press his luck, but the slimy bastard I wouldn't touch with a ten-foot pole makes the wise choice to keep his mouth shut and return his attention to Samantha.

I'm almost out the door when I hear Trevor's command for me. "My room, Ember. Not yours."

"I think you have all the entertainment you need tonight. I'm sure Candy will be happy to keep your bed warm." She looks up at him with a hopeful expression.

She gives me a triumphant sneer over her shoulder when he seems to agree and unbuttons his pants.

"No teeth, sweetheart." Thank god! I can't help the grin sliding over my face as I spin to exit the room. In my head, I'm lifting my arm in victory, confident I just dodged a bullet, but he erases my glee with three words just before I arrive at the door. "My room, Ember!"

I slam through the exit before storming to the fucking room I have no damn desire to stay in tonight or any other night for that matter. For the millionth time, I contemplate grabbing my shit and Sophie to get the hell out of dodge, but I have a reason to be here.

And my reasons differ vastly from that of the ones who believe they are in charge or the men and women who join up. For the majority of the people here, they joined for any semblance of safety this group could offer them. They believe living within a group of people will keep them safe. But I have to question their logic because, let's be honest, when these riders find out what this group was created for, I don't imagine it will be long before they come here to shut it down. For me, it's about killing a rider; for this reason alone, I'll stay. But more importantly, it's why I permit this asshole to treat me like shit....

All so I can bring a soon-to-be-dead rider straight to me.

Chapter Nine: Choices Have Consequences

*N*OT BEING ABLE to see what happened to her drives me crazy, and every time I shatter the walls holding my restraints, Michael and Gabriel move me to another cell. They enchant each one with a stronger spell than the last.

I now regret not asking War to protect Avalon. I figured because Pestilence understood she was unlike the other mortals in their realm to me, he would be the one to look after her. The issue is I don't know what fate befell Pestilence. If he were able to return here to update me on their status, I know he would have. He must have sensed my growing apprehension as they raced to retrieve his chosen. Or did he? It is possible his fear for the woman he cares for may have overshadowed everything else.

And Avalon must question why I have not come to her. It has been a year since I invaded her dreams when she was held in the camp and months since her soul traveled to me. I know it is unfair of me to hope she yet remembers the time we shared together since I have repeatedly declared I want her to find happiness in her mortal life, but a large piece of my heart cannot help the desire to feel her lips upon my own.

I also realize at this rate, I will be called back to her realm soon, but this time, it will no longer be to judge. It will be to reap. Something I am still desperate to halt.

"Thanatos, you should refrain from breaking your chains," Raphael quietly advises from the other side of the cell door.

"If they wish me to stop, they only need to remove them."

"I must beseech you to halt any further attempts; if you do not, Michael will be granted his wish."

"And which one is that? Because when it comes to me where Michael is concerned, there are many."

"The one which puts you in the deepest of prisons. You will be left to toil in darkness until the lamb beckons you forth to begin your task or time has erased all thoughts of their world. It is a lonely existence, not one I would wish on any being, least of all the reaper who has been loyal to our father since the beginning of time."

"I do not fear Michael."

"But he fears you, and he always has. It is this fear that drives his motives to have you chained, bound, and far from our father's grace."

"I will not—"

"Thanatos, please. I promised your brother and one of my oldest friends I would look after you. This is me fulfilling this promise."

Raphael is both a good and just being. The fact he is begging me to halt any further escape attempts, specifically knowing the promise he made War, is something I cannot ignore. The sympathetic sigh I give must confirm I will honor his request; however, if I am to do this, I have a request of my own. "Will you tell me the outcome of Pestilence's battle? The one which ended in my brother's release."

"He is alive and well. The lamb saw to this." Relief washes through me, knowing not only did my brother survive, but so did Avalon.

"I don't understand if Pestilence is well; how is it that War's seal was opened?"

"The lamb was forced to make a choice."

"A choice?"

"Either break the seal and release War upon her world, or Raum would claim Pestilence's soul."

"What! How is this permitted by our father and your brethren?"

"Our creator will not involve himself in any of the outcomes; you know this, Thanatos. As for Michael—the brethren I will assume you are referring to—wishes the mortals to be removed from our father's grace. He does not share your or Pestilence's view of them. He believes there is no hope of redemption. As such, he has cast them aside, which means he will offer no aid to a rider who has embraced their world."

"It is not his place to decide this. It is ours," I growl as I slam my arms forward, raining bits of stone, dust, and debris down on me. Raphael's eyes slipped closed, believing I had reached my limit of remaining their prisoner. It is only because of the respect I hold for him that stops me from bringing the walls holding my chains down around me. The noticeable relief covering his face when the cell remains intact is apparent, but his responses for the remainder of our conversation are given much more cautiously.

"And he believes your decision was swayed not by the populace as a whole but by one soul alone."

"Is one soul not enough to display they are capable of greatness?"

"For most of us, yes."

"But not for all."

"I'm sorry, Thanatos." When I dip my head to thank him for his honesty, he returns the gesture before leaving me to contemplate everything he revealed. It seems the seal to wake War was purposely broken this time, but unlike the last time when she was tricked, this one was a choice she made. A decision to bring another rider to her world to save my brother's soul. Something I will forever be grateful for and something Raum....

Will soon regret.

~Avalon~

We have been traveling for a few weeks now, and I admit to being astonished by the number of willing people joining his ranks. If I'm being honest, not all of them are here of their own accord; some only joined after he destroyed their community.

The one thing I will say about him is he gives them an option. It's a shitty one in my opinion, but a choice is still better than outright death. Any who accepts his offer becomes a soldier among his ranks, and those who cannot fight are given other duties. Something tells me this will not be granted to those men and women rising up against him and his brother.

The other thing is War doesn't let me stray far from his side. And I still think there are times he is flirting with me. I would have said I was being ridiculous if not for Pestilence's eyes searching the sky anytime he overhears his brother's comments. And I swear he is cringing, almost like he is waiting for the sky to open up to allow heaven's warriors to rain down upon us.

I don't know what he's looking for; it sure as hell isn't Thanatos since he has shut me out and Pestilence as well. Something I only know because I asked him. The one time I tried to slip the inquiry into a conversation I was having with War, he gave me a side-eyed glance before replying, 'I have my task... and my brother has his,' with the damn smirk that irritates the shit out of me covering his face. What kind of damn answer is this? But it served its purpose since I haven't brought Thanatos up to him since then.

Tonight is the first night we will be alone since Pestilence joined us. War and I rode out to investigate a

100

town some of the newest soldiers advised us the militia stayed at for a time. Since these men joined his ranks of their own volition, War felt it best to follow up on their information. Not sure why I had to come, but as previously stated, I'm never far from his sight.

For the last hour, he has told me more than once I should bathe in the pond we pitched camp by. While I don't disagree that I could use one, it's too damn cold tonight to do this. Especially since we will be sleeping under the stars on a handful of blankets with nothing more than a campfire to stave off the cold. No tent means no bath for Avalon.

"So your answer remains the same?"

"If the request hasn't changed, then I suppose it means my answer is still a no."

"And this is final?" Again with this question, I don't know why he thinks the answer will change because it hasn't the other fifty times he asked it. So, instead of giving him a verbal response, I arch my eyebrows and tilt my head, hoping he understands the sarcasm the look represents. The 'What do you think my answer is?' expression, which, in my opinion, is universal.

"I suppose you have the right to decline my request," he tells me calmly, which has my previous expression changing to one of confusion. I find it hard to believe he is giving up on this so easy, and apparently, my doubt is well founded because before I can question it, he scoops me up and deposits me into the pond. "While I reserve the right to disagree."

"What the hell, War," I sputter as I scamper to my feet, pushing my wet hair out of my face.

"While I appreciate what my horse does for me, it does not mean I wish to sleep next to one of the beasts of this realm."

"Your point?"

"You have the unpleasant odor often associated with a wet dog, Bella Agnellu. It is a pungent odor that should never be connected with a woman as enchanting as you. Nothing should ever be permitted to detract from the allure of the woman before me."

"I DO NOT smell that bad."

"Are you certain of this because, once again, I reserve the right to disagree. So, for this reason, it is past time you remove the stench."

"No!" I yell as I pull the hair clinging to my neck away.

"As is my way, I will give you a choice. You may wash yourself, or I will do it for you." His uncompromising response is only slightly less infuriating than having him toss me a bottle of shampoo.

"It's fucking freezing, War!"

"Then may I suggest you wash fast." With no other option left, I slam my hands down into the water, splashing the irritating rider standing on the bank with his massive arms crossed over his chest. Which only causes him to laugh.

"One of these damn days, I swear I'm going to knock you on your ass," I mumble as I pull the sweatshirt I was wearing over my head and throw it at him.

"Provided you are clean when you do it, you are welcome to try tonight."

"Go. Away!" I snarl as I lift my shaking hands to my hair to get this freezing-cold pond bath over.

"I have left clean clothes for you over here on the bank. If you require help washing, I will be right over there."

War flicks his head in the direction of the campfire. Did he do this to mock me? He sure fucking did. Which is abundantly obvious as he strolls back to camp while whistling some stupid I dumped the lamb in the lake fucking song.

By the time I finish my forced bath, my fingers are pruney and have taken on a bluish hue. I have more goosebumps covering me than I would have thought possible. And to top off this shitty night, some damn goose keeps swimming by me, and I swear the damn thing is looking at me like I'm an idiot. Although I can't say I disagree with this sentiment. Thankfully, War thought to bring something for me to dry off with; otherwise, my clothes would be soaked in seconds.

I fully plan on ignoring him after returning to camp, but it doesn't seem to be an issue since he is lying on the blankets he has spread out by the fire, fucking sleeping. Nice to know one of us is all warm and toasty, I think while plopping down next to the fire as I begin vigorously rubbing the blanket he provided me to dry off over my wet hair. Here's hoping that the friction from my action and the heat from the fire will have this mop dried soon because the lack of food and water, not to mention the cold makeshift bath he tossed me into, have all converged together to make me tremble, and no amount of heat from the campfire will cease it.

"Much better," he says without removing his arm from over his eyes.

"Fuck off."

"Now-now, Bella Agnellu, I was only attempting to help."

"Next time, don't." My answer is more growl than response. Something I've picked up after traveling with these riders for so long.

"Would you forgive me if I apologized?"

"Probably not."

"That is not a no, mouse."

"It's not a yes either, asshole." I don't miss his chuckle, but he remains silent as I return to drying my hair. When I believe we're done talking, he has to ruin our peaceful surroundings.

"Tell me everything you know about the ones who shot my brother."

"What do you want to know? They are a bunch of assholes. Kind of like a certain rider I know. Hey, maybe you all might get along. Never know, they might become your B.F.F..... You all can form your own club, the assholes who annoy Avalon Alliance."

War laughs, clicks his tongue, and says, "Okay, mouse, you had your fun. Now tell me about the assholes you're so confident I'll get along with."

"Like I said, they're a bunch of jackasses who think they can take on you riders."

"Truly?"

"I wouldn't have said it if it wasn't true." This has him pushing up on his elbow to give me his full attention as we continue our conversation.

"As they have not been at any locations we have looked so far, can you tell me where I can find these brave men?"

"Since I tend to travel with the ones they oppose. And I sort of shot at them during our last meet and greet; they haven't asked me to be a part of their inner fucking circle, War."

"Which means?"

"I have no damn idea where they are," I snap as another shiver passes through me, causing me to tremble violently.

"What is this?" he asks.

"What's what?" I snarl as I put my throbbing head in my hands.

"This thing your body keeps doing."

"It's called shivering, asshole. Something I wouldn't be doing if you didn't toss my ass in a freezing cold pond."

"I would not have had to toss your ass in a freezing cold pond if you had bathed as I instructed."

"Piss off!" This time when a shiver rocks me, my teeth join in, chattering loud enough that the goose who kept me company takes flight.

"Come here," he instructs, and since he is not used to any mortal defying him, I know my answer will only piss him off. I couldn't care less if he's irritated right now since I have been pissed for the last fifteen minutes.

"Hard pass."

"This was not a request, Bella Agnellu."

"Don't know what that means, but my answer is still no."

He sighs, mumbles something under his breath, stands up, marches over to where I am sitting, and scoops me into his arms. He does this so he can carry me over to the bedding he put down before depositing my shivering ass on it. And as confused as I am when I thought he was giving up the place he set up for himself to sleep, it shocks the shit out of me when War lies down next to me and pulls me against his warm body.

"What the hell are you doing?"

"Correcting my grievous error which led to these noises."

"What noises?" I asked through chattering teeth. He looks at me as if I have already answered the question.

"Who knew you humans have such fragile bodies."

"I'll fragile you," I mutter. Although I should have just said it outright since his rumbling chest confirms he heard me, and he's laughing at me again.

"Go to sleep now, u mo Bella Agnellu. We have a long day ahead of us."

"Are you ever going to tell me what the hell this means?"

"Depends."

"On whether I'm a good little lamb or not," I snarl as I flop over, pull the covers over me, hoping they are enough to help me from freezing and tuck my hands under my head. But his response results in the chill slipping away, replaced by heat building from the inside as my eyes fly open.

"On how good you are at convincing me."

Chapter Ten: Growing An Army

*F*URIOUS! THIS SINGULAR emotion explains how I feel about the humans who wish to rise against us. Usually, I would pay them no mind. There will always be those who oppose us. I would expect no different, but if you are going to spread this propaganda inferring you beat back the riders, then at the very least, dare to attempt the feat on the field of battle.

Yet not these mortals. It seems for them, merely perpetuating a falsehood suffices as action. The little human boy my brother protects has more backbone than these cretins. Although, I believe this has more to do with who he is to my brother since I sense Pestilence's essence upon him. It didn't take me long to figure out this was the little one responsible for putting Thanatos into chains. I admit I like him too, except during the times he continues to ask me what I want when I have asked for nothing. The entire conversation is tiresome and frustrating for both of us. Even more when my beautiful lamb laughs at me. Although I enjoy the sound of her laughter, it's something I won't disclose to anyone. Pestilence, in particular, since his face morphs to sheer panic every time he hears me speak about or to the lamb.

The problem is that I have been in a foul mood since learning how I was beaten back by a handful of mortals, a victory I can assure you never happened. Pestilence even uses caution when speaking to me, doing his best not to further rile my ire. If not for my insisting the lamb stay close, she would also avoid interacting with me, which only serves to annoy me further. Something about her calms me, a feat few can claim.

Then there is Pestilence, who keeps asking me what Thanatos told me of his time here. Each time, my response is the same. Nothing. He told me nothing. This always prompts him to ask what he said about the lamb. At first, I advised him he said nothing about his time here, lamb included. This garners a creased brow, crinkled nose, and tight-lipped frown as he stares at the ground. Yet it is his ceaseless chin scratching while he contemplates what to do next that provides me a clear sign he is uncomfortable.

So apparently, this is his way of telling me it is a conversation that should have happened, but since it didn't, the prudent path forward would be to inquire about it, just not from him. My brother Pestilence is many things; peacekeeper among his brethren amongst them.

I can tell you one thing, all of it is compiling together to irritate this rider. This does not bode well for building my army since the last couple of communities we crossed were not offered the opportunity. I destroyed them before any could object, and had I not delayed entering this encampment, they would have suffered the same fate. Instead, I am staring at one pissed-off Bella Agnellu.

"What are you doing? Stop it!" the lamb's face has turned an alarming shade of red.

"Avalon, this is how I build my army."

"It doesn't have to be this way. You could give them a choice."

"They have a choice. They can either submit or die. The choice is theirs. Besides, it is poetic justice since the mortals who accept will help me destroy the humans who oppose us. All of which is still in line with my task."

"Yeah, so what happened in the last three communities? Because I'm pretty friggin sure you didn't give them a damn option," she snaps as she repositions herself to keep me on this side and my quarry at her back.

"Mouse, it is time for you to move aside."

"Do I look like a meek damn mouse to you right now, rider?"

"Brother, I think we can allow—"

"Pestilence, it would be best not to interrupt me while I discipline, u mo Bella Agnellu."

"Discipline?!" Avalon yells as the color on her cheeks intensifies.

"I also think you should refrain from calling her this," Pestilence mumbles as his hand finds the back of his neck.

"Would someone tell me what the hell this means!?"

"Yes, it—"

"NO!" My growled response as my glare settles on my brother has him swiftly rethinking what he was preparing to tell my beautiful lamb.

"NO?" Pestilence corrects with a question.

"Don't press me on this, Brother." My anger is misdirected. It is the mortals who garnered my fury. My brother is nothing more than the unlucky being I'm directing it at.

"Where the hell is Google when you need it," Avalon mutters as she pushes Pestilence and me away from the gate used to mark the entrance to the encampment I was preparing to destroy.

"What is a Goo–gal?" I ask.

"Wouldn't you like to know? Not so fun when the '*you can't understand what the hell this person is saying*' shoe is on the other foot, now is it, rider?"

"I also did not comprehend this. Are you speaking an actual language? Why would I put my shoe on another foot? And what foot are you speaking of? Your foot, Pestilence's foot, whose foot?"

"Your horse, smartass."

"Ha! My horse has no feet, Bella Agnellu."

"Or does he?" she snaps. The lamb believes I do not realize what she is doing, which would be a mistake if not for me enjoying the playful banter between us. At least it is playful for me. I think she is just pissed. This is why I have allowed her to push me further away from the camp. A camp of mortals who should fall to their knees and thank the lamb for saving them.

"Hey, Rider," I whip around to face the man who must not realize what she has done for them, nor does he seem to value his life since he is stalking in our direction. Snaking my arm around Avalon's waist, I pull her behind me. However, my brother must not feel it is sufficient distance between her and the advancing son of Adam since he has now placed himself between my lamb and me.

"You are either incredibly brave or extremely stupid," I tell him as I advance on him. Perhaps this encampment will fall today after all.

"Neither. I wanted to make you an offer," he responds, lifting his hands to show absolute submission while wisely halting any further progression.

"Speak!"

"The word is you're looking for the group who's building an army to oppose you." He stops to await my response. The issue is I have no intention of giving him this. The first rule of battle is never to allow your enemy access to valuable intel. Since I have yet to decide if this son of Adam is a friend or foe, I feel no need to gift this mortal such a boon.

"Okay... well... they have moved southeast of here."

"Where?"

"Alabama."

"Why?"

"They didn't share this with us. I imagine for the same reasons you opted to hold your tongue." Again, I remain silent. He is welcome to come to his own conclusion. "Anyway, they passed through about a week ago. I think they originally thought we would be easy pickings, and when they discovered this wasn't accurate, they wanted us to join them."

"Did any of your group accept?"

"Yes?" he says, drawing the word out in a questioning tone as if unsure if he should provide this information. He shouldn't of course, but his ignorance may be the only thing that prevents me from tearing their world apart.

"How many?" I keep my tone calm and my posture relaxed. There is an art to warfare, one I have perfected since the time of my creation.

"Fuh-five," he stammers, only realizing now he has said too much.

"Five sons of Adam thought to take up arms against my brother and me."

"We-we don't have any-anything to do with it."

"They came from this community?"

"They did."

"The rebels were permitted to leave from here with these sons of Adam?"

"We have women and children."

"As do I." I lift my hand, presenting the women and children who accompany me.

"We-we didn't force—" When I tilt my head, the rest of his thought dies abruptly on his tongue.

"So the rebels were here but remain no longer. Five of your community members decided to leave with them. They are making their way to Al-la-bam-ah, yet you do not know where. And you are freely offering us this information to... what? Appease my brother and me? Do I have the stated facts understood correctly?"

"Ya-yeah," he mutters as he looks over his shoulder before deciding it might be better to voice his response with more authority. I will say he gives a valiant effort even though it remains a monumental failure. "Yes."

"I will assume this information was not granted to me out of the goodness of your heart?"

"Well... um... we were thinking... uh, actually hoping you and the other rider would leave us in peace."

"Ah, so there it is. There is always a catch with you mortals. Am I not correct, brother?"

"I would have to say yes."

"War, they didn't have to tell you anything," the lamb hisses through clenched teeth.

"Correct. And he could have remained within his camp and waited for us to leave. Since you had convinced me to do so."

"Because they knew we were leaving!" she growls as she finally pushes past my brother. "And in case my words were unclear to you, that was sarcasm."

"Historically, when one walks away instead of toward, this constitutes the very meaning of this word, Bella Agnellu."

"I'm going to Bella Agnellu all over your ass," she grumbles more to herself than me. But when I tilt my head while grinning at her, she mumbles something about having no idea what she just said she planned to do to my *ass*.

"No, you do not," I tell her with a laugh. I will accept her face's scarlet color as her way of recognizing this mistake. With my eyes still delighting in her frustration, I provide my response to the mortal who had enough courage to face me. "Five."

"Five? I-I-I'm sorry, I don't understand."

"I will require five of your strongest men to offset the five who left with the rebels."

"War!" Avalon snarls as she lashes out to grab my hand, but Pestilence quickly wraps his arm around her waist to pull her away.

"I… we… the community cannot spare any more."

"How many are within your walls?"

"Roughly fifty families."

"See, you have more than enough to spare a minuscule five. Five fighters who will ensure this community's ongoing survival."

"We—" Before the negotiator can argue his point, an arrow is released. These fools believed I did not see the archers taking up defensive positions. This is the first mistake this group will pay for. The projectile most assuredly meant for me goes wide to the right. If not for my brother's quick reflexes, the damnable thing would have found its mark dead center in Avalon's chest, which is their second and, in my opinion, most dire misstep during this interaction.

Pestilence's howls of pain as the arrow impales his arm rather than the heart of our lamb are only outdone by my furious growls.

"Wait, please," the man implores as his arms fly out from his sides. His hope to stem the increasing wrath burning within me is misguided. Almost as much as his desire to halt any further aggression from his camp. With a roar that sends him to his knees, I jerk my sword from my back while Pestilence nocks his first arrow.

"You think to harm u mo Bella Agnellu and believe there will be no retribution?"

"He. Didn't. Do. Shit!" Avalon again hisses as she struggles to push past my brother to reach me, something I can assure her will not happen because he fears my fury more than hers.

"The arrow embedded in my brother's arm would imply how incorrect this assessment is, mouse."

"He'll heal. Won't you, Pestilence?"

"I—" My pointed glare has my brother falling silent. Somehow, my little mouse slinks past Pestilence and positions herself between the riders preparing to rain heaven's fury down on these fools and them.

"War, leave it alone. Let them live in peace. They gave you intel about where your actual fight is. It's time for us to go. Right. Now!" Could I refuse her request and raze this community? Yes, and she knows it. She understands an army could not stop us if this was our desire, yet she stands there in opposition anyway. Which is the only reason I return my sword to its rightful place.

"You are most fortunate she speaks for your salvation. You should fall on your knees and praise her." The man's eye slid from me over to a seething lamb. Yet he makes the wise choice to accept my directive as non-negotiable when he lowers himself to one knee to bow his head to the woman whose mouth has dropped open. A deed that causes the exact reaction I was hoping for. Her fierce protectiveness rears up and shows me what she is capable of.

"Stand up! You don't bow to anyone, least of all me. War, stop being an ass," she barks as she pushes Pestilence's bow, which he only drops when I nod my agreement.

"There must be some way we can work something out," the man says as he slowly reaches full height.

"Ten."

"What?"

"For attempting to remove the life of someone I value significantly more than any of your lives, you will give me ten of your strongest warriors, or your annihilation will begin."

"They have families!"

"As does the one you shot at, and if not for her, your entire community would have fallen before you stepped out to greet me."

"They have children."

"I don't care. Oh, and I will require the one who shot the arrow. You have ten seconds to decide."

"Please, she's only a child," his desperate pleas hold no sway over me.

"Then you should not have allowed the young one to act as a warrior."

"She is not a warrior. And I think you know it!"

"Yet she shot at one who travels within my army. An act you did not discourage and your poor decision to allow a child to take up arms and position themselves on the wall as two riders stood outside your gate would indicate you condoned the action. Reparation must be made. You now have two seconds."

"Or?"

"Or I will destroy your community while my brother grants you the gift of a lingering death. And you are now out of time."

"Fine! Just don't destroy our homes or take their lives."

"What?!" Avalon yells. Apparently, she is livid that this mortal agreed with my demands, but he had no choice.

"This surprises you, little lamb. These sons of Adam will always offer other people's lives to save their own. You, of all people, know this," Pestilence calmly informs her.

"Who are the ten you are sending?" The gathering crowd anxiously awaits to hear the names of the ones who will no longer call this place home after today.

"George... Ted... Theo. Sam. Frank—Ray—Nate...." He pauses for a second, closing his eyes as if the following three will be the hardest three words ever to cross his lips. "Beth... Julie." The naming of two women I find fascinating, but the last one he speaks shocks me the most. "And me."

"You?"

"You didn't believe I would send the men and women I have lived with, fought with, and bled with this entire time to face whatever you have planned for them while I hide behind these walls, did you?"

"It is precisely what we thought."

"I guess you don't know us *mortals* as well as you thought you did." His retort requires no response from me. I nod once at the man who holds a modicum of worth. Worth I have found lacking in so many others in this realm.

"Will you allow them time enough to say goodbye to their families?"

"War?" Avalon murmurs as she places her hand on my arm, her eyes begging me not to do this. Even if every part of me would like to grant this to her, I require an army, and this is how I achieve it. Yet I can make concessions I believe will partially satisfy her request.

"Bring them. They need not leave their families behind. I will protect your warriors and their families within my ranks. Furthermore, my brother and I will leave the remaining occupants of your community unharassed. Is this acceptable?"

"I'll tell them," he says, slowly turning to speak with the gathered men and women at the gate.

"And I will still require the inexperienced archer."

"Please, she's just a kid, rider. It's only her and her baby brother."

"Then she will bring him with her because this is neither a request nor something I will negotiate about." After this, I turn to mount my horse, who grows impatient at this delay while Avalon attempts to argue her point to my brother in a low tone, hoping I won't overhear their conversation. Yet it is my brother who wisely tells her this is all the concession I will grant this day. A fact he is not mistaken about after the attempt on her life. They are fortunate this place still stands.

Chapter Eleven: Two Brothers

I KNOW I must journey to where Thanatos waits for word about the lamb and my outcome. I should have gone long ago. The problem is I am uncertain how to handle this situation. How am I to tell him of War's growing interest—dare I say—attraction and affection for her... for his Apple?

I have made several subtle attempts to make my militant brother understand who she is to Thanatos, but he simply refuses to hear it. I cannot tell if this is because he covets what our brother should have claimed or if she fascinates him much as she did me upon meeting her. Our fascination manifests in distinct and different ways, albeit I had preconceived notions about her importance to our brother. A brother who will not find War's comments as amusing as War does.

"What could put this stern scowl on such a handsome face?" Greer asks before she grants me what I need most by wrapping her arms around me. I waste no time reaching behind me to pull her into my arms to bring my lips against her head once I have her body tucked against mine. An action that brings with it a calm I have only ever felt when she is near, and my son is close at hand. Something I still have yet to share with the woman who has captured every piece of my heart. I cannot explain why I hesitate. Is it because I fear she will not want this for our son?

"Let me guess, War did something stupid again."

"When is my brother not acting impulsive?"

"Something I have noticed only Avalon somehow stops."

"As have I." A sigh accompanies the sentiment, something she mirrors when I sit down and pull her onto my lap. Although the reaction I gave was out of frustration, hers was to display her contentment. Something that makes me smile while my hand glides along her back. The back I wish was not concealed from my touch or eyes by this irksome piece of cloth she calls a shirt.

She spins to straddle me as her lips brush along my jaw. I cannot say what I enjoy more the feel of her skin when I slide my hands under her shirt, her tongue gliding along my neck and jaw, her breasts pushed against the hard planes of my chest, or her fingers threading through my hair.

"Meva bella temptació, you will soon find yourself pinned against the wall if you continue tempting me."

"And how do you know this wasn't a part of the plan all along?" she whispers against my ear before pulling it into her waiting mouth. Something I have discovered I enjoy. Immensely. But not as much as the feel of her dragging her core across the erection, growing harder by the second. I growl while ripping open the shirt, keeping me from her perfect breasts.

"Pestilence, I liked that shirt."

"So I shall have to find you another," I tell her before smashing my mouth to hers, swallowing up any further protest she has concerning a moot issue. If she did not wish it to be destroyed, she should have thought to remove it before tempting a being who has been without her touch for far too many days now.

The soft moans she releases when my thumb circles the nipple pebbling from my attention inform me it will no longer be an issue she wishes to discuss. My hands slide down to her ass. She protests with a groan, displaying her dissatisfaction that I am no longer teasing her pebbled nipple, but this fades when I drag her along my erection. The erection that's twitching in anticipation of her sliding around it.

"Pestilence, are you going to keep teasing me?"

"I enjoy watching you writhe under my touch. Something War has kept me far too busy to fully appreciate as of late."

"Yeah, please talk with him and inform him I need you as much as he does." When my tongue glides across one of her stiff nipples, she cries out before correcting her previous comment in a breathy rush. "Actually, more. I need you more than he does. OH FUCK!"

The excitement I feel increases upon hearing her speak the words only I can pull out of her, crushing the final bit of my reserve. Without further delay, I wrap my arms around her, pulling her against me as I come to full height. Her legs coil around my waist while she carries on with the sinuous movements against the erection stimulated by her actions and warmth. If I do not claim her soon, I will lose all control.

We make it no further than the table before I lower her to it and waste no further time removing her pants.

"Your turn now," she pants while tugging at the button on my jeans. I no sooner have the offending garments off before she wraps her hand around the shaft of my throbbing erection to stroke the length, driving me insane with the need to claim her once more.

"My beautiful temptation, I cannot describe the sensation of what you are doing to me."

"Not good enough, my handsome rider. Now tell me how fucking good it feels."

"It feels fuckin' good."

"Tell me how desperate you are to slide inside the spot, pulsing with a desperate need to feel you filling it."

"I am frenzied by my aching need that will only be satiated when I slide within you."

"Not exactly what I said to say, but I'll take it because it was sexy as fucking sin." She groans when she strokes me against her slick folds. Wet from her growing anticipation of me taking her body over and over again until my love is so satisfied she falls asleep in my arms. "Fuck me before I lose my godforsaken mind."

With her last plea, I slide inside her. The feel of her clenching around my cock almost buckles my knees. Which would be nearly as satisfying since it would lower my mouth so it was in line with her core. A place where I would dine on the essence only my beautiful temptation can provide me.

"Oh, fuck... faster... fuck me faster, Pestilence," she begs while digging her nails into my back, her legs wrapping around my waist, "Harder. Faster!"

"It has been too long since I have known the pleasure of my chosen."

"Much too damn long," she pants before claiming my mouth. My tongue drives between her parted lips the instant she grants me access. Her taste is sweet, like honeyed nectar straight from the hive. The moan escaping her vibrates along my lips straight to my cock, thrusting inside her before I swallow it in my desperate need to claim all she has to give.

"Oh, my fucking God!" she screams. I attempt to hide the rapture we are experiencing from the other men and women we travel with as I place my hand gently across her lips. I despise having to silence her since my only desire is to hear her scream my name. Running my hand between my body and hers, I do not stop until I find the sweet spot I know will have her crashing soon; my thumb finds the nerves of her engorged clit. I circle it with slow, sensual swipes, pushing her over the edge. "Oh 'uck ee. 'm umin'."

I cannot halt the grin this evokes as I smile against her breast before I pull a taut nipple between my teeth as she pulses around me. The feel of her finding her release pulls my own seconds after.

With my cock still seated within her, I carry her to our makeshift bed. One she has made much more comfortable with the addition of a mattress she made from cloth and feathers.

"To godforsaken long," she pants with her mouth pressed against my neck. Reluctantly, I withdraw my erection, still stiff with the need to claim her so I could tuck her against my side. With her head resting on my chest and my hand skimming the silky skin on her back, I allow my thoughts to return to my brothers.

"Babe, why don't you tell me what's bothering you," Greer encourages me with her loving words and gentle caresses.

"How could anything bother me when I have such an exceptional beauty in my arms?"

"After all this time together, you think I can't tell when something is weighing on you. Now if it was me being all somber, you would want to help, so why don't you share the burden and let me do for you what you have always done for me?"

"How am I so blessed to have found such a caring soul?"

"Just lucky, I guess. Now spill," Greer says before twisting to push up on her elbows so we could have a proper conversation. I want to tell her, but this is a heavy weight to bear. One I should carry alone. It is unfair to pass my concerns to anyone else, especially when that someone is the woman I love.

"Do you need an incentive to share?" she asks before lowering her mouth to my chest to allow her tongue to circle around my nipple. I tilt my head to give me a better view of her face and the grin she wears. When I do not reply, she shifts her body to straddle mine. Since we both still lack any clothing, this position places her warm core against the erection, demanding I claim her again.

Greer's fingers glide along my arms and across my chest while she continues kissing from one side to the other. Delivering a quick bite to each peck.

"So here is how we play this game, handsome. Every time I make you moan, groan, or squirm, you tell me one more detail about the massive weight you carry on these delicious broad shoulders of yours."

"And if I don't give you any of these reactions?"

"Then I will have to try harder," she tells me with her lips pressed against mine before shifting her hips to slide against the erection I am frantic to drive into her. In fact, I want this more than I want air. Even though I want to protect her from what I suspect is happening with my brother, I cannot help the moan she pulls from me.

"There's one, love."

"It's my brother."

"Okay, I will safely assume the brother in question is War."

"Ah-ah-ah, beautiful, this constitutes a question you have not yet earned." Her lips find my neck just before she shifts to bring the head of my dick to the warm wet entrance I pray she will grant me access to, but when she denies my desire, the groan this time is more from frustration than gratification.

"So why are you worried about War?"

"Did you skip the previous question, the one where you made assumptions about which brother I spoke of?"

"Nope, I don't need to because when you answer this one, I'll know," she tells me while her teeth pull my earlobe into her mouth before she runs her tongue against it.

"Umm," the sound slips out before I can stop it. My hands find her hips to pull her against me harder.

"That's two answers you owe me now, love."

"So it is," I tell her before deciding it's my turn to run my lips along her neck.

"That's not an answer to my question, handsome," she advises just prior to her lowering her chest to mine, letting her nipples graze against me.

"I fear he may not be aware of something."

"What would this something be?"

"With regard to another."

"You are going to make me pull every answer from you, aren't you?"

"As I thoroughly enjoy your method of extracting information, my answer is yes. I plan to make you work for every detail."

"I do like the way you think." This time when she shifts, it is her moan she extracts. A sexy fucking sound that causes a growl deep in my chest since the only thing I can think of now is making her scream my name.

"Who is the other?"

"The lamb," I confess as I claim her mouth in a heated kiss. One I pray will have her forgetting this little game she plays and allow me entrance to her body.

"You don't fight fair, my handsome rider."

"Nor do you, my beautiful temptation."

"Do you want me, rider?"

"Yes. More than you could ever know."

"Do you want to fuck me until I scream your name?"

"Yes." my reply is both heated and filled with need as every part of me now demands I take her.

"What about A? What is it about Avalon you believe he doesn't know?"

"You did not earn this ans—" Prior to me finishing my sentence, she shifts her hips once more, sliding down my erection which halts my previous thought because not only does she make me groan, she makes me roar one word that echos off the walls and fills the room.

"Fuck!"

"Yes… fuck now. Answer after," she moans against my chest. The shift from her being on top to me taking control is swift and demanding, and I cannot halt the punishing pace at which I invade her. And fuck Greer is precisely what I do until she has screamed my name three times and begs me *no more*. It is only then I allow my own release. No longer caring who hears us, I roar her name as I spill every drop inside her.

With her tucked against my side once again, she asks in the sexy, sleepy tone I know means she is both satisfied and content, "What about A?"

"I fear he does not know who she is."

"He knows she's the one who is responsible for breaking the seals."

"No, my beautiful temptation. I mean, who the lamb is to my brother."

"Who is she to War?" Greer asks, lifting her head and showing me the confusion my unfinished thought has caused.

"Wrong brother, my love."

"What?"

"Not War. I am talking about who she is to my other brother. Who she is to…."

"*Death!*"

Chapter Twelve: Stepping Up

I DON'T KNOW what is more irritating… the way War keeps trying to push my buttons. The confused look Pestilence continues to give his brother and me or Thanatos refusing to answer my pleas no matter how many times I beg it of him.

I just want to know if it was all in my head. If I meant nothing to him, which I am now beginning to think is probable, or if this realization only came to him once he returned home. Does he have someone else, a being who he cares for in his own realm? A heavenly version of a girlfriend or wife. I would have said no damn way a year ago, but now…. Now, I don't fucking know anymore.

Damn, I hate being this insecure about what I once believed was everything.

And to top it off, I have some overbearing rider dictating what I can and cannot do.

"Do you think you're going to stop me?" I snap at the infuriating rider, whose grin grows each time I lash out. This fight is centered on me leaving camp without *his protection.* His fucking words, not mine, as if I need some overbearing asshat trying to be my damn dad. I've got news for him I've survived since birth without one of those or a rider looking over my shoulder; I'll be damned if I want one now.

The only friggin thing I wanted to do was take the two newest kids to join us fishing. The young girl who shot the damn arrow at War and her little brother. They are having difficulty adjusting to their new life, and I can't say I blame them. The girl, Ellie, looks ready to jump out of her skin whenever War is near. And her little brother, whom we only know as Duck, senses his sister's fear and refuses to leave her side. They just need one damn day of not fearing for their lives to see that we aren't the worst people they could be stuck with.

From what the previous leader of their group, Joe, told me, the kids had only been in their community a few weeks when they were forced to leave with the rider she shot at. Something I can only imagine scared the hell out of her. Especially since he was outside the walls bellowing like some macho dumbass on a power trip, which I guess he kind of was doing.

I had almost made it out of camp when his booming voice halted our progress and sent Ellie to her knees. Like she needs to bow to him. Hell goddamn no, she will not bow to anyone, riders included.

"Stand up, Ellie, and you back off, War. I'm taking the kids fishing."

"No."

"You think you can bark this one word, and I'll concede?"

"I believe not only can I, but I did," he says, covering his stupidly handsome face with that irritating little smirk he gives me. A face I'm thinking about punching right now, but something tells me this would only lead to a broken hand for yours truly, and little more than a red mark, if anything, for the asshole rider.

"So you say." I snap back.

"No, u mo Bella Agnellu, so I know."

"Oh look, snookums, it's a dick-measuring contest." Suki squeals when she and Xander stroll over to find out what all the shouting is about.

"No, it isn't, Suk," I snarl, bending over to pick up the fishing poles.

"Why the hell not, A?" Suk asks, her eyes shifting between the rider and me.

"Yes, A, why not?" War asks while he attempts to halt the grin I know he wants to give me, but I can see the sides of his lips twitching ever so slightly from his damn delight. How did we go from arguing with one another to him trying to rein in his amusement? Oh, that's right, because of my little stick her nose where she shouldn't be involved, friend Suki.

"You be quiet. And you know why, you big ox."

"Well, if you ask me, I think you could totally beat the red rider over here. Hell, he just needs a red cape, and we could change his name to the Little Red Rider." Suk giggles at her joke while War's eyes assess if he wants to continue the playful banter or deal with the woman smacking her boyfriend's chest as her giggles morph into roaring laughter. A boyfriend who is swallowing hard, knowing if War takes offense to this shit, he's the one who will be left to deal with it since there is no damn way he'll let War hurt Suk.

"Go ahead, Bella Agnellu, tell the small one why you refrain from this."

"Because clearly, you have and are the larger dick out of the two of us." an expanding grin stretches over War's face while he crosses his arms over his expansive chest.

"How very astute you are, my little lamb."

"I wasn't finished. I'll concede you have the larger dick since you are a guy, and I am a girl, which means I don't possess a penis by default. However, I do have the bigger balls of the two of us. So shall we move on if we're done comparing dick sizes?"

"Oh snap, she schooled you, War." His reaction is not what I was prepared for when a booming laugh erupts from the burly man in front of me.

"And a personality to match. Didn't you call this, A?"

"Call what, Bella Agnellu?"

"That you were the fun one. I'm pretty sure I remember a story you told me, Avalon. You know, the one where you informed Death that War was the fun one."

"This I shall like to hear."

"No!" I shout, unwilling to share this memory with him and regretting I disclosed it to Suki.

"No?"

"It's what I said, is it not?"

"Fine, I shall ask my brother. I'm sure he will enjoy telling me all about it."

"Pestilence won't be telling you shit because he doesn't know," I say with a smug confidence I should have held until I had all the facts.

"Who said I plan to ask him?"

"Then what brother are you talking about?" the question no sooner passes my lips when I realize which brother he intends to ask. "Oh, hell no!"

"Yes, I shall go straight to the source. The brother who was present when the comment was made."

"No!"

"Again with this word, tell me why the denial this time."

"Because I don't want you to ask him."

"Why?"

"Are you three?"

"No." I know he is only mimicking the response I had given him twice before. Even so, it's damn annoying.

"I only said it to piss him off."

"Imagine that. I only plan to repeat it to piss him off."

"Damn it, War." Seeing my frustration is getting me nowhere, I try another approach. "I take it back anyway."

"It's impossible to take back words once they have been spoken. Their echoes always ring in one's ears. And these will most assuredly remain in mine."

"You're being an ass."

"But a fun one. Right?"

"Nope, pretty much just an ass."

He throws his head back and releases a booming laugh at the same time Pestilence and Greer walk up hand-in-hand. The flush of her cheeks and messy hair all screams I just got laid. And confirms the roar we all heard earlier was Pestilence and Greer making up for a lot of lost time. Thank goodness Nehra took Wren out to play with a few of the kids whose parents opted to follow War and Pestilence rather than remain in the camp.

"Brother, something you wish to share?" Pestilence says while his eyes remain fixed on me.

"I wish I could, yet the lamb refuses to share the story. No matter," he says as he walks over before leaning down to deliver the rest of his response so only I can hear. "I will find out one way or another. It might be wisest if you were the one to disclose the tale to me. I'll be in my tent if you are feeling loquacious."

"I'll loquacious your ass," I snarl over my shoulder, but his response has my cheeks heating, and I am unsure if it is from embarrassment or something else entirely. Something I would rather not think about.

"Or we could explore all the things you would like to do with my ass. Since there seems to be quite a few you have mentioned. Yet still not as many as I would like to do to yours." After this, he winks at me before retiring to his tent. The one he most certainly will be waiting for me in. The same one I am forced to sleep in every night since he refuses to let me out of his sight for longer than a few damn minutes. "Ensure the lamb finds her way to bed before the night grows too late, brother."

We are all left stunned by his response while heat courses through my veins, one fucking traitorous pump at a time. I have no damn idea why he can't just let it go. I've told him more than once nothing is going to happen. Not now... not ever. And as much as I mean what I said, it is hard to pretend that having someone as handsome as War flirting with you doesn't stir some emotions you never plan to explore. Hell, even the way he looks at me like he knows what I look like under all my clothes is enough to have me biting my lip.

"Holy hot rider, batman, I think War is hitting on you, A."

"You don't say, Suk," I snap, irritated he said this shit in front of everyone.

"Lamb, a word," Pestilence says as he walks by, which tells me he does not wish to share this word with everyone else like War did. Damn his stupid brother. As irritated as I am at War, Pestilence is my friend and someone I respect, which is the only reason I follow him without protest beyond earshot of the others in our camp. We walk for several minutes in silence until I can no longer stand the oppressiveness of it all.

"So you and Greer are doing well?"

"We are," he says as he looks at me from the corner of his eyes.

"What? I know you want to say something, so spit it out, Pessy."

"Again with this name?"

"Hey, blame Hope, not me, since she's the one who came up with it. I just happen to think it fits you perfectly, Pessy." mentioning her name brings a new thought crashing around me. I know she possesses the rock that will protect her from beings like Pestilence and War, but what about raiders? That fucking rock isn't going to do shit to protect her from a band of assholes. "Do you think we should have asked Noll and Hope to join us?"

"Perhaps, but I am not sure he would have agreed. Noll likes his solitude, and camp life would not grant him this. I will keep tabs on them though, little lamb."

"Promise?"

"Have I ever said something I did not intend to see through?"

"No. I know you will."

"Can I ask you something?"

"I don't know why he keeps saying the shit he says to me." Pestilence doesn't respond, but the intensity of his gaze confirms this is what this private little conversation is all about. "It's what you wanted to ask, right?"

"In part."

"Okay, sooo, what's the other part?"

"Do you believe Thanatos would approve?"

"I don't know what he would or wouldn't approve of. But if I am being honest, I don't think Death cares either way."

"Death?"

"It's his name."

"It is. I have just never heard you refer to him as this."

"I decided it's time to make some changes in my life. I need to let go of some… some childish fantasies."

"Avalon," the sympathy spilling out in this one word makes me feel weak. It's an emotion I despise over all the others. I am many things; helpless isn't one of them, but with this one damn word spoken by someone I care for, I am reduced to the little lost girl cowering in the dark corner of some shithole bedroom, praying Calvin's wondering hands won't find me tonight.

"Pestilence, don't! I need you to let this one go."

"Avalon, I want to—"

"I can handle War, Pessy. What I can't handle is the way you're looking at me right now and the pity I hear in your voice, so please let it go and let me forget what my heart held out hope for. Hope doesn't do anything but cloud your judgment; it's another emotion I have no use for." With my head hung low, I turn to trudge back to camp. I feel the weight on my shoulders and the silent echo of my words when I quietly say….

"At least not anymore."

Chapter Thirteen: Push

I TRIED TO do as she asked and leave this for her to handle, but the overwhelming sense I was betraying my brother weighed heavy on me. When I tried to speak with War on more than one occasion, he refused to hear anything I had to say about Avalon. I even attempted to slip it in during a different conversation, but he was swift to interrupt me, advising me to leave it.

I recognize War can be hard-headed when he sets his sights on something, but I also know he is loyal. If he knew what had happened between Thanatos and the lamb, he wouldn't say the things he continues to express when he believes no one is close enough to hear. A step up from him blurting whatever was on his mind, regardless of who may be near. I imagine this was the only compromise Avalon could elicit from him.

Thankfully, he has been so focused on building his army for the last couple of weeks that he hasn't had much time for anything else. Well, apart from quietly fulfilling the task they sent him to do. Something else I believe he does to appease Avalon. Using the *'what she does not know cannot hurt her'* mentality.

But time does not relieve my troubled conscience, knowing I have not returned to check on the fate of my brother nor to ask about what he told War. So it is becoming too much to bear. I know part of this is because I suspect whatever keeps him from this world is related to what I asked him to do. A punishment I alone should face for saving my Wren, not him. But today is the day I face what fate has befallen him.

His room has been stripped of all his possessions except one book that is supposed to chronicle our ride across their world. A damnable book in which the horsemen prevail while humanity falls, a harsh read for someone like me who has a vested interest in their survival.

"A final insult of a gift from my brother to yours."

"Michael is responsible for this?" I ask in a huff while throwing the book at Raphael's feet.

"I have made many attempts to reach him, hoping to ascertain why he is so remiss to allow the mortals of this world a chance, but he refuses to speak of it."

"Is my brother…." I drop my head, already knowing the answer. Even with this, saying the word feels as impossible as removing my beating heart. Thankfully, Raphael does it for me.

"Imprisoned? Yes."

"Because of Wren?"

"Because he returned a soul who had passed from their world."

"A soul that was stolen."

"No, Pestilence, none of our kind took it. He lost his life to the humans you now try so hard to save. It is a cruel twist to both love them and hate them equally."

"It is not without its difficulties, but the humans I protect are worth every sacrifice I make."

"I suppose so."

"Will you take me to my brother?" Raphael dips his head before guiding me to the cell they are holding my brother in.

Upon our arrival, we find one warrior positioned in front of a cell door, and I know without question this is where I will discover Thanatos. It's a mistake on their end if they believe one warrior will halt my brother if he decides he no longer wishes to remain here.

I should also point out it would be a grievous error if this warrior believes they will keep me from him. Yet this jailor is not standing guard as one would expect. They are pressed up on tiptoes, peering through the small window into the cell. It is not until the guard looks in our direction I discover why they would risk Michael's wrath when Ariel's red, heartbroken eyes look back.

Ariel is one of our father's chief warriors, and someone I have long suspected cares more for my brother than one in her position should. This in part, is why she has guarded this information and kept it close to her heart. The weight of sadness pressing down on her as she stands outside his cell is evident, even at this distance. I cannot imagine that watching someone you care for suffer is easy.

"Why is Ariel placed as his guard?"

"Michael intended her to serve as a warning to others who may wish to follow their heart and speak out on behalf of any soul my brother has set his sights against."

"She spoke out in favor of releasing Thanatos?"

He smiles while tilting his head. I assume this is to suggest the question is ridiculous since I already know she would speak out in his defense. "Unfortunately for her, Michael saw this as an attempt to overrule his command and question his authority."

"What was she hoping would happen?"

"Ariel spoke in favor of allowing your brother to continue his task of ferrying souls to their next life. Something Michael obviously stands in opposition to."

"She only did it because—"

"Because she loves him. Yes, and Michael is aware of it. Yet another reason for him to enforce his might over her."

"Our father allows this?"

"Our father is… preoccupied with other affairs at the moment."

"What could he possibly find more pressing than the unjust jailing of his son and the fall of his favorite children?"

"There are many things. These two are merely a drip in the bucket he is balancing." Raphael turns, and I know I will get no further information from him, but none of these issues matter because this is not why I am here. So we traverse the length of the hall in silence.

"Ariel."

"Pestilence," she states, promptly following her greeting with a humble head bow and averting her eyes.

"My brother?" I nod toward the door. Her eyes slip closed before she gives me her quiet confirmation.

"Perhaps you would like to take a break, young soul?" Raphael asks while gently placing his hand atop her shoulder.

"Yes, I think it would be best. Thank you." She takes one fleeting look over her shoulder before disappearing in the same direction we came from.

I realize my every fear with only one glance through the barred window. My brother is chained, but the glowing glyphs are what I find most disheartening since these alone will cut him off from the world he has watched over and protected for more lifetimes than any other soul can claim. It hurts me to see him like this, and I realize each false reason I spoke or thought so I would not feel guilty about not returning here sooner proves how selfish I am.

"Take all the time you require," Raphael says before his armor slowly takes form over his body, encasing him in a material no mortal sword could penetrate.

"Brother." Thanatos' eyes fly up to meet mine, and I see the hope of what news I can give him within them.

"You survived the battle to retrieve your chosen?"

"I did, but only barely, and only with the aid of Avalon. Because of her, I am not toiling in hell as Raum's favorite torture toy."

"I heard some of this, but I don't understand how she could have stopped him."

"Because she is fearless, Thanatos. When it comes to protecting the ones she holds close to her heart, she will stop at nothing."

"Yes, this I remember. Tell me what happened, brother," his request is more a plea than a demand. I believe there is only one thing he really wants to ask... if she is okay. So rather than delaying what I think will comfort him, I tell him what he is too afraid to ask for.

"She is alive, well, and just as stubborn as she has always been." He releases a heavy sigh. My words seem to act as a balm to heal the fear of what became of her. For the next hour, I tell him everything that happened, from my arrival to falling in love with Greer. I told him about when she fought against the men who invaded their camp and how she refused to allow me to go after Greer alone. Ending my tale with her breaking the seal and damning humanity to face another rider only to save the soul of one.

"So this is the reason our brother was called there."

"Yes. Raum captured me when I was weakened by one of their arrows. He further debilitated me with a blade dipped in his essence, pierced my chest, and stopped just short of ripping through my heart."

"It pleases me to hear she is doing well."

"She blames herself for much of what has occurred in their world, and as such, she carries more burden than she should."

"You will help her shake this off. Help her see this was not her doing."

"Can I ask you something?"

"Of course."

"Do you regret any of it?"

"I regret I was not able to stop our arrival."

"I meant with Avalon. Do you regret any of your time with Avalon?"

He drops his head so I cannot see the pain filling his expression, but I do not miss the tick of the jaw he has clenched tight. "I only regret leaving her."

"If this is true, why did you not tell our brother?"

"Tell War what?"

"What she meant—means to you."

"It no longer matters, brother, because I am here, and she is there. I only confess my true feelings to you because you alone can understand them."

"You still should have told him."

"Why?"

"Because he is—I think he may also…."

"Tell me why!"

"You might want to talk to our brother."

"I am talking to you." His tone may be calm, but the hard lines of his rigid muscles belie the indifference he wants to portray. His forceful yank rips one chain from the wall when I remain silent. "I chose not to tell anyone else to protect her, but if what you are implying is true, I may have failed to do this."

"War would never hurt her, Thanatos."

"War will not be as cautious with protecting her identity. He will allow his emotions to rule his choices."

Raphael rushes into the room with his hand on the hilt of his blade. "Thanatos, I must beseech you to halt any further attempts to remove your restraints. Please, my old friend, please do not force my hand."

My brother's eyes drift from Raphael to mine, giving us his answer. "Tell War that I wish to speak with him. He has twenty-four hours to comply before I come for answers."

Looking from Thanatos over to the warrior who will be honor-bound to stop my brother at all costs, the angel gives me a cursory nod. But when I prepare to exit this plane, he grasps my arm and murmurs a plea of his own.

"Make haste, rider. For I fear your brother will not comply much longer."

*****

When I return to camp, I waste no time rushing to his tent, knowing I will find him there. I am shocked when I discover the lamb in his bed while he sleeps in a chair across the room from her.

I slip over to wake him, but his hand snatches out to grab my wrist since I am too distracted, ensuring I have not disturbed the lamb. He thankfully does not question or argue when I nod for him to follow me out of his tent.

Once outside, frustration replaces fear when he does not want to listen to reason. Had I known it would be such a damn fight, I would have knocked the big bastard over the head while he slept and ferried him to Thanatos without his consent. There are times when it truly is better to ask for forgiveness than permission.

"I'm sure he does."

"Brother, it would be best if you travel to him before he comes here."

"You mean when Bella Agnellu breaks his seal?"

"I mean, before he tears the veil apart."

"Why would he do this?" This is the first time I ever want to growl because of how you elect to speak to his Apple, the one soul he cares for as much as his brothers. And now you, one of his brothers, are trying to claim her. How am I the one who continually finds myself in these difficult situations?

"Did he not speak to you about the lamb?"

"My answer has not changed since you last asked me this."

"You need to speak with our brother."

"Fine, we will travel there together."

"I should return to Greer and—"

"You will come since you felt so inclined to interject yourself in a situation that neither needed your attention nor benefited from it."

"The benefit is keeping the veil intact," is my mumbled response, which causes a huff from my militant brother.

I have no other option if I want to halt what I know is about to happen, so I agree with a simple dip of my head. After this, we leave this world for our own. I only pray we are not too late.

When we arrive, Raphael is doing his best to calm our irate brother, who has ripped another chain away from the wall.

"If you halt any further attempts to remove your restraints, I will grant you the ability to communicate with your brothers," Raphael tells him as he keeps his hands raised defensively.

"Did you call me here to help break you out of this cell? Because it looks like you are doing a fine job alone."

"What the hell are you doing, brother?"

"Waging war," our militant brother declares as he leans against the wall and tucks his thumbs into the jeans he opts to wear rather than what we are provided before our descent.

"I mean with Avalon," Thanatos growls, and for not the first time since War's arrival, I fear I may have to step in between two beings I care for.

"I don't see why you concern yourself with my interaction with the lamb." Thanatos yanks the chains holding his wrist free from the wall, lashing out at War, who only scarcely steps out of his reach before he can grasp ahold of him.

"Is there anything you want to tell me? Something I should know about you and her?"

144

"No!"

My head whips in Thanatos's direction. What the hell? I must have misheard him. This was his opportunity to tell War.

"Thanatos!" I growl, not wanting this dissension to continue between my brothers.

"Are you certain, brother?"

"Apple—I mean, the lamb has a task. It is our job to protect her while we fulfill ours."

"Which I am."

"You can do this without touching her."

"Who said I have touched her?"

"You haven't?" for the first time since I asked him what he told War, I see Thanatos visibly relax.

"Not yet."

"Yet. What the fuck do you mean? YET!"

"What I said. Unless, of course, there is something between you two you are not telling me." Thanatos's eyes roam the room, almost like he is searching for something that War and I are unaware of. Could there be some device watching and listening to our every word?

War's relaxed posture as he continues to lean against the wall, waiting patiently for our brother's response is unsettling, but when Thanatos shakes his head, the grin on War's face broadens.

"I guess if this is all you wished to talk to me about, I will return to—"

"Just ensure you continue to guard, not touch, the lamb who doesn't always use her best judgment, little brother."

"Uh-huh."

"What?"

"I'm just wondering how much longer you will continue denying there is nothing between Bella Agnellu and you?" Oh shit, did he have to use this nickname when referring to Avalon? Thanatos goes from mad to enraged. The issue is War has opted not to look at him, picking this time to clean his blade rather than watching the brother he is trying so hard to infuriate; he doesn't see the subtle shift in his eyes. However, I do.

"You are my brother. A being I trust and would protect with my own life, but if you call her this again, you will not like my response."

"So there is something between you and the lamb."

"I have already answered this."

"Okay then, brother, until you are ready to admit to me how you feel, your Apple is fair game."

Fuck, this is about to turn so damn bad.

Chapter Fourteen: Cowboy

I CAN TELL you not knowing where these riders are and worrying if they will find us before we reach our destination is more than just a little nerve-racking. Especially since we are still days away from this damn fort Wayne keeps telling us will save our asses.

When the idiots who call themselves our exalted leaders told a select few of their plans the night of the meeting, I stayed only long enough to get the details outlining their strategy. I didn't remain for the after-party. After witnessing one of the triple bitches preparing to service Trevor, I returned to his bed, but the hope Candy would keep him busy all night remained. I thought the big guy may have answered my prayers as the hours ticked by and my eyelids grew heavy. I figured the bitch was good for something after all. This was the dumb-ass thought playing on repeat in my head until he came in stinking of sex and not from one, but two of the triple bitches.

I assumed there was no way in hell he could need me to satisfy anything because when I walked out, it looked like Candy was doing a bang-up job, but with his hand skimming along my bare legs I'm left with one thought.... I should have left my damn clothes on. Hell, none of this would be an issue if my ass had been sleeping in my own damn room... in my own damn bed.

He wasted no time ripping my panties off before rolling me to my back and slamming his face between my legs. Ordinarily, I wouldn't object to this kind of attention, but right then, the only thing I could think of was if my legs were the only ones his face had been buried between.

I didn't like the idea of having a tongue working me so fervently if it was doing the same thing to one of those bitches. In the end, he refused to relent until he made me come. Only after he licked away the proof of my orgasm and made sure he left his fucking evidence of ownership calling card, a damn hickey on my inner thighs, did Trevor flip me over, yank my ass in the air, and fucked me harder than he had ever done before. I would have even enjoyed it if not for the thought of Candy on her knees with his dick in her mouth when I left the war room.

Not that I cared he screwed someone else because I don't; I just cared that it was *her* he decided to fuck. A worthless bitch who makes it her mission to antagonize all the single women in camp. With one exception... me. I'll give her some credit; at least she's smart enough to ensure she doesn't say anything about yours truly. Especially when no one else is around to save her sorry ass because she knows I would have no issue beating the shit out of her.

I also notice how often I find Candy pressed against him, with her hands not so subtly copping a feel of the dick I know has been in her almost as much as he has tried to fuck me.

"Tonight, Ember. I don't give a flying fuck if you are exhausted or if your head feels like it's going to fall off. Tonight that sexy little ass is mine," he whispers in my ear while patting the ass he claims belongs to him, and apparently, so does my vagina since his hand has made its way from my ass to between my legs while he bites my neck. Pulling away, I'm furious he thought it was okay to do this shit. I don't know why this prick thinks I'm a fucking piece of meat for his enjoyment, but somewhere along the way, this is precisely what happened. I lost myself and became his property. Something I have no intention of remaining for much longer.

"Don't you have plans with Candy?" I ask, hoping he just forgot and will leave me in peace.

"Don't you worry about what I plan on doing before I come to bed! Just remember this ass, my bed, all fucking night long."

"Candy would be only too happy—"

"Don't say it, Ember. Candy won't be in my bed. You will be. So not another word."

I know what you're thinking. It's not anything I haven't thought a million fucking times over. Why in the hell would I continue to subject myself to this miserable prick? Why not just tell him to take a long fucking walk off a short damn pier? The answer is simple since I have already told you that people who defy Wayne and Trevor either come up missing or get left behind.

If I have any hope of taking out the damn rider who killed my parents, I need this group, and if it means I have to suffer a little humiliation along the way while I wait to do it, then I suppose this is my life until my goal has been accomplished. In the meantime, I will continue to hold on to my last hope that Candy can pull his focus for good, or it looks like night patrols will be a regular part of my foreseeable future. Because it's only this assignment keeping me away from him and out of his bed at night. Something Wayne will never allow him to pull me from.

The only reason I didn't volunteer tonight is that I thought he would be busy with the sucker-twirling dimwit.

The size of our group and the age ranges of the people with us keep us from moving any faster than we are now. Since it appears we are still a couple of weeks away from reaching this almighty fortress in Bama, there are few options to make this trek go any faster. I almost wish they would have sent a smaller group out to set up and fortify this place. That way, it would be ready for them when they finally arrived. And since I would have been one of the people to volunteer, it would have served as a reprieve from Wayne's second. But alas, none of these dipshits would listen to me.

"Did you get the shit done I asked you to do?" Wayne's gruff voice never gives you the warm fuzzies. I can't believe the triple bitches like him. Arrogant asshole.

"Yeah, it's done," I curtly reply before returning my attention to unloading the supplies we will need to make camp for a few days to let the oldest and youngest among us rest and recover.

"Do you have plans tonight, Em?"

Em? Since when did this prick start calling me Em? Regardless, he can call me the Queen of England or whatever the hell else he wants if he's going to demand I go out on patrol, which will save me from sleeping in the same bed with Trevor. But I have to tread carefully here in case this is a test. These two dicks love their little test of loyalty.

"I do, but if you need me to do anything for the camp, it's nothing I can't postpone."

"I want to increase patrols."

"Yeah, no problem. Put me down." Inside, I'm doing a little happy dance. Fingers pointed in the air, ass-shaking without a care. Nothing sexy about it. Happy dance.

"Come see me around six so I can fill you in on the details," Wayne says, pushing past me like I'm no longer worthy of his precious friggin time. No matter. He just saved me from having to deal with Trevor tonight. Something I'm sure his best friend will have an opinion about. Too damn bad if he doesn't like it, he can take it up with asshole numero uno. Who said wishes can't come true? If I could leap up and click my heels together without falling on my face, I would so be doing that shit.

With the looming dread for the night Trev had planned for me off my shoulders, the rest of the day was much more pleasant. I'm out with a scouting party, and the people in the group aren't the 'I don't give a shit if they need it because we're taking it' kind of people. We only take the stuff that appears to have been abandoned. What the hell is the point of saving humanity if we can only accomplish it by destroying everyone else? How is doing shit like that any different from what the riders are doing? They just plan their annihilation on a more widespread

151

kill 'em all kind of level. One thing for sure is these riders don't think small scale, not like the morons running this group.

The house I am raiding has some amazing stuff, and the thick layer of dust is good enough for me to believe it's free for the picking. We need most of this shit, so I'll call this excursion a monumental success.

I almost have the cupboard emptied when someone clears their throat behind me. The sudden arrival of the ninja—a nickname given on account of the asshole sneaking up on my unaware ass—has me smashing my head into the frame when I jerk out from under it.

"Oh, damn. Are ya okay?"

"Ow," I grumble while rubbing the spot I imagine will be a decent-sized lump by the time I return to camp. "Does it look like I'm okay?"

"I reckon it was a stupid question."

"Ya think." I snap at the newcomer like it's his fault that I have zero depth perception. When I turn to see who is on the receiving end of my irritation, I find a burly man filling the doorway. A beefy man not from our group. If his size wasn't enough to intimidate me, the damn big-ass spear strapped to his back surely fuckin does. Realizing how precarious this situation is, I grab my knife, leap to my feet, and angle my body into more of a defensive position.

"Whoa-whoa-whoa, hang on there, little missy. I ain't plannin' on hurtin' ya none," he says, putting his hands up and stepping away from me.

"Yeah, 'cause if you were, you would sure as shit tell me. Right?"

"Chalk it up tuh another—"

"Stupid response," I interrupt, not caring if this was what he was planning to say. No point in dragging this out any longer than we need to. The single-step distance was a brilliant idea, yet nowhere near the space I needed and wanted for my comfort.

"Why don't you take a couple more big steps away from me, cowboy." This wasn't a request, so he'll oblige if he knows what's healthy for him.

He complies, which shocks the shit out of me since if this had been Trevor stumbling upon some lone woman in a house chock-a-block full of great supplies, his response would have been to charge her and take everything she had before telling her that her best chance of survival is with our group. Of course, her survival would hinge on the way she responded to this last part.

"Are ya out here on yer own?" He answers his own question for me when I tilt my head, giving him my 'you have to be shitting me if you think I'm answering that,' face. "I reckon I don't blame you much for not wanting to answer me."

"Where are your people at?" I ask as I grab my bag and take several more steps away from him. It won't do anything other than give me an extra second if he decides to charge me, but a second may be all I need to come out of this shit in one piece.

"I think I'll just be takin' a page out of your book and say it is best if I keep this tuh myself."

"Is this your place?" I can't help but notice if he only stumbled by me when he was passing through, he's doing it without much in the way of supplies.

"No, ma'am, just looking for a place tuh put my head down for a spell."

"Uh-huh, well, how bout I make you a deal then, cowboy? You stay right where you are, and I won't have to dirty up my pretty new knife."

"Well now, that would be much appreciated, ma'am." I slowly begin backing out of the room because my momma didn't raise no fool. "Oh, and miss, if ya don't wanna be comin' face tuh face with those riders, ya might wanna be headin' out soon."

"The riders are coming this way?"

"Yep, 'bout two days behind ya."

Fuck! Without waiting for further information, I sprint from the house, whistling for the rest of our group. When Phil walks around the corner, I tell him in a rush to gather up the rest of our members and get them back to the base. I also warn him about the helpful cowboy before racing back to where we set up camp. I am not worried about pissing Wayne off when I bust into his tent.

"Ugh... what the hell, Ember," Mandy squeals before yanking her top up. At least this dumb ass makes a half-ass attempt to cover the parts of her body I could have gone a lifetime without seeing. Wayne, not so much. If it hadn't been for Mandy jerking away from him, I'm not even sure he would have stopped. As it is, he stands beside her with his dick on display, looking at me like I'm the one with no morals. And while I'll admit when it comes to sex, high society might consider my moral standards loose. At least I'm not getting laid in the middle of the day when we have the horsemen of the fucking apocalypse breathing down our necks. It's nice to know camp life is so generous to him.

Asshole.

Fucking asshole.

"We need to talk... alone," I bark, tossing Mandy's pants at her. She could have broken her pelvis if she had slammed her hands on her hips any harder. Oh, wouldn't that be a shame for one of the triple bitches to be sidelined from their sexcapades? Whatever would the other two do without her? Poor little hoes would have to work overtime.

"Time to go, Sandy, Candy, whichever one you are. Chop-chop." Yes, I know it's Mandy, but I get my digs in where I can. Especially since they have no problem talking shit about me.

When Mandy makes no attempt to leave or Wayne to put on a pair of damn pants. I toss the shorts belonging to him at his head and give her my one-word warning. "Now!"

"Wayne," Mandy screeches. The level she manages to get her shrill voice to would have any dog in the vicinity howling in agony.

"Take a walk," Wayne tells her, which only serves to piss her off further. It might be petty, but I can't help getting in one last dig... a self-satisfying little wave as she storms by. "You wanted me alone. I'm alone."

Okay, when he puts it like that, it makes me wanna scream about how I did not want him alone. Especially since he refuses to put his dick away. In fact, I would rather gnaw my own arm off than be alone with this prick. If it had been anyone other than one of the triple bitches, I would have told him no problem. Hell, if it had been any other chick from camp, he could have kept screwing her during my debriefing. I am pretty sure a guy's ears still work when screwing. I just didn't want the big mouth in here while disclosing what the cowboy told me. There is no sense in causing panic to roll through camp. Something the dimwit would have done the second she ran from the tent.

"The riders are only two days behind us. If we don't get moving, we will never reach this damn fort before they overtake us."

"And how is it you came across this information?"

"When I was scavenging. I met a man—"

"Ah, I see. Some random ass man offered you this vital intel… for free?"

"Well, I didn't give him anything, so yeah, for free."

"And you believed him?"

"Not exactly sure what he would gain by lying to me. So, again… I'm going to go with, yeah, I believe him." Almost on cue, Phil and Jon enter the tent. Which is a blessing since it forces Wayne to put on the damn shorts he had flung over his shoulder. After I told Phil about the cowboy, I'm sure he would have gone into the house to check out my story about the guy. With any luck, he was as open with Phil as he was with me. "Ask Phil."

"Now, why would I do that? Was he with you when you had this conversation?"

"No," I say hesitantly. I hate how this asshole dismisses me just because I'm a woman. I have a brain. Perhaps if he listened, he might get some insight other than the testosterone-fueled kill-everyone advice he receives from most of his council. "But before I returned, I told Phil, and since I can't imagine he would have left without checking the guy out, I'm sure he can fill you in on the details you seem so hellbent on ignoring from me. Tell him, Phil."

"Yes, tell me, Phil." Phil shuffles his feet and refuses to meet my gaze.

"What the hell is going on?" Trevor's deep voice is unmistakable and happens to be the last damn thing I wanted to hear today. I was hoping to avoid him altogether so I wouldn't have to tell him his plans for

156

tonight are... well, postponed... permanently if I can swing it.

"Your crazy ass girl came storming in here, interrupting me when I was in mid-fuck with Mandy," Trevor's eyes shoot to mine, and I don't miss the anger brewing within them. I don't know if it's because I came in here without Wayne or Trevor's permission or if it's because I walked in on Wayne and one of the triple bitches mid-fuck as Wayne said. Whatever it is, I know Trev will give me an earful the second I walk out of here.

"Ember," he hisses, storming in my direction.

"Phil, tell them," I mumble under my breath.

"I would love to, Ember, but we didn't find any guy when we went inside."

"Did you wait too long to go into the house? Could he have slipped out the back door?"

"Sorry, Em, but we didn't find or see anyone."

What the hell? There's no damn way they could have missed him. The dude was like six foot four inches tall and built like a damn tank. Needing to confirm I didn't imagine this guy, which I have no idea why I would, I run my hand across the back of my head. The second it comes into contact with the lump, I wince, which confirms at least this part of my memory is correct.

My eyes wander from one man filling the room to the next while they all continue to stare at me. From Jon looking at me like I am a lunatic to Phil's pity-filled eyes — which, by the way, I detest much more than the rest of the emotions I find assessing me. You can feel about me any way you want as long as it is not pity. Who the hell in their right mind would choose to be pitied? To Trevor's fury-filled one, and finally to Wayne, whose stare is the worst. What I see in his eyes makes me question what his plan really was for me tonight, because what I find in Wayne's is pure lust. Making me wish I had let him finish up with Mandy before storming in uninvited.

Chapter Fifteen: Pushing Limits

I *CAUGHT ELLIE* trying to sneak out of camp with her little brother again. But unlike all the other times they were discovered, I finally got her to talk to me last night, and what she said broke my heart.

Ellie is a twelve-year-old little girl going on twenty because she has been forced to care for her three-year-old brother, the one she still only refers to as Duck.

She told me her parents left her and her brother one night about a year ago to scavenge, and they never came back. She believes raiders caught and killed them. As awful as this may sound, I hope this is what happened and not the alternative: they left their kids behind to save their own skin. It's not out of the realm of possibility since this is precisely what Wren's mom did to him, but at least she left him with Greer, a woman she knew would protect him. If Ellie's mom and dad split, these assholes left their kids to die. So for my sanity, I'm going with Ellie's version of the events, making myself believe they died trying to feed their kids.

Ellie and Duck were taken in by a few groups, but either they got separated, or things didn't work out. My guess was when things didn't work out, it had something to do with Duck not talking. Realistically, it's almost impossible to comprehend how Ellie could have made the time to teach him how to talk when she was putting so much energy into keeping them alive.

I guess the safest they ever felt was when Joe took them into his community. They had only been there a few weeks when we happened. And by happened, I mean War's army showing up outside their gates.

She apologized profusely for shooting the arrow, stating she didn't mean to release it. They were all scared, and who the hell could blame them after discovering two riders of the apocalypse outside your camp. Who wouldn't get a little jumpy waiting while these horsemen decided your fate?

This sweet kid also told me she wasn't aiming for me; she thought she had War sighted. Okay, so note to self: get Pessy to teach her how to defend herself and how to properly aim a bow. I mean, I can use one if I have to. When push comes to shove, I can land my mark, but if you had your choice between just okay and the greatest fucking marksmen in the world when it comes to shooting a bow, who the hell would you choose?

When I pressed her about why she would risk leaving us, she retorted with, 'Why would she risk staying with us?' especially since she was confident War wanted to kill her for shooting me. When I reminded her she didn't hit me, Ellie said she didn't think War saw the distinction. I guess she had me there. And even if War was willing to let it go, Pestilence had to be pissed since she shot him.

I assured her Pestilence didn't hold grudges, and I knew he understood why she did what she did. I somehow convinced her to stay but still elected to double the patrol and had Xander watch her tent so they couldn't sneak away while I went and talked to the one causing all her fear.

A conversation that might be a whole lot easier if this rider would put on a damn shirt.

"What would you wish me to do with them?"

"I don't wish for you to do shit. What you are going to do is stop acting like an asshole. Tell Ellie you understand why she did what she did. Then I want you to explain they will always have a place with this group, and the last and most important thing is I want you to protect them."

"And why would I agree to do any of this?"

"Because you're not an asshole."

"According to you, this is precisely what I am," He declares as he leans against the table in the center of his tent.

"Well…."

"Bella Agnellu." War's use of this dumb nickname is meant as a warning not to push my luck, and since I want something from him, I suppose the prudent approach isn't to insult him straight away. I can refrain from calling him an asshole until this little negotiation concludes.

"War, she's a kid. A kid who is trying to raise a nonverbal toddler." His reaction to this is to lean back against the table. Okay, so he doesn't believe in giving the youth of this world a break; maybe I can play on his emotions.

"She's as scared now as when you forced her to come with us." Now the cheeky bastard has crossed his arms over his massive tattooed chest while quirking his eyebrow. Alright, asshole, you may have no issue dismissing a kid, but let's see if he can ignore a request from me. "And because I'm asking you to give her a damn break."

"Children are as culpable of their poor choices as any adult. She should be scared. She shot a fucking arrow at you. As for you asking for me to do this, convince me."

"Convince you? You've got to be kidding me." Oh my friggin god, now he's grinning at me. I swear this rider can be so damn infuriating sometimes. I thought Death and Pestilence were bad; let me assure you, this opinion has shifted. Drastically. Even more when he acts like this.

"What do you want?"

"This is not how I conduct negotiations concerning war crimes."

"War Crimes? She. Is. A. Kid. War! Damn it, it's not like I'm talking about fucking Hitler here."

"Is this how you convince me?"

"I asked you what you wanted!"

"Why would I tell you this?"

"Because it was your damn idea. I believe your exact words were 'convince me,' correct? I am simply asking what I need to do to convince you."

"Yes, but why would I limit myself?"

"What the hell are you rambling about?"

"I'm willing to bet what you are preparing to offer me differs vastly from what I might think to ask for. So if I tell you what would convince me, I may lose out on something better."

"Okay… then, how about this? You'll do it because you don't want my size nine foot up your ass."

War lumbers toward me, forcing me to step back. When I stupidly back myself into a corner, War presses in on me prior to his hand wrapping around my waist to secure me against his hard body. The other hand grasps my chin so I cannot look away from him. "Is this the offer you wish to give to convince me, u mo Bella Agnellu? Because if it is, how do you know this is not something I would enjoy?"

My mouth falls open. This rider has done something I never thought any being could ever do… he stunned me silent. More than stunned, he stole the retort I had planned right out of my damn mouth. After taking in the shock covering my face, he continues. "You are always welcome to try, but I promise you this, Avalon. If you do, I may find my reason ti pigliò cum'è u mo sceltu cuncubin."

Snapping my mouth closed, I force myself to swallow the lump in my throat. I had hoped my comment could be delivered with my typical Avalon attitude, but it came out way too rushed and sounded altogether way too damn breathy. "Wha—what?"

"I said," he moves closer, forcing me to step back. At least, if I want to keep any semblance of space between us. "you are always welcome to try, but I promise you this, Avalon. If you do, I may find my reason ti pigliò cum'è u mo sceltu cuncubin."

Even though I don't understand what he said, the last word sounds pretty damn similar to another word I know all too well, and this one word smacks me out of my heated haze. "I don't know what the hell you said, but I'm pretty fuckin sure I heard the word concubine in that sentence."

"Because you did, and when I claim you, I will have found my reason to invade this sweet little body of yours." His eyes slid from my face to my chest, which is rising and falling much too fast. As hard as I try to rein in my racing heart, I must have done a shitty job. Because after his eyes meet mine again, he drives home his point by pressing the unmistakable bulge of his hard erection against my lower belly before patting my ass.

I am so fucked right now and not in the happy 'oh god yes, don't stop Thanatos' sort of way.

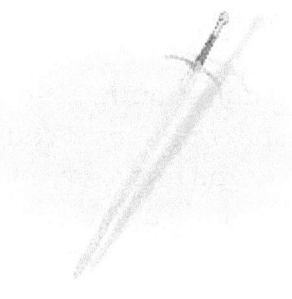

~ *War* ~

When I pulled the beautiful lamb against the part of my anatomy that responds to her each time she is near, it only reinforces my desire to explore her, making it almost intolerable not to touch her. Especially when her face heats to this shade because this makes me believe her body and words are not in agreement.

164

The bigger issue, and what has stopped me thus far, is that I need to know who she is to my brother. Pestilence has alluded to the fact that when it comes to Avalon, Thanatos has taken extreme interest and is often unyielding in his need to protect her. This leaves me to wonder if he had chosen her as Pestilence had done with Greer. Yet when I pose this question to him, he denies it. But it seems he has something to say about her being this close to me because I can feel him invading my thoughts. Something I am contemplating ignoring in favor of exploring this color on her face further.

What are you doing, War?

Ah, I see my old friend upheld his promise and granted you access to your brothers.

I did not ask you for insight regarding my current predicament. I asked you what the hell you were doing!

Tsk-tsk, brother, our father would not be happy with your choice of words. My cavalier attitude has pushed my brother past the point of reason, as evident by his increasing growl. Rather than risking him tearing the veil apart, I refrain from replying with any further snarky comments. It would be most prudent not to press this issue too far, as he seems to be on the verge of not only ripping the veil apart but tearing my ass to shreds with it. Instead, I opt to find out why he is this invested in the lamb, so I give him this short one-word answer. *Responding.*

Responding does not require you to be on top of her.

I'm not on top merely against the source of what seems to be riling your ire.

Nor does it require your hand to be on her ass.

Admit the truth, and I promise it will no longer happen.

What truth?

That this mortal means more to you than she should.

She is the lamb. We are obligated to protect her.

I'm fairly certain that no one will harm her while held against my body as she is now.

You are pushing an issue that you should not be so keen to continue forcing.

Why? Because she is important to you? He growls louder than before, and I hear the unmistakable sound of a wall crumbling, yet he still refuses to confirm or deny my question.

Why are you unwilling to answer this? I wait to give him the opportunity to finally reveal what Pestilence has suggested; however, when he remains reticent, I figure my wait is done, and I have my answer. *No? So be it. I will take your silence to mean she is nothing.*

War! His furious growl causes me to shake my head at his stubbornness.

"Are you talking to someone?" Avalon asks while she struggles to put some space between us.

"No one."

You are pissing me off, brother. You should not consider me as no one, and why are you still pressing your shit—

Shit?

Groin, dick, cock, take your damn pick, War. Whatever you want to call it, the question remains, why is your shit still pressed against her? I laugh at his observation but permit Avalon to step away from me.

"What are you laughing about? This is no laughing matter. Ellie and Duck need—"

"You may keep your prisoners within my camp. There is no need for them to fear me."

"Prisoners? They're not prisoners, War. These are kids we're talking about."

"Then assure your kids they are safe, but keep in mind these kids are your responsibility now," I tell her, tapping her nose as I turn to leave her in my tent. With any luck, she will be willing to explore those "convince me" comments when I return.

"What the hell do I know about raising kids, War?" she yells, to which I shrug before confirming,

"You will need to figure that out, u mo Bella Agnellu." Which results in another low growl from my brother. I will assume he does not like my pet name for the lamb any more than he approves of my body pressing against hers.

*****

Since the day in the tent, my brother has gone silent. Making me wonder if his ability to witness and connect with Pestilence and me while we are in this world is limited. Avalon has also made every effort to avoid me when no one else is around. Unfortunately for my beautiful little lamb, she will have no option but to spend time with me because I have insisted she travel with me today.

My army has grown quite large, and during the time we continue our trek to find the ones who oppose my brothers and me, I will require supplies to sustain my forces and the ability to haul everything as we travel to Al-la-bam-ma. This is my plan for today, and since I grow tired of the lamb avoiding me, she will also come. With her perched upon my horse, she will be unable to evade me and will have little choice with regard to conversing with me.

"Come, Bella Agnellu, the day has gotten away from us."

"I'm not going."

"This is where you would be mistaken because you will accompany me during my travels."

"Listen, I get that I keep pulling you horsemen's asses out of the fire; it doesn't mean I want to keep doing it."

"I do not understand the meaning of pulling our ass out of the fire. When have my brothers ever placed their asses in a fire which would require your assistance in removing them?"

"It's a saying... as in, I rescued them."

"Rescued? You rescued my brothers?"

"Yep, and I don't intend to do it for you."

"Care to share with me how one female mortal saved not one of my brother's lives but two?"

"Okay, let's start with you reeling in the skepticism, big guy."

"Big guy?" I question.

"She likes to provoke. It is best to ignore the moniker if you do not wish to retain it for a time," Pestilence interjects as he walks his horse to the stable we set up for our companions.

"Yeah, what Pessy said." Avalon wastes no time walking up to them and begins stroking his horse's mane while speaking to him in what I can only describe as a tender, loving tone. I don't listen to everything she says, but I don't miss her calling him Storm. Something I have heard her reference during prior conversations when talking to others about his horse or when speaking to him. I will have to inquire what this means.

"Pessy?"

"Yes, the name she has taken to calling me." He says with an exasperated sigh while removing the saddle from his companion.

"She will not call me this *big guy* moniker."

"How do you propose to stop me?" She asks, crossing her arms over her chest while leaning against Pestilence's horse.

"I am not my brother."

"What the hell is that supposed to mean?" The lamb may have posed the question, but the furrowed brows and scowl covering my brother's face confirms he is as interested in hearing my response as she is in gaining it.

"Simple. It means I am not so forgiving. I do not permit disobedience within my ranks."

"Your... ranks?"

"This is what I said, is it not?"

"Let's get one thing straight, asshole. I am not among your ranks."

"Are you sure because the other sons of Adam and the daughters of Eve who have crossed paths with me and are not in my army did not last long in your world. And as you are still alive, it means I count you among my legions."

"Bullshit!" she snaps as the shade on her face changes. It has morphed into the deep red that only appears when she is enraged.

"Protest all you wish; it changes nothing, u mo Bella Agnellu."

"Someone better tell me what the hell this u mo Bella Agnellu means. Right now, damn it!"

"My beautiful lamb," Pestilence informs her before stepping back, knowing the shit storm the lamb is about to unleash. Yet he should be more concerned with me as I turn my angry glare in his direction. If I thought her face was red before, it has now become an alarming shade one can only associate with fury.

"Listen, asshole, you can call me Avalon, Ava, or A—no fuck that, not A. You can't call me A either.—but if you refer to me as this Bella Agnellu shit again or anything other than what I just told you to call me, you will find out how a mere mortal was capable of saving both your brothers' lives… the hard way."

She cuts me off the instant I open my mouth to offer my retort. After all these weeks of traveling together, her fiery response proves she knows me quite well. "And don't say 'how do I know you wouldn't like it' because I promise you won't!"

Again I lift my finger, but she has already spun on her heels to storm away while advising over her shoulder, "You won't."

I cannot hide the growing smirk crossing my face while I stalk behind her, so I can toss her over my shoulder before depositing her on my horse. Once seated behind her, I lean forward and murmur, "I suppose it is a good thing we will have plenty of time to find out… my beautiful lamb."

The sharp inhale as her breath catches appears to be her only response. With a satisfied chuckle, I click my tongue to signal to my companion it is time for us to be on our way.

Chapter Sixteen: Rope

~Avalon Winter 2026 ~

*I*NFURIATING. *THIS IS* the only word I can think of to describe this rider. He drives me insane with his cryptic flirty shit. I have no damn idea why he keeps doing this crap other than to frustrate me. Here's the thing: I'm not sure what bothers me most, the fact War thinks he can get away with it or that Death permits it. I thought he would have something to say about one of his brothers treating me like I'm fair game. I know Pestilence would never allow War to speak to Greer in this manner. At least, I don't think he would. I suppose there is one way to find out.

"What do you think Pestilence would do if you talked to Greer like you speak to me?"

"And how do I speak to you, Bella—"

"Nope! Absolutely not. I already told you not to call me that shit any longer."

"You don't seem to mind my brother calling you little lamb."

"Yeah, well, his nickname doesn't hold the same connotation as yours." I can feel him chuckle behind me, and I want to spin around to hit the asshole. My problem is there's a genuine possibility he would like it.

"So be it, mouse—"

"Really? This is what you're going to call me."

"Since you have advised I am no longer permitted to refer to you as my beautiful lamb, what else would I call you?"

"You could try—I don't know... maybe my name... Avalon."

"No, I think not, mouse."

"Whatever, just answer the question."

"If I spoke to the daughter of Eve my brother has chosen as his mate the way I speak to you, he would not like it, nor would he permit it to continue." So I suppose this is my answer. Right? Death allows it because he doesn't care. "Why do you ask?"

"Doesn't matter," I mumble before letting the hurt of his admission fully register, which makes me slightly more than just a tad irritated, so my next question is more bark than inquiry. "Where the hell are we going?"

"I told you since my army continues to grow, and if I wish to follow the mortals who want to remove my brother and me, we will require supplies, not to mention a way to transport them. I believe I know where we can obtain something to help with this. Our trip also affords me the opportunity to scout out the surroundings, something I cannot do when I have an army at my back."

For the rest of the ride, neither of us speaks. I don't know why War remains so quiet—lord knows he normally has no problem saying whatever shit is in his head—as for me, I needed time to let his confirmation settle. I guess I've known for a while now, but this just cemented it for me.

The further we go, the landscape changes from metropolis to rural, and the snow begins to fall. Great. Just fan-fucking-tastic. This is the exact opposite of what I need. The damn snow could have held off another day because one thing is for certain, we are hours away from camp, and I have no intention of having a repeat performance from the last time I got stuck in a snowstorm with a rider.

The bigger issue—yes, there is a bigger issue than freezing—is my ass has gone completely numb. Even after traveling with Death and Pestilence, my backside has not become accustomed to this constant riding. No hardened rider ready bottom for me, which is an issue since this rider seems hellbent on dragging me everywhere he goes. Even though I interfere with his task more than help him accomplish it.

Today seems to be the worst time I have experienced while accompanying a rider. The last thing I want to do is start squirming around in front of him because, let's face it, War would probably see it as something sexual. Not the real reason for doing it… ass pain. So when he finally pulls the reins on his horse to stop us, I say a silent prayer of thanks to whoever the hell is listening.

"Stay here, mouse," War demands.

"Piss off," I snap back.

"It would be prudent for you to mind my directive, Bella Agnellu. Unless you wish me to tie you to my horse," he said, taking a commanding step in my direction. Even having this big-ass rider crowding me, I would have argued for several reasons if not for the burning need to rub my sore butt. Something I positively will not do in front of him. Why did his comment piss me off? First, I hate being told what I can and cannot do. Like I'm some damn obedient dog. And second, he called me mouse, followed by beautiful lamb… again.

After waiting for him to return for what felt like too long, I ventured into the wooded area near where he had left me to gather some wood. Otherwise, he might return and find a frozen damn mouse lamb seal breaker. I would not have dawdled if I knew what awaited me back at camp.

One extremely irritated rider.

"Why the sudden change of heart?" Change of heart? Oh… wait, he thought I took off. Well, I see an opportunity to teach him a lesson. Maybe get a little retribution for the beautiful lamb shit.

"Believe me, it wasn't easy coming back, but I figured I could keep going, which only would have pissed you off further, or I could come at this from another approach."

"This was a wise choice."

"Thanks, I'm smart when I want to be," I reply, giving him a cheeky grin.

"Because otherwise, you would have found yourself chained to me tonight." He says, tapping the saddle bag.

"Wait, you were serious about that shit."

"Only one way to find out. In fact, I'm hoping you will run."

"Why?"

"Because I would enjoy the hunt," he says with a wink before he steps closer, pinning me between his enormous frame and his horse. "And having you chained to me all night, my beautiful lamb, is very appealing."

"Ahhh…. No," is the only thing I can mutter. He backs away when he is sure I have nothing else to say, and I don't intend to take off, chuckling at my obvious discomfort the whole time. So much for me teaching him a damn lesson since the ease with which he turned the damn tables on me is frustrating. Asshole.

"You wouldn't dare."

"Wouldn't I?"

"Not if you want to keep your manhood intact." Big, big mistake on my part, and the problem is the longer he contemplates it, the more he seems to like the idea, especially when I attempt to leave to gather more wood. This is how I ended up being tethered to this damn bullheaded rider because no matter how many times I tried to convince him I never wanted to run, he liked his version of the events better. Since it puts me right where he wants me. And telling him Pestilence would never be such an asshole didn't help my plight.

"It doesn't surprise me. My little brother always had an affinity for you mortals."

"And you don't?"

"Are you asking me if I love you? If this is what you're asking—"

"I wasn't, but since you brought up the subject, why don't you tell me what you want?" He moves closer, bringing his mouth to my ear before murmuring.

"I would not be opposed to fucking y—"

"Don't finish that goddamn sentence."

"Fine. Provided you do not take my father's name in vain, Bella Agnellu."

I've reached my limit on trying to be friendly with this rider, so I flop down before irritation wins out, but rather than yelling at this being who couldn't care less what I have to say, I sit up and punch my makeshift pillow, hoping to fluff it up. When I flop back this time, I can feel his eyes on me. I can also hear the sound one makes when trying but failing to silently laugh at someone, specifically when you don't want them to know. I flip over on my side so I don't stab this asshole. The problem is, he rolls with me, pressing his body against mine. Playing the part of the big spoon. No. Absolutely fucking not.

"What are you doing?"

"It is cold tonight. I am simply trying to save you from freezing. This is still a thing with you mortals, is it not?"

"I'll be fine."

"No point in taking any chances."

The exasperated sigh I give him only amuses him more. Wonderful. Now he's not even trying to hide it. I try again to forget about the obnoxious asshole until I feel the unmistakable bulge of a growing erection. Pulling away, I look over my shoulder before growling, "Could you maybe rein that thing in?"

"It seems to have a mind of its own. Specifically, when I am lying so close to one of Eve's beautiful daughters."

"If you unchained me, we wouldn't have to lie next to one another. And guess what? By doing this, you wouldn't have to worry about shit happening below your waist from being so close to me... Avalon... not Eve's daughter."

"You are a daughter of Eve, and my answer remains the same. No."

"Why not?" I ask, no longer trying to hide my irritation.

"Because as much as I would enjoy chasing you, I don't feel like doing it again tonight. The only thing I would like to do now is rest. And may I remind you that you dared me, mouse."

"Then can you at least stay over on your own side?"

"It's my bedroll. The entire thing is my side."

"Why can't you be more like Pestilence?"

War props himself up before leaning next to my ear to whisper his response. "Because I am the fun one, Avalon. Do you not remember?"

Once again, I wish I had never uttered this stupid statement to Death. Talk about something coming back to bite you in the ass.

Chapter Seventeen: Fool

I KNOW HE was here. He fucking talked to me. Told me the riders were coming. Damn it, I couldn't have imagined it. Could I? It's not like the shit I went through when mom and dad died. The phantom images that haunted me day and night, the ones that made me relive their death every time I closed my eyes. These are all the thoughts plaguing me while I walk from room to room.

I could tell by the looks on the men's faces they didn't believe me. Trevor tried to stop me when I bolted out of Wayne's tent, but I had to check it out for myself. The only thing he wanted to do was bitch at me anyway because I embarrassed him, not because he was worried about me or wanted to check on me. In all fairness, he didn't know how awful things were for me when I first joined this group. The only one who knows about the torment I experienced is the woman running up the road.

"Em," Sophie yells from the main floor. It didn't surprise me when I saw her coming down the street since she was one of the abundant witnesses standing there when I stormed out of Wayne's tent.

"Up here, Soph," I yell while I remain with my head pressed against the cool glass from the window. It makes for the perfect vantage point to observe the road while I try to piece together how the hell some random ass guy somehow got in and out of the house without anyone seeing him.

"Ember, what the hell happened? Richard Cabeza and Limp Dicklet—"

"Limp Dicklet?" I ask as I roll my head enough to take in Sophie's face.

"My new name for Trevor. Ya know, since he is el suck-o in the boudoir."

"Yeah, Soph, he's definitely going to know what you're getting at if you call him that, and something tells me he won't appreciate you calling him a limp dick."

"Floppy Member?"

"No."

"Unit B Saggin'?" Okay, I can't help but laugh at this one while shaking my head. Leave it up to Soph to pull me out of my thoughts.

"I'll keep working on it, but for now, Richard and Limpy are plenty pissed that you took off, and I'm pretty sure Limpy Saggin'...." She gives me a side-eyed glance. Again I shake my head as a little chuckle escapes me. "Tough crowd. Anyway, I think he's looking for you."

"Correction, he found me," I tell her as I watch Trevor storming toward the house we are in.

"Ember! Are you fucking in here?" The asshole apparently doesn't understand what a door knob is for since it sounds like he kicked the door in rather than twisting the damn thing to open it.

"Sophie, you should probably go."

"And leave you here alone with Pasture Johnson ... hard pass."

"Alright, this one you might have to explain.... Later," I quickly add when I hear him bounding up the steps. Her response is to give me two thumbs up. While I roll my eyes at her. She is so damn corny, which is what makes her the perfect friend for me.

"What the fuck did you think you were doing?" Trevor snaps when he barges into the room.

"I thought I was warning our camp of an impending danger. Because if the riders are close, I can't imagine they won't attack."

"Nobody is paying you to fuckin think, Ember."

"Nobody is paying anyone to do shit anymore," I snap.

"Knock off the damn attitude."

"Trev—" Sophie doesn't even get out his full name before he whips around and silences her with a deadly glare.

"Next goddamn time you think you have news, bring that shit to me first. I'll decide if it's important enough to take to Wayne."

"The fucking horsemen of the apocalypse! You don't think this subject qualifies as important?"

"Since your source for this all-important intel seems to only live in your damn head. No! No, I don't think it qualifies!"

"Whatever," I huff before pushing past him. There is no point in staying here any longer. After a thorough search,

I could not find any evidence to suggest that the guy had been here, and at this point, I'm not interested in hearing any more shit from Trev.

"Besides, I gave you the very specific order to have your ass in my bed tonight, so I'm trying to reconcile why you were out scavenging to begin with."

"Take it up with Wayne." I grab Sophie's arm before storming out of the room.

"I will, and while I do, you better take your ass back to my tent and wait for me to get there. Like I told you to do earlier today." This time, it's Trevor pushing past me. He hates letting anyone think they have the upper hand, and while I have no intention of going to his damn tent, I figure it's easier to let him think I'll be there than deal with his mouth all the way back to our camp. Besides, I'm more interested in learning what Sophie's latest nickname means. We wait until he disappears from view before Soph speaks up first.

"Well, he's a bundle of fun."

"Yeah, to say the least. Okay, dish." When she just looks at me with a puzzled expression, I add. "Pastor Johnson?"

"Oh, not my best material. I had to come up with something fast, and since you already poo-poo the other awesome names, I had to give you this shit. So what I said was pasture, not pastor, as in putting him out to pasture and Johnson as in dick, put it all together, and you get...."

"Retire his dick."

"Now you're getting it, but I think I have something better, although I'll have to come up with an acronym 'cause it's entirely too long to say all the time."

"I'm all ears."

"Well, actually, you have small ears, but your eyes are kind of freakishly large."

"The better to see you with, my dear," I said along with a Bha-ha-ha laugh.

"Whoa-whoa, you know I hate that damn fairy tale. Freaks me the hell out having a damn wolf eating Red's granny and then dressing up like the stiff all so her farsighted granddaughter can end up as dessert." She shivers before mumbling, "Gives me the damn chills."

"I don't remember any portion of the story claiming the granddaughter was farsighted."

"Well, how the hell else would you describe it? I mean, the chick was right next to the damn wolf and couldn't see it wasn't her grandma. And don't even get me started on her obvious lack of an old factory."

"Old factory?"

"Yeah, her sense of smell."

"Olfactory?"

"Yeah," she says, dragging out the word with wide eyes while wobbling her head around like I'm the idiot. "…it's what I said."

"My mistake."

"No worries," she replies before falling silent while I keep looking at her, waiting for her to tell me the better name. When she finally realizes I have been staring at her, she turns to look at me. I raise my eyebrows and tilt my head, hoping she'll take the hint. "Oh right, Trevor's new name."

A beaming smile crosses her face before she giggles. "Captain Spankless Johnson. I'm thinking we can call him Spanky or Cap for short. It's either this or Gimpy Johnson."

I burst out laughing, unable to contain my amusement, while I wrap my arm around her shoulder. She's corny as hell, but she's the only damn person in this world who can pull me out of my head and make me laugh no matter how foul of a mood I'm in. It's a rare and wonderful trait if you ask me, and something that makes my following statement so much more than some half-hearted sentiment. "I love you, Soph."

"I know," she sighs before joining me in my revelry.

~*War*~

The sound of voices carrying on the cool night air was the only reason I left Avalon to her peaceful slumber so I could investigate.

"Remain with the lamb," I instruct my companion. A soft sigh pulls my attention back to the lamb, who rolls to the space I just vacated while tucking the blanket under her chin prior to inhaling my scent. "Keep her safe."

With as much caution as my gigantic frame can manage, I creep through the thickest part of the tree line. Moving closer to the source of the conversation, which is apparently about my brothers and me.

"You got that shit straight."

"Hell yeah. We're going to put those fucking riders down."

"Well, first thing's first, we have to catch up with Wayne's group. After we find them, we'll need to fortify, stock the stronghold, and train everyone." Thank you for sharing your plans. It will make destroying you so much simpler. I continue circling the group of men to assess their weaknesses. Twelve sons of Adam surround the fire. Two are sleeping, five hold weapons, and one has only seen sixteen summers. Too bad he will not make it to seventeen since it was he who advised they would put us down. Which I will assume means he plans to attempt the impossible and kill us.

"We shouldn't be taking these riders lightly. Especially since we know their entire reason for existing is removing humanity."

"If you're so damn scared of these fuckers, why don't you hide behind your momma's apron strings, Kenny?" This young one has grit, yet little else. And if the glare he receives from the one he called Kenny is any clue, I believe he is about to discover bravery is not everything, nor will it take a rider to put him down. Fortune seems to shine on this fool since it appears he has a brother of his own. One tasked with watching over this naïve son of Adam.

"Baby steps, little brother." His brother positions himself between Kenny and the mouthy one. If I had to guess the way Kenny withdraws when the fool's brother advances, I would say he may represent a worthy foe and one with both fortitude and intellect.

"Fuck that. I wish one of those assholes was here now because I would have no issues ending him. Painfully." If this is how he feels, then far be it from me to deny this foolish mortal his wish. Their heads all whip in my direction as I step out.

"Yes, please, by all means… tell me how you plan to kill my brother and me." Every son of Adam jumps to his feet, and the ones with weapons draw them to level in my direction.

"Who the fuck are you?" the worthy foe demands, bringing his sword up from his waist, making me reconsider my previous assessment of him. In war, it is best not to take such an aggressive stance until you are aware of who you are dealing with and what their arrival represents to your survival. In this case, it is a mistake and one I will take immense satisfaction in demonstrating to these mortals the error of such a misstep. My travels with the lamb have ensured it has been far too long since my blade has seen battle. A situation I plan to remedy straight away.

"I am the rider you wish to remove."

"Bullshit, you're no rider," the young fool yells as he attempts to move around his brother. Once again, fortune smiles upon this dullard since his brother's arm snaps out to halt his approach.

"You don't look anything like the fucking riders," the fool shouts from behind his brother's outstretched arm. Since a simple appendage is not an adequate deterrent to halt anyone set upon their goal, I would say the young fool doesn't want the fight he proclaimed.

"Is this so?"

"Yeah!"

"By all means, please enlighten us with your vast knowledge regarding what these riders look like, young jester?"

"Names not Jester, and sure, I'll tell you right after we beat your fucking ass for sticking your nose in our business."

"Brian," Fool's brother snarls through his gritted teeth.

"You are welcome to try, young jester."

"Already told you, asshole, my name's not jester."

"Perhaps you prefer fool then?" the clueless lout snarls before trying to push past his brother, who seems to understand who they now face.

"Shut up, Brian!"

"Fuck that. Everyone knows the riders are bigger, older, and ugly as fuck."

"Are you coming on to me, Brian?" I know my taunt will bring the little fool scrambling. I will enjoy killing him first. He dips below his brother's arm, twists from the grasp of another, spins, and brings the blade in his hand up with only one intention in mind… to remove my head from my shoulders. Too bad for him; this does not align with my plan.

My stance never wavers while I watch him advance. To an untrained warrior, his approach may appear to be that of a skilled swordsman, but a trained fighter never gives his back to his opponent if they can help it. Which will spell this son of Adam's demise because the second his blade slashes toward my throat, he finds my blade impaled in his torso.

His brother's eyes grow wide as all words fail him. His sharp inhale is my only indication this battle has begun. Shoving the fool's body off my blade, I widen my stance, square my hips, bring my sword up, and wait for their assault.

The first comes from my right, causing me to lean back before I bring my elbow up, shattering his nose with the impact. The fool's brother has arrived, intending to seek retribution for his slain sibling. I parry his first attempt, block the second, and disarm him on his third. When another member of his group attacks, I grab the man before me and spin to allow his own ally the privilege of removing him from this realm.

With the blade sticking through his chest, his eyes drift down to the object responsible for ending his life. His cough brings with it the telling signs of his looming death. I wait until his focus returns to mine before I tell him, "Your mistake was in threatening my brothers."

*****

Even though I made every attempt not to rouse the sleeping lamb, she woke the second I returned to the spot next to her.

"War?"

"I apologize. I did not intend to wake you."

"Did you go somewhere?"

"Where is it you believe I would go?"

"When it comes to you riders," she yawns and pulls the blanket out from under her so she can offer a portion to me. My preference would have been for her to retain the entire cover for her comfort. "...only your dad knows." Her choice to rephrase this comment from only god knows to my dad makes me laugh.

I settle next to her, allowing my eyes to slip closed. She will require additional rest before we set out on my horse. When she is silent for several minutes, I assume she must have returned to sleep until she clears her throat to ask her next question.

"Um, War?"

"Yes."

"Is that… blood on your arm?"

Chapter Eighteen: Tell Me

*W*AR NEVER ADMITTED what happened the other night, although I have suspicions. Since returning to his army, I have also noticed Pestilence and him having some pretty intense conversations, like the one they are in the middle of right now. Oh, I could leave them alone and allow them to keep their secrets, or I could do what everyone knows I'm going to do… find out what the hell these two riders are up to.

"Does she know?" War asks Pestilence.

War reclines against a tree next to where their horses are kept. And as has become his custom without a damn shirt on. It's difficult to rein in my wandering eyes with his chiseled abs, sculpted tattooed chest, and muscled arms out on display for the silly mortals of this world to marvel at. Especially since these things all look like they were carved from granite.

I've also noticed how many women this little army has collected over the last month. Women who leap at the chance to join his ranks and have no problem outright gawking at him. And even though he is constantly flirting, I'm not sure he realizes their come fuck me eyes are directed at him. I wonder if this is because, like Death and Pestilence, he doesn't understand how insanely hot he is. Or… is it possible this rider doesn't yet realize the pleasures he would have if he decided to experience the temptation only our flesh can offer him?

Not that I intend to show him. I would put money on the fact this rider—like his brothers—does not realize how devastatingly handsome he is. If you ask me, God kinda sucks. I mean, it's distressing enough he created beings whose sole purpose is to kill off his other creations, but he had to make them all look like this. Muscled, toned, tan, tattoo-covered golden skin that screams to be touched.

Not by me.… Been there, done that, had to pick up the broken pieces by myself. Although, in all fairness, Death never promised me anything, and it's my fault, I didn't think to inquire if there was a future or current Mrs. Death back home. I should ask Pestilence; maybe it would make moving on easier if I knew the truth.

As beautiful as the riders are on the outside, what I find most appealing about them is that they will go to any lengths to safeguard the people they deem worthy. I also admire how much these riders genuinely care about each other.

It's not until Pestilence pulls his eyebrows together that I realize I've been staring for far too long. Especially for someone who has told War time and again it will never goddamn happen. The issue is he's not the only one who saw it, and now War is grinning at me with his damn infuriating "I know what you were doing," smile.

My weak attempt at pretending I wasn't gawking at the half-naked rider is an epic fail. Because clearing your throat to pretend you weren't doing exactly what you were just caught doing ever fucking worked! Real damn believable.

"Jesus Christ, Avalon, pull your head out of your ass," I silently chastise myself. Hoping to stem off the heat crawling up my cheeks, I try to divert their attention back to the conversation I walked in on.

"Know what?" It's clear Pestilence is uncomfortable with my question. Which tells me whatever secret they have, I won't like it.

"Know what?" I asked again with more convictions. This time it's also less question and much closer to a command.

"When we discovered Wren, he was no longer living." Pestilence's gaze refuses to meet mine.

"Yeah, I know. I was there, remember?"

"Yes, but what you do not know is he was past the point of returning, little lamb," Pestilence says cautiously.

"Then how did he come back?"

"Thanatos was the only one who could restore what the mortals took."

"You already told me Death brought him back."

"I did," Pestilence shifts uncomfortably. He's not telling me everything.

"That's not all though... Is it, brother?" War says with a smirk as his eyes remain on me.

"What's he talking about, Pessy?"

"I never grow tired of hearing this name, brother," War tells him, making Pestilence groan in frustration. If I want him to tell me what has him so conflicted, I better hold the Pessy shit for a minute.

"Pestilence, what are you not telling me?" He exhales before his hand finds the back of his neck to rub it. A clear sign he isn't comfortable discussing this subject.

"To bring him back, Thanatos required the essence of an immortal being."

"And," I snap, becoming angrier with each half-response he gives me. Why the hell won't he just tell me what happened when he took Wren's body? And I swear he better not tell me Wren is some clone… or pod person… or whatever else these riders are capable of.

"I gave him some of mine."

"You did what?"

"In order for Thanatos to restore him, I provided him with a piece of my immortality. It was the only way to bring Wren back."

"So this is the big secret that it wasn't only Death who brought him back. You saved him as well?"

"In part." I rush forward, which causes him to flinch. I believe he thinks I did this to hit him, but when I leap into his arms to hug him, the tension in his muscles melts away. When he pulls back, he lifts his eyebrows in a questioning manner. Which has War asking his own question.

"Does she do this often?"

Okay, so I think it's safe to assume the 'she' part is a reference to me, and the 'do this' part refers to the hug I still have wrapped around one of my favorite rider's necks. But he doesn't seem to mind, which is evident when he replies with a chuckle. "Only when she is pleased."

"Now I wish I had told her," he mumbles, but when I glance at him, he winks before continuing. "I should love to see what she will do when you tell her the rest."

"What rest?" I ask as I pull away from Pestilence so I can see his eyes.

"In doing this, Wren became my... my son. He is forever bound to me, and I will let no one ever harm my son again." I leap at him again, but this time I hit him with enough momentum; it knocks him backward over the log he had been leaning against so I can pepper his face with kisses.

"Again, I wish it was I who told her." War's timbre is steeped in a sensual, lustful quality that I have grown accustomed to whenever he is trying to make me uncomfortable. Too bad for him; I'm too busy hugging Wren's daddy. Even though I thought of the rider as his dad after seeing how close they had become, knowing he is Renny's dad is another thing altogether.

Ignoring the overly lusty rider, I ask, "So, is he immortal now? Is he like you?"

"I did not condemn my son—"

"Your son." I can't help the girly giggle his comment elicits from me.

"Yes, little lamb, my son," he replies with a grin. Even though I can't tell if the grin is from my amusement or him confirming he is Wren's dad, it doesn't matter because what I see is pure happiness. "I did not wish to sentence my son to a life of loneliness. He will never be a rider like me or my brothers."

"Does Greer know?"

"Yes, brother, does the little one's mother know?"

Pestilence grits his teeth and narrows his eyes at War's teasing, "No, not yet."

"But you plan on telling her, right?" I can't keep this from her. I don't have many women I consider a friend in this world—no, she's more than a friend. She's my family—so I won't risk losing her trust.

"Someday soon, but not now, because I am unsure if my chosen is ready to hear the truth of his return yet."

"Your chosen? You mean Greer's like your wife now?"

"For as long as she will have me."

After promising Pessy I wouldn't say anything to Greer, I excuse myself. I need a second alone because even though Pestilence is the one who gave up a piece of his immortality, it was Death who brought him back. And even if he doesn't care about me or what I think about him any longer, he deserves to hear my appreciation as well. I prefer to do this alone, so I walk far enough out of the camp to ensure I have the privacy to thank him.

I choose what I believe is the perfect spot before tilting my head toward the sky to look at the stars like I have done hundreds of times when I want to talk to him and prepare to thank him. But all the thoughts swirling in my head refuse to come out. The gratitude I planned on expressing feels insufficient for what he did. How do you thank someone for the gift he gave Greer? As ridiculous as my sentiment may be, it doesn't feel right not to tell him. So here goes nothing.

"I don't know if you can hear me or if you even care what I have to say. Thank you for saving him," I say as my eyes slowly lift to the sky to allow me to search the heavens. I don't know what I thought I would see up there, maybe a star shining brighter than the others or some other cosmic event like a shooting star. Hell, a lunar eclipse would be great, but none of these things happen. So I can't help but wonder if he is still watching us. I suppose it's possible he finally decided we are no longer worthy of his time. This would explain why he's gone dark.

"He cannot hear you right now," War says when he walks up behind me. His sudden arrival from his silent steps causes me to jump as I place my hand on my chest. After taking a few exasperated breaths to ensure my voice doesn't give away my racing heart to this cheeky bastard who will never let me live it down, I inquired what he meant by this.

"Why not?"

"There was a price to be paid for what he did with Wren." I remember Pestilence telling Greer as much, but he would never confirm the price or what the hell these ambiguous words meant. "But I can help you reach him. You only need to take my hands." With a hint of apprehension, I reach out to accept his outstretched hand. I admit being on the receiving side of this softer, more gentle mammoth man who seems to live for the battle is nice.

"I don't know if you can hear me, but thank you for what you did for Wren. Of all the souls you could grant this to, he was the right choice because he is the best of us." The last part is more whispered than spoken because my words have become thick with the emotions overwhelming me.

War's eyes move from me to the sky while I await his response. Especially since it appears that War is conversing with someone I can't see. What I don't understand is why his thumb is rubbing small soft circles on the back of my hand or the wicked grin blossoming across his face. "He said to tell you that you are most welcome."

"All that silence for four little words," I said with a chuckle, trying to hide my disappointment.

"And he asked me to give you this." War bends over and gently presses a kiss against my lips. I pull away until his arms wrap around my waist, drawing me closer. The strength in those arms and the tender way he holds me is so familiar that it takes me back to when Thanatos did this for the first time. And for a second, I forget this is not the rider I wish was here. When my senses return enough for me to withdraw from his embrace, I admit I am left feeling slightly breathless but ashamed of letting it happen. I'm also confused about why Death would ask his brother to do this. I guess it doesn't represent a betrayal since it has become clear to me he doesn't think of our time the same way I do. Maybe this is him confirming he has moved on, and it's time I do the same.

War straightens before a slight chuckle slips past his parted lips. "Worth every second."

"What?" I ask, now confused about what the hell he means by this, but before I can make my inquiry and further complicate things, his subsequent statement only confuses me more.

"And every bit of his fury."

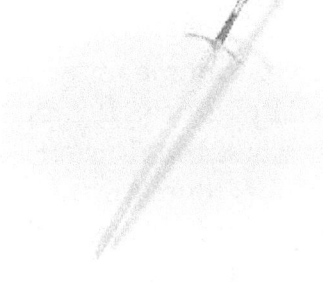

~ War ~

As much as I would have preferred staying with my beautiful lamb, my brother's insistence that I come and speak with him directly has pulled me to our realm. I can feel his anger mounting the closer I get to his cell. A cell he is only in because he allowed Michael to place him there. I'm sure part of this is because he will always do as our father asks of him, but I sense this isn't the only reason he consented.

The instant I open the door to his cell, his head snaps up, permitting me to see something he does his best to hide.

His demon side.

I'm sure it comes as no surprise for all his similarities to his brothers; Thanatos is different. A difference that becomes clear in moments like this because in order for him to fulfill his task of ferrying souls, our father made him equal parts angelic and demonic. A necessity for times when a soul must be delivered to Lucifer's realm. It's what makes him so powerful and why Michael has always been jealous of my brother. But for Thanatos, it is a side of himself he struggles to suppress because, in his eyes, it is a mark of shame.

Most beings would not risk his ire. I am not most beings.

"Why the hell did you do that?" His growl is low and dangerous, telling me how close to the edge he is. The wisest amongst us would not risk pressing him further, but I think he needs perspective. So I don't plan to just push him; this time, I shove.

"Just admit it, brother."

"Admit what?"

"If I must tell you, then you're not ready to be the man who is worthy of her."

"War!"

"Yes, Thanatos."

"Don't fucking do it again."

"I won't, but only if you are prepared to lay claims to her."

"Claiming a mortal even if the being is our lamb is not our purpose."

"It doesn't change the truth of my words."

"Why are you doing this?"

"To force your hand since you refuse to admit what the lamb means to you. I will either force it out of you or claim her for myself."

"No!"

"No, what? No, you will not permit me to claim her, or you will not admit how you feel? Which No is it to be, Thanatos."

"I will not allow you to manipulate me, brother. Now quit fucking playing with the lamb."

"You still don't get it, Thanatos. So be it. Just remember, you could have stopped this."

"War."

"God be damn, brother," he yells as I walk away from him. I have a lamb to show some remarkable things. "WAR!"

"Admit it, brother, and then she will only be under my protection."

"As opposed to?" he yells.

"Me," I tell him just before I close the door.

"FUCK!" I hear him yell a second before he slams against the door. If not for the runes holding him at bay, I believe he would do something he had never done before. Hit one of his brothers.

Chapter Nineteen: The Lies We Tell

ICHAEL'S SELF-RIGHTEOUS expression when he enters my cell informs me he is already aware one of my siblings has been here to see me. After my conversation with my ill-informed brother, I am in no mood to deal with this irritant.

Only through our father's mercy does he remain blissfully unaware of the reason for War's visit. This is most fortuitous for me because I will not have to disobey my father. Lucky for him since Michael will not be tempted to use her to bring me to heel. A situation I will never allow. Making it fortunate for all else involved for one straightforward reason... I will not have to kill the warrior standing in front of me.

As he strolls around the cell they hold me within, I know he is searching for the reason War came to visit and to inspect the damage I caused following our infuriating conversation.

"When will you learn not even the infamous Death is capable of breaking the bonds holding you?"

"When you realize it is only with my consent, you are able to restrain me."

"You always have thought too highly of yourself, Death." With his exploration of my cell complete, he stops directly in front of me. His focus remains on the wall to my left, and with his hands clasped behind his back, he attempts to display indifference, but his wing's rigidity tells a different story. He is as frustrated that he has yet to break me as he is afraid of what I will do when I decide I am done being the dutiful son.

"Stating a truth does not equate to any feelings of superiority, Michael."

"Why was your brother here?"

"Why does it matter to you? Are you jealous my brothers care more about me than your inane decree?"

"I'm told you two were discussing a mortal." For once, I am glad he is not looking at me; otherwise, he would have witnessed the shift in my posture. It appears one of my guards has been more spy than jailor. By the time his eyes swing to meet my gaze, my expression has returned to one of bored indifference.

"It seems not just any mortal either, but the one who has swayed the riders. The lamb who does not understand her sole responsibility in this is to call you and your brethren forth... not bed the horsemen."

"Avalon has not bedded the riders," I growl even as I attempt to hold my fury in check. If he continues to push this, they will leave me with little choice but to ensure he cannot hurt her. An act my father will surely see as treason and the catalyst that will bring about the end of my long existence.

"Huh, I thought you riders were incapable of this."

"Of what?" I hiss while clenching my hands as I prepare to shatter the shackles containing them.

"Lying." He wisely steps away because I feel my demonic side pressing for release. It is a piece of myself I keep locked away. Pushed down so deep most of the time, he cannot appear because it confirms I am not as divine as the beings around me. When he believes he has put enough space between us to keep him safe, he asks the one thing I prayed would never be questioned.

"Are you in love with that mortal?"

"You know as well as I do, Michael; we were not created to know of their love."

"Yet, all the same, I believe you do. Which proves how weak you truly are."

"Weak? I am many things. Weak is not one of them."

"How else would you describe it when one mortal lamb accomplished what none ever believed possible?"

"Enlighten me, Michael."

"She taught the reaper of souls how to love, and in doing so, she has brought the riders to their knees."

"I kneel to no one other than our creator. As for the lamb, she taught me what it means to be human, nothing more."

"And what is the one thing all these mortals want?"

"You believe I know of their desires?"

"Yes, because it is also what you covet. One of our father's favorite sons so easily swayed by a pair of breasts, the curve of her hips, or was it—"

"I advise you that finishing this sentiment will not bode well for you. Besides, the riders covet nothing." He is why I could not tell War my true feelings for Avalon. Since War's return, Michael's watchful gaze is never far. He claims this is only done because I gifted my brother a soul who should have been our father's when I granted him the return of his son. He believes I overstep, but why would our father give me the ability if he did not intend me to use it? But this angel does not see it that way, and I know if he finds out the truth about Avalon, he will use her against me to gain whatever he wants.

Michael believes if he can find something I desire, he can force my hand to choose his side in this coming war, and he's right. I would give him anything he wanted to save her. Avalon's life is in peril with her own kind because of who she is, and with mine if they ever find out how much she means to me. And because the only beings I trust with this information are our creator and my brothers, I must continue to use caution where she is concerned. Therefore, I permit them to believe she merely represents a physical attraction. An exploration of the flesh and nothing more.

"We are not meant to desire anything—"

"Yet it seems our father gave us the ability to do just that."

"Do you truly believe he wishes his greatest creation's demise, Michael?"

"No. But I intend to prove to our father his faith in these creatures is misguided."

"Why?

"Because they are unworthy of his forgiveness and we… his warriors and the protectors of paradise, not they, should be his favorite. And I intend to prove what your affections for one mortal woman have granted you."

"This will be a difficult undertaking, as I hold no love for any of them."

"Gabriel, please show this rider what his beloved lamb is doing."

"With pleasure." Whatever they are preparing to show me will most likely torture me in a way none have ever been able to claim before. Because knowing the games Michael plays, this revelation will no doubt include showing me she has moved on and found comfort in another man's arms. I would never have permitted him to touch me if I knew what Gabriel was preparing to reveal.

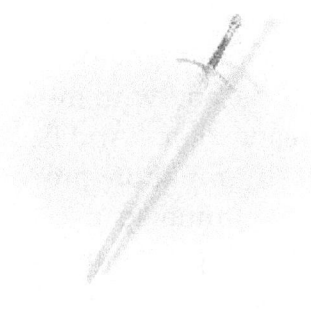

~*Avalon*~

Shortly after War helped me reach out to Death, he disappeared, leaving me to question if his brother was the one who was mad and if so, why. It's not like he's pining away for me. I can smell the faintest hint of campfire smoke in the air as I pace around his tent while I wait for him to return. I don't know why having this question answered is so damn important to me; it just is. After all, I gave up on the notion that I was as important to him as he was to me a while ago.

When the heavy footstep of someone approaching his tent echoes around me, I believe I will soon have the answers I need. But when the flap to enter his tent is flipped back, Pestilence—not War—enters.

"Little lamb, I did not expect to find you here."

"I was looking for your brother. Do you know where he went?"

"Um… I believe he had to return home."

"For good?" Seriously, could my voice get any higher or squeaky? It's damn frustrating. I should be happy if he has returned home, not…. What? Uncertain? Sad? Confused? Why does the possibility of him returning home cause a mix of emotions?

"No. Are you well, little lamb?" Pestilence asks, moving closer to where I am standing.

"Yeah. Why?"

"Because the color has drained from your face." When the hell did I become this—this pathetic person? I've never let anyone have this much control over my emotions. Damn it, why did Death have to go and fuck with my head? Not that I expected forever or that what I had with him could come close to Pessy and Greer, but I thought, at the very least, I was a little more than a friend.

Pestilence being Pessy can sense the turmoil brewing within me, and true to my favorite rider's style, he appears at my side to place a hand on my shoulder. He didn't do it to stop my incessant pacing. He does it hoping his action will offer some comfort. And it does. Being around

Pestilence is like being with Suk or Greer, but better because he understands me without me having to say a word and does it without judging me. Which is a paradox since it's precisely what they sent him here to do.

"I'm here if you need to talk, Avalon."

"I know, but I'm good."

"Why don't you come back to my tent to visit with Greer and me? I know Renny would love to see his favorite aunt."

"You mean one of his favorite aunts?"

"My words were not misspoken, little lamb." His confession causes a little chuckle, as does the growing smile he grants me.

"Just let me grab my stuff." He nods before he turns to leave; however, before he can exit the tent, War arrives.

"Brother." He may be talking to Pestilence, but his gaze is on me.

"Brother." Pestilence's cautious reply implies he may have been a little more aware of where War disappeared to than what he led on.

"I believe you were on your way out, Pessy." War's use of my nickname causes Pestilence's shoulders to stiffen, only to sag shortly after. Yet he takes the opportunity to look at me over his shoulder, and the look he gives me says it all. A look that screams he wishes this little nickname would have remained between Hope, him, and me.

"Come, little lamb, my brother requires a time-out." I can't help the chuckle his little joke caused. Even War laughs with us. When I move to follow my new favorite comedic rider to his tent, War's arm wraps around my waist, stopping me in my tracks.

"She will stay." Pestilence's face is panicked as his gaze shifts from me to War to the top of the tent. Is he afraid the creator will release lightning to strike him or his brother down? Did their father declare me off-limits? What the hell could have him so shaken?

"Avalon?" His subtle question tells me the prudent choice would be to follow him, but I still have questions, and currently, there is only one who is capable and willing to give me what I seek. So, I lay my jacket down rather than following the sensible path.

"I believe my Bella Agnellu wishes to remain with me."

"Keep that shit up, and Pessy will have a permanent roommate."

"But when would he have time to make his chosen scream his name if you remain there?"

"I know what a sock on the doorknob means."

"Um… a what?" War may have asked, but it seems Pestilence is just as lost by my comment as War is. Huh, I figured after spending so much time with Suki, this would have been a no-brainer for this rider.

"You heard me."

"Yes, but I am unsure why you would place a sock on a doorknob or how this relates to my brother bedding Greer."

After I refuse to answer him, he turns to escort his brother out of the tent, but when he turns his attention back on me, the heat I see in his amber eyes makes me rethink this whole staying in his tent… alone… with no one else around us thing. Remind me why I thought this would be a good idea. Especially when he begins slowly stalking toward me, making me feel more like prey than anything else.

For each step he takes, I retreat two until he has me backed into a corner with his hands on my hips and my body pinned tight against his.

"Ah... War?"

"Yes, Bella Agnellu."

"What are you doing?"

"I plan to kiss you again."

"Why?" With this last comment, my heart, which was already pounding wildly, has become a damn jackhammer in my chest. While my lungs refuse to function as they should. Not to mention my mouth wants to compete with the damn Sahara. I almost leap out of my skin when his mouth presses against mine. The action was so unexpected I gasped, allowing him the chance to sweep his tongue across mine.

"Because I wanted to see if you taste as sweet as you smell," he tells me with his lips still against mine.

"You can stop now," I breathlessly tell him, something he instantly picks up on, making him growl. So if I had to guess, he knows how flustered he has me and likes it.

"Did you talk when my brother's lips were against yours?" What the hell? How does he know Death kissed me? And more importantly, did the rider I once shared so much with encourage this shit. I start to ask his question until another thought occurs to me... what if he's testing me to see if I would admit what happened between his brother and me? If this is the case, then I should feign ignorance. Damn this rider, why does he have to twist me up so much? Regardless, I have to decide, so I choose the safer path. Lying, but with good reason.

"Umm, I don't know what you're talking about."

"Truly," he says as he drags his lips across my cheek down to my neck. It's been a long damn time since anyone has kissed me like this. This explains how I so easily get lost in the sensation and heat his touch is causing. I know it's a shitty reason, but I'm only human, and he is very skilled in his exploration. When a soft moan inexplicably escapes my parted lips, his mouth is back on mine faster than I can move while his hand tangles in my hair to hold my head at the angle he wants it. Another startled gasp again allows his tongue to sweep against mine. For a brief second, I forget he is not the brother I have longed for as my hands tighten on his arms.

"I like the way you taste, my beautiful lamb. I understand why my brother covets you." With the mention of Death, my wits return, allowing me to wrench away, but does nothing to alleviate my guilt about what just happened between us. I'm ashamed I allowed it to go on as long as I did.

War backs away with a wicked grin plastered on his face. His eyes lift to the top of the tent, much like Pestilence's did before. His abrupt laugh causes me to jump before asking, "What?"

"It seems my brother does not approve of me kissing you." Great! Just fuckin fabulous. Not only do I have to contend with this big oaf in front of me, knowing I let him kiss me, but Death was watching the entire thing from his realm. This is rounding out to be a fan-friggin-tastic day.

"You will remain with me tonight."

"I-I can't do that, War."

"I will not force you to remain, but I want you to…. And I promise to be on my best behavior. I wish only to talk to you." I suppose the prudent choice here would have been to deny him before finding somewhere else to sleep, but I would be lying if I didn't admit I missed feeling connected to someone. Besides, he promised me he wouldn't try anything, and I know these riders always uphold their word.

Chapter Twenty: Pain Can Be A Powerful Motivator

~Death Late Winter 2026 ~

THE INDESCRIBABLE AGONY filling my soul as I watch War kiss her is undeniable, but watching her reciprocate his affection crushes me. Does she now feel for him what she once felt for me? It appears my desire to push her away has worked. She no longer desires me, which would be fine if the one she now wanted was not my brother.

But I did this. I pushed Avalon away, and worse, in my attempt to safeguard her, I neglected to tell War how important she is to me. Even if he has his suspicions, I cannot fault him for this choice; the sole blame lands at my feet.

As difficult as it is to bear witness to this, I steady my features, slow my breaths, calm my heart, and rein in my darker side before looking from the images that will haunt me for the remainder of my days to the ones who hope this will torment me. I have no intention of letting them know they accomplished what they set out to do. Instead, I force my heart to accept what my mind has known for a while now.

"This," I lift my hand to cut through the mist that forms their entwined frames. It was the only way to remove the scene before me. Something I know has not occurred yet but will happen soon, quite possibly when he returns fully to her world. "This is what you wanted to show me. My brother embracing the lamb, you accuse me of loving?"

"The one we know you care for more than you should."

"She means nothing to me. This display between my brother and the mortal means nothing to me."

"If this were true, then you would not object to Gabriel ending her life?"

"I would, and if he attempts, you will require stronger chains than the ones on me now."

"If the lamb means nothing, why are you so quick to defend her?"

"Because she never asked for this, and her path is hard enough without having to deal with a miserable prick of an angel whose only wish is to make an already insurmountable task more difficult." Michael's unrelenting glare morphs into outright rage, which tells me I accomplished what I set out to do. For now, I have convinced him Avalon means nothing to me. With his fury burning bright, he pushes Gabriel toward the door, and if she was ever in danger of them discovering the truth, it was with his subsequent statement.

"I suppose it is only fitting."

"What is, Michael?"

"For the lamb who wakes the rider to also be their whore." Don't react-don't react. Whatever you do... Do. Not. React. This is what he wants from me. He wants to push me to make a mistake, but I won't. It is our responsibility to keep her safe, and since I cannot physically protect her without outright defying my father, I have to do it from here. These are nothing but words. Words meant to provoke... to push... to force my hand. All things I will not give in to. Gabriel grants me access to Avalon's current location as a parting gift. The instant the image flickers to life, I know their plan is to force me to witness their growing affection for one another.

I want nothing more than to yell my brother's name. To beg him not to do what I know is about to occur. If Michael hoped to lock me in a hell of my own making, he has accomplished his goal, and I am powerless to stop it. The laugh from the angels filters down the hall and circles around me, bouncing from one wall to the next as War escorts Pestilence from his tent.

The instant he takes her face in his hands, my world shatters around me, and the roar of pain shakes the already crumbling walls.

*****

I do not know how long I remained with my head dropped to my chest or my wings extended behind me, but the pain in my shoulders and wrists confirms it has been much longer than I realized. After they left, I ripped my legs free as I prepared to enter her world. My only choice was to tear the veil apart to accomplish it. The very thing put in place to keep them safe from beings like me. Doing this would mean I had defied our father and his warriors would come. I would have no other choice but to kill them, and if they somehow managed to subdue me, she would be in even more danger. Following my baser desire could hurt her more than my arrival there could help.

Something I cannot and will not risk.

My brother will have a momentary reprieve as I contemplate other ways to return. Ones that do not include destroying her world to do it.

The easiest way to return to her world is for my Apple to call me there. By this, I mean break my seal, but there is a risk with this as well because when I arrive, it will be to reap, not judge. Besides, to break my seal, she has to break Famine's first, and well, let's just say this brother is not so keen on keeping humanity alive. In fact, if she releases him, I fear no amount of supplication will keep Famine from fulfilling his mission. Not by me or by our other brothers, and certainly not by my beautiful Apple. No, I need to do everything in my power to keep him here. Tucked away from Avalon and her world, safeguarding the only woman I care about. Which means returning to her because of a broken seal is no more an option than tearing the veil apart.

A key clicking in my cell door announces the arrival of who I can only guess is my tormentor. I know Michael and Gabriel were well beyond the confines of my prison when I released the first of many agonized roars these images caused. But if I remain as I am, they will realize they succeeded, so with the last of the strength I possess, I retract my wings and stand upright before lifting my gaze.

"Thanatos." Not Michael or Gabriel. Ariel. A soul I never thought would be a part of such a thing, but what else could her arrival here mean? She is an honored warrior who reports only to our creator and Michael.

"What do you want, Ariel?"

"To help you."

"Help me what?"

"Tell War the truth. Tell him what your Avalon means to you."

"She means nothing."

"She means everything. Do you think I cannot see how you suffer? I know what it is like to love a being you cannot have and does not share your feelings."

"You expect me to believe this folly? You are Michael's warrior."

"I am our father's warrior," she quickly corrects. "I merely report to his guardian."

"You do not share in his belief?"

"No, but I agree with your brother." I lift my brow, hoping she will elaborate on this.

"He is a prick," she says as she glances at me through her lashes. I cannot help but laugh. Which is something I have not done since leaving my apple. Ariel delights in my amusement as a slight giggle accompanies mine. When she looks up at me again, her beaming smile has lit up her entire face. She looks every bit like the angel she is. This is the first time I realize how beautiful this being is, making me wonder who could ever be so foolish as to reject her.

"You are in love with someone?"

"Yes."

"And they do not reciprocate your feelings?"

214

"No."

"Then he is a fool, Ariel. You deserve someone who sees your value."

"I'm sure he would disagree," she tells me as her eyes drop from mine. "But honestly, I don't think he knows."

"How could he not?"

"He is... busy. Our creator asks much of him, and he always does what is asked of him."

"Huh, sounds like we have a lot in common." I meant it as a joke, but her smile confirmed my statement was not far from the truth. "You should tell him. He would be fortunate to have the affection of someone like you."

"That's very kind of you to say, but I don't believe there is a future for us."

"Why?"

"Because he loves another, and I believe this being is the only one who will ever make him happy." Avalon flashes through my mind, making me realize Ariel and I may have more in common than we think. She loves someone who loves another, and I love a woman I will never be with again. In many ways, I suppose our shared experience makes us kindred spirits.

"I can guarantee you a secure space to talk to War, so you can speak without fear of being overheard."

"Why would you do this, Ariel?"

"Because I don't agree with what they have done to you, and I know if War understood the truth, he would never covet the one who holds your heart."

"How would you do this?"

"I can bypass the runes to send you to Purgatory and block them from knowing you are gone."

"You possess this ability?"

"Yes, but you will not have long. I can only hold the block and gate open for so long. So you must hurry."

"How long could you give me?"

"Five to ten minutes at the most. Provided you are back by then, none will be the wiser." Five minutes is all the time I require to tell my brother the truth and halt what appears to be happening between them. When I nod my agreement, she smiles before placing one hand on my head and the other one against my chest.

"Whoever this being is, he's a fool." These are my last words to her before I arrive in Purgatory. A place where I can reach my brother, but above all, it offers me a space where I can tell him what he needs to hear without interference.

*****

With my arrival in her world complete, I am struck by the reality I am too late. She lay wrapped in my brother's protective embrace. Lost in the peaceful slumber, my brother War, not me, provides. Seeing her like this is a dagger to my heart. I cannot say if discovering her like this or watching her give in to his kiss is more difficult. The kiss was something that took her off guard. Sleeping in his arms was a choice she made. One I pushed her to and something I would do anything to rectify.

My brother's eyes flutter when he senses me looming over him. The initial shock of finding them like this evaporates, replaced by a fury I can no longer contain. The instant he registers who has awakened him, the realization of what my arrival here means crosses his face as I grab him to yank him into our realm. With him here, I can now concentrate my energy on explaining the error of his ways.

"Hello, brother. If you wanted to speak with me, you only needed to—"

I suspect my response is not what he believed it would be when the first thing I do is smash my fist into the mouth he had pressed to hers not long ago. The impact catapults him back several feet against a wall, where he lands on his ass in a crumpled heap. I am on him before he finds his footing to hit him again. Until today, I had never struck one of my brothers, but he pushed me beyond the point of reason.

When I finally manage to pull myself away from him, he forces himself upright, spitting out a mouth full of blood before rubbing his jaw.

"I will assume this is retribution for Avalon?"

"You will not touch the lamb again. Do I make myself clear, brother?"

"I told you if you wish me to stand down, you only need to—"

My wings explode behind me as raw fury courses through me. For the first time since returning to their world, the smug grin he has worn when talking about my Apple melts away. I believe he realizes his misstep, but to ensure this, I hit him again before jerking him off the ground to hold him suspended in front of me. Hoping my next statement will put an end to this shit, I slam him against the wall so I can give him the answer he seeks.

"I claim her. Apple. Is. Mine!"

"Are you sure?" He asks while turning his head to spit out the blood filling his mouth.

"When I release you, you will return to their realm, where you will continue to protect her. You will do everything in your godforsaken power to keep her from breaking any further seals. You will halt your

217

extermination except for anyone who would harm her or the ones she loves. You will discover what I found because they are worthy of our forgiveness, and you will do these things because you are my brother."

"Okay." He calmly confirms as his eyes meet mine.

"Also, if you ever fucking kiss her again, you will not like my response to it. She has been through enough in her life, and you will not make this any more difficult for her than it already is. Avalon deserves to find happiness, and by our father's name, I will ensure she damn well gets it. Do I make myself clear?"

"I don't think it will be that easy, brother."

"Make it that easy, *brother*, but do it without putting your fucking hands on her. Because otherwise, pain can become a powerful motivator. One that will bring my full fury raining down on her world."

"So you do love the lamb."

"Do not make me rip the veil open to prove my love for her, War," I snap as I drop him and retreat toward the hole I created. I need to return before anyone realizes I am gone. But I need to make one additional stop before I return.

"Hey, brother."

"Yes, War."

"That wasn't so hard, now was it?" His smirk is back, and as much as I would like to hit him again, I have little time to spare.

"Protect *my* apple, nothing more. Find your own beautiful lamb if you wish to experience all they offer. Leave mine the fuck alone!"

"Thanatos, how did you escape the prick and his dipshit brother?"

"I had help."

"By who?"

"Ariel. She understands how loving someone you know you will never be with feels. Something I sympathize with."

"She should."

"What are you talking about, War?" I ask with an exasperated breath.

"Because, my clueless brother, you are the one Ariel is in love with." Before I can push for further details, he returns to her world. Surely, my brother is mistaken. I cannot be the one Ariel spoke of. Can I?

*****

My last stop is the most important because it affords me the chance to speak with her. Something I have not done since she nearly died. My fingers slide down her cheek as I am desperate to touch her. A soft, contented sigh slips through her parted lips. Lips I have thought about often since I left her world. I sweep a strand of her hair from her face. Leaning forward, my lips brush over hers as I slip into her dreams.

"Death?"

This is not the first time she has used this moniker, but after everything we had experienced, I wanted to be more to her than a rider sent to judge her. I wanted her to look at me as she used to. My only desire is to be the rider she once longed for. I aspire to be her Thanatos. The being who yet holds a piece of her heart, but I fear in my attempt to give her a mortal life, I have failed the only soul I never wanted to let down. And in doing so, I have lost her. Which is why I cannot halt the shattered exhale escaping me.

"Apple."

"I don't… don't understand what are you doing here?"

"I wanted to see you."

"Why?" I can tell her it is because I miss her. I love her. That being away from her is a torture I never dreamed possible, but I know this will only hurt her, so in the end, I tell her a half-truth.

"War will no longer bother you."

"He doesn't bother me."

"His destiny is for another. He knows this now, but my brother will continue to protect you, as will Pestilence. I am sorry this existence has been thrust upon you."

"There was a time I would have disagreed with this sentiment."

"You would have?"

"Yes, when I thought there was a possibility of more."

"More what?"

"It doesn't matter because I know it isn't possible."

"So, now?"

"Now it's just nothing. A hole left in the middle of my chest that I cannot fill no matter how hard I try." I drop my eyes from hers; this is what I wanted, was it not? For her to live a human life without the distraction of what we both longed for. What I still long for.

"It will get easier, Apple. With time, you will return to a life you alone control."

"Pestilence has told me the same thing, but no one asked me what I wanted."

"This is the way it must be."

"Yeah, I suppose it does," she tells me before dropping her gaze from mine to the floor. Ariel's waning strength tells me I am out of time. I have given her the only thing I can now… a life free from us riders.

I allow myself one last second of contentment when my knuckles graze skin I will never touch again before I dip my head. Even though I know this is necessary for her safety, turning from her is one of the hardest things I have ever had to do. Especially since I know this will be the last time I invade her dreams. As I move to withdraw from her mind, she stops me to ask one last question.

"Was any of it real? Between you and me was any of it…. I have to know if what I thought we had was all a lie?"

Knowing the lengths the beings around her will take to obtain my loyalty, it is imperative no one discovers my only weakness. The one soul I will tear this world apart to protect. So I prepare to answer her question the only way I can with the truth, but one which will not grant her the answer she seeks.

"It was." As much as I wanted to tell her it was real, I couldn't. Instead, I leave before she can clarify whether my response was regarding her wish for it to be true or my acknowledgment it was all a lie. An answer I cannot grant her, no matter how much I want to tell her. Because the simple truth is, to me, she is everything. The only soul I have ever desired and the one I will love for all time.

I leave, taking with me the memory of this dream.

*****

When my eyes open, I am back in my cell as Ariel steps away from me. Her hands are shaking, and her skin is pale, almost dull. What she did for me took a lot out of her. Could War's revelation be true? Am I the one she longs for? I pray it is not the case. She is a beautiful, kind, and caring soul, but I have already given my heart to another. There is nothing left for anyone else.

"Did you talk to your brother?"

"I did. Thank you for aiding me, Ariel."

"You are most welcome. Did you... did you go to her—to the lamb while you were there?"

"Only to tell her she would remain under Pestilence and War's protection."

"She is very fortunate to have gained the respect of the riders."

"She is special and a soul who has suffered enough in her short existence. My only wish is to protect her from any further harm."

"I understand wanting to protect the ones you care for," she quietly tells me before slipping out of my room. I will have to speak with Raphael. They will no longer force Ariel to be my jailer. At the very least, I owe her this.

Chapter Twenty-One: So This Is What I Have Been Missing

WE FINALLY REACHED the fort that Wayne was convinced would be our saving grace. I am not so confident. It needs a lot of work, and if the whispers we keep hearing are true, the riders are not far behind us.

Wayne wasted no time assigning duties to everyone except him and his best friend. Somehow, these two are not a part of the damn list. I don't know why these pricks think they are above what they believe is menial work. I'd like to menial their ass.

If these dumbasses care about the people they proclaim they are *'protecting'*—yeah, this word is absolutely said while doing air quotes—they should try leading by example. Not by the damn iron fist made famous by every cruel leader this world has ever had to endure.

Speaking of cruelty, Trevor only became colder toward me after the whole cowboy thing. I don't know if he was pissed when I bypassed him and took my information straight to Wayne. If it embarrassed him when the intel couldn't be corroborated or that Wayne has taken an unhealthy interest in my backside since his hand tends to wander there whenever I'm near. What the reason is for his anger, I don't care. What I care about is when things first started between us, it was closer to a relationship. A screwed up, non-healthy relationship but a relationship all the same, but now it is closer to… ownership. I've had to fight the prick off me several times. Most of the time, he overpowers me, but other times—far fewer than I care to admit—I can stop him. I have contemplated leaving this damn group a million times since our arrival here, but in the end, I stay, and not for the reason you may think.

Oh, I still intend to have that dance with a certain rider. One that concludes with my knife sticking out of his heartless chest. But right now, it's more important to safeguard the people who have put their faith in Richard Cabeza and Cap—yep, the name stuck.

It was after a conversation with Phil. He told me something I was ill-prepared for; it seems I am the person most of the nonviolent people in the camp look to for guidance. As shocking as it was to hear how the people in this camp felt about me, it blew me away when Phil admitted he and Henry counted themselves among this group. I mean, these are Wayne's trusted council members. At first, I thought it was another test, but after careful observation over several weeks, I saw how often they respectfully disagreed with Wayne and Trevor. They constantly sought any path to keep the people in this community out of danger where the dipshits thrust them headlong into it.

After one particularly vicious encounter between Trev and me, Phil caught Soph and me trying to sneak out. I was past the point of having enough. He told me that if I was leaving, they would follow. In fact, he begged me to take them with us. But I didn't have the means to care for these people. Since I have no desire to let them down, I chose to stay, and by doing this, I have also elected to continue eating the shit Trevor dishes out for me.

We've made a lot of progress over the last couple of days toward what I hope one day will be a new start. A place where people can live in peace and find sanctuary from the assholes... like the Richard Cabeza and Caps of the world.

"Ember, you need to get out of here," Sophie pants as she pushes me toward the exit.

"Why?"

"Trevor is looking for you, and it doesn't look like he wants to tell you what a stellar job you're doing here."

Soph may be a corny jokester, but there is no way she would exaggerate about this. She knows how bad things have become between Trevor and me, so I don't hesitate when she pushes. Unfortunately, I don't move fast enough.

"Ember, my fucking room. Now!"

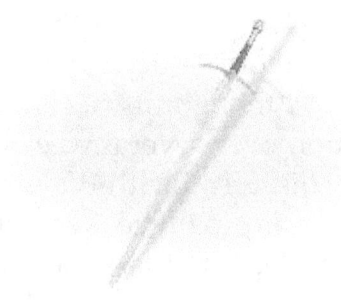

~ Avalon two weeks prior ~

I don't know why War had a sudden change of heart. One minute he was kissing me and pulling me into his bed; the next, he became a perfect gentleman. Well, almost perfect. He still makes some comments, but this is where it ends.

Not that I'm complaining, because something shifted in me too. Coincidently, it was the same night he stopped all his advances. I can't shake the feeling I'm forgetting something. Something big and that something is what shifted everything. It's like a memory you are desperate to retrieve, but it remains just out of reach.

Regardless, I'm happy to remain nothing more than his friend. A none kissing, none hugging, none bed worthy friend. Because if I'm being honest, even if Death is done with me in some ways, I still felt like I was betraying him.

War even gave me a tent of my own. It's situated right between his and Pestilence's tents, but it's all mine, so I'll count it as a win. And since they have decided we are close enough to the ones who oppose them, I don't have to worry about tearing it down and putting it up every other damn day.

"Game night tonight, A?" Ellie asks while walking by on her way to breakfast. War's army—albeit calling the men and women who have joined him an army is a massive stretch—continues to grow. And my fear he would use them regardless if they were too old or too young was utterly unfounded. He's a worthy leader. Good to the people who follow him. Lethal to the ones who oppose him.

"Absolutely. I'll see you and Duck after dinner."

"You know Duck is just going to sing nonstop, right?"

"Oh, I'm counting on it," I laugh. Duck still doesn't talk much, but he sings all the time. The problem is you can't understand him, but when he gets going, his voice carries directly over to a particular rider's tent. Which usually forces the rider over to mine, where he becomes a horse for Duck to ride.

You heard me right; this giant, fierce warrior gets down on his hands and knees and lets little Ducky pretend he's his companion. Much to the rider's chagrin, I've even named Duck's horse. I don't think the big bad rider approves of it, but since Duck likes it, the name stays. This means General Twinkle Toes will most likely make an appearance tonight.

The riders are the only ones who tend to their horses, but they have been so busy planning their siege of the fort thirty minutes east of us that it leaves them with little time for much else. So I figure I can give it a go. I don't think Storm will have any problem with it. The issue is War's horse has yet to warm up to me. But I won't give up because he still needs a name, but in order for me to do this, I need to get to know him. Here's hoping today will aid in this endeavor.

An hour later, I have Storm washed, brushed, fed, and I'm leaning my head against him while I talk quietly until War's booming voice startles me.

"Why do you keep calling Pestilence's horse Storm?"

"It's his name."

"His name. And who decided this name?"

"I did."

"Why do you do this, mouse?" I have to say, while I'm glad he knocked off the beautiful lamb shit, I hate his new nickname for me.

"Because, as I told both Death and Pestilence before you, they deserve a name too."

"Alright then, you will name my horse."

"You actually want me to name your horse?"

"Of course, since you have named my brother's horses, it is only fitting his should come from you as well. After all, he deserves what they have. Isn't that right, my old friend?"

"Yeah, but not with their consent and certainly not at their request."

"I am not like my brothers, mouse," he says, leaning over to bring his mouth to my ear. "I'm the fun one. So name him."

I look forward to the day when he doesn't remind me of this every two damn seconds. "It doesn't work that way I have—"

"Name him." He repeats with his carefree, sexy grin covering his face.

"Okay, buttercup." I can tell he's not fond of the name I rattled off. Of course, even I have to admit it's not my best stuff, but hey, this is what you get when you force this shit.

"What is a buttercup?"

"It's a flower," one of his soldiers interjects.

"Or, in some cases, it can be more like... suck it up, buttercup."

"No mouse, try again."

"For someone who said I should do the naming, you're very demanding. Okay, what about Rain?"

"No, he doesn't like this one either. It's too close to Storm."

"He doesn't like it, or you don't like it?"

"Does it matter? He is an extens—"

"Extension of you. Yeah-yeah, I know."

"As such, he likes what I like, and we dislike this."

"Now you're just being an ass! How are you feeling about... Goliath?"

"Did you make this word up? I believe you are making things up."

"Or I'm just giving you words to prove how colossal your horse is," I grumble.

"You are not as good at this as I thought."

I groan while an exasperated huff escapes me before I dramatically proclaim, "Sarge!"

"What does this word mean?"

"Like a sergeant, as in the military, something you should be able to get behind."

"Agreed. Your name will be Sarge moving forward," he tells the mammoth beast as he pats his side before strolling away. I wait until he moves out of earshot before I turn my attention back to his horse. His enormous eyes are focused only on me. It's the first time I have ever taken the time to see how beautiful he is with his rusty red coat and dark mane. His size detracts from these things, but like his rider, this horse is so much more than what they created him for.

"Don't worry. After I get to know you, I'll figure out a better name. We'll switch it then," I tell his horse as I pat his snout, and I swear he snorts his agreement.

*****

~Avalon one week prior~

I don't know what the hell or heaven is up with War, but he's been kind of a mopy brutish a-hole for the last couple of days. I suppose if anyone is able to tell me what is going on with him, Pestilence can.

"He's just frustrated. He is the rider of battle and strife. My militant brother is unaccustomed to waiting." Pestilence tells me while tossing Wren into the air, who giggles each time he reaches the highest point before he drops back down into his dad's waiting arms.

"Soooo, what can we do to… fix him? For lack of a better word. I miss the old War."

"Back to the rider who flirted with you mercilessly?" Pestilence looks at me from the side of his eye after sitting Renny down and patting his bottom to send him to play with Duck. Most people would believe with Wren's limited vocabulary and Duck being nearly non-verbal, they wouldn't get along as well as they do, but somehow they have learned to communicate without words.

"No. No, I don't need War to flirt with me, but I miss hearing him laugh. So how about it? How do we fix your broken brother?"

"He's not a toy, little lamb. He doesn't need to be fixed, but I suppose if you really want to help, you just need to figure out how War can work off some of his pent-up energy; perhaps this would help."

"Hmm, pent-up energy. I think I know what can help with that." I leave Pestilence behind me, shouting my name after spinning on my heels to find what I need to put this plan in place.

"Why do you keep looking at me like that, mouse?"

"You've been broody lately, so I think I have a solution to fix all of this," I say, circling my hand in the typical wax-on wax-off motion to demonstrate he is the problem I intend to fix.

"Broody?"

"Yes, as in moody, grumpy, sulky… cranky."

"Are there any other E's you would like to add to this growing list?"

"Nope, think we covered all of them." War goes back to cleaning his blade, which he's done four times today already. When I continue staring at him, even going so far as to lean over, forcing him to look at me, he sighs before setting his big-ass sword down to give me his full attention. "Okay, let's hear it. How do you plan to deal with this travesty?"

"You need to get laid." A wicked grin crosses his face, and I realize my mistake with how this statement was worded pretty damn fast, even more so when he leans over to bring his mouth to my ear.

"Are you volunteering, mouse?"

"No-no," I stammer and cue the flushed face. The rest, I tell him in a rush. "But she is?"

War's eyes move from me to the beautiful brunette who eagerly volunteered for the job. As surprising as it was when I first set out on this—deflower the rider named War—mission, it doesn't take long to understand why half the single women and a few married ones lined up. It could possibly have anything to do with his flawless body.

231

Nope, not at all, until one look at his muscles and tattoos out on display has me swallowing the heat creeping across my chest. One volunteer even gave it a name, declaring the assignment the *take one for the team* task. Although calling something a job when they all but fell over each other to sign up may be inaccurate.

"This daughter of Eve wishes to lie with me?"

"Well, she would probably prefer you call her by her name… Nora." I say her name a little slower, hoping it will help him remember it. When the side of his lip tips up, followed by him looking at me from the corner of his eyes, I raise my eyebrows before continuing. "You know, as opposed to Daughter of Eve."

War peers past me again to a grinning Nora, who lifts her fingers to wave. Two hours and several 'Oh, God's' later, War flings back his tent flap, appearing without a stitch of clothes on. Damn, it seems the rider is enormous all over. The rest of the women who had offered their services all let out a collective sigh at seeing him standing there, all golden and glistening and glorious.

"Did you forget something, War?" I ask as I lift my eyes toward the sky, trying not to look at his well-endowed exposed man bits.

"She left." He pants.

"Yes?" Did he think she was going to stay forever?

"I was not finished."

"Uhhh…. What?" Did I hear him right? Because I know I heard her screaming his name and God's name at least eight times. How the hell could he not be finished?

"I want to do that again."

"Umm, she left. Very satisfied, I might add."

"For this, I will risk his wrath. Come, little mouse. I will satisfy you next."

"Ahhh. Nooo."

"Why?" he asks as he positions his head, hoping to capture my eyes that I still have plastered on the sky.

"Because."

"This is an answer?"

"It's the best you're getting. Now go put that away." I say, trying to ignore the erection he seems unaware he is sporting.

"I shall require some assistance. Which you can help with."

"And I said no. I'm not what you want."

"You are female?"

"I think you are already well aware I'm a woman."

"You have all the parts of a female?"

"Yes."

"Then you are precisely what I want," He said, grasping my hand.

"Not going to happen, big guy," I tell him as I pat his chest before walking away.

"What should I do about this?" he yells, and I can only imagine he's pointing at the enormous erection several women in the camp are now captivated by.

"I'm sure you'll figure it out," I reply over my shoulder.

"But not with you?"

"Nope," I laugh as I wander over to their horses.

Before he can protest any further, three women speak up, confirming they would be happy to help... and help they did.

All. Night. Long.

*****

The following day, Pestilence and I wait a respectable amount of time before we venture into his tent, only to find him surrounded by not only the three who spoke up yesterday but several other naked women.

"You have created a monster, little lamb."

"Hey, at least he's not moping. And they seem... very happy and satisfied," I say while grinning at the rider who doubted my mad — pull a-pissy rider out of his funk — skills. I can't help but glance at him, only to find him shaking his head.

I suppose it's a good thing I showed him what this world has to offer when I did because in the coming weeks....

My entire world will be turned upside down and fall to shit.

Chapter Twenty-Two: Run-Run As Fast As You Can

*T*REVOR SLAMS THE door closed entirely too hard since the wood is rotted and warped from years of sitting unused. Frankly, I don't know what I did this time to rile this asshole up so much. Most of the time, I know exactly why he's pissed, but I'm at a loss this time.

"What the fuck have you been doing with Wayne?"

"I haven't done anything with Wayne or anyone else, for that damn matter. But even if I had, what the hell business is it of yours? You have your dick stuck in Candy, Mandy, or Sandy every goddamn day." His eyes shoot up to meet mine, and the rage I find in them has me taking a decisive step back, now very aware of his looming proximity. I'm not ashamed to admit I wanted to put as much space between us as possible.

When his hand clenches into a tight fist, I know no amount of space in this room, let alone this fort, will put enough distance between him and me. I guess I should have seen this shit coming. He's the typical alpha macho do as I say, not as I do asshole. In simplest terms, it's okay if he fucks his way through every woman on the eastern, and quite possibly the western seaboard, as long as my legs only open for him.

"What the fuck did you just say to me, Ember?" Okay, I totally could have and should have gone with I'm sorry... I didn't mean it... I was just mad... forgive me, but my dad didn't raise his daughter to cower... to any man. Least of all, a man who would raise his hands to a woman because he didn't like what she had to say. Besides, if I can't stand toe to toe with this prick, how the hell will I ever be able to face down the rider I fully intend to kill?

"I said, what the fuck—"

"I heard what you said. What part of my response are you having difficulty with?" I see the shift a second before he lunges, but it's enough. I turn the instant before he barrels into me so I don't take the full brunt of his body slamming into mine. As a result, when I stumble back, his forward momentum causes his right side and head to slam into the stone wall.

In the span of him trying to shake off the impact, I spin out of his grasp. If I can make it through his door, out to where other people are milling around, he won't do shit. He doesn't want witnesses when he acts like this, and something tells me this interaction isn't for others.

His hand snatches out, catching my hair in his iron grip as I rush past him. The sudden jolt as my head reels back causes my feet to sail out from under me, putting me on my ass. Hard. And this time, I'm not fast enough to avoid his next attack.

Before I can block or move my head, Trevor slams his fist down against my jaw. Copper invades my mouth as pain explodes across my face from the impact. I lash out, smashing the heel of my hand into his nose as my dad taught me. The hit delivers the desired effect as blood erupts from it.

When his eyes snap back to mine, the normal brown I am used to seeing has been replaced with black. Rage from my assault surfaces, and for the first time in my life, I'm terrified of the man looming over me.

The second hit stuns me and momentarily takes me out of the fight, but when he rears back, preparing to bring the full force of his weight and wrath with his next hit, I roll my head. Trevor's hand grazes my cheek, and pain flares to life, but it doesn't knock me out as he wanted. His howls of pain confirm his fist took the brunt of this attack when it impacted the stone floor.

I sputter a cough because blood from his first assault coats my throat, making it impossible to take another breath without inhaling the thick liquid.

With Trevor nursing his injured limb, I jerk my legs out from under him and wrap them around his neck to twist, using my fear and his momentum to put him on the ground with me on top of him. His hand flies out, but the dumbass already forgot he broke it from his last attempt, which means even though it hurts, it doesn't incapacitate. I know hitting him will not do the kind of damage I need to grant me enough time to escape this room, and even though it is already pretty banged up, my head is the option I go with, bringing it down to shatter his already wrecked nose.

I don't waste any time leaping to my feet. I lose my balance for a brief second and stumble into a wall, but since I know this golden ticket is a one-time deal, it means I get my wits about me pretty damn fast so I can rush out of his room. Here's the thing, I know if I stay now Trevor will never let this stand, so I don't just stop after I exit his room; I rush into the tree line close to this stupid fucking fort they brought us to.

Once I know I am well out of view, I collapse to the ground, panting and spitting out the blood still filling my mouth. With the adrenaline subsiding, my hand shakes while I wipe my face.

"What the fuck did I do?" I mumble while sucking in another lung full of air. I'm homeless, with none of my shit or any supplies. I left everyone who was counting on me behind, and I did it all because I couldn't keep my fucking mouth shut.

"Damn it!"

"What did I fucking just do?" I don't know who I'm posing this question to. Certainly not the almighty since I still blame him for my mom and dad. I mean, it is his rider who destroyed my life. Swiping my hand under my nose to clear away some of the blood, I sit back on my knees while contemplating my next move.

I need to get word to Phil somehow, but first, I need to find a safe place to take the people who want to leave. Something tells me Wayne and Trevor will not be happy I'm taking people away from their numbers. It's imperative to ensure Phil, Henry, and I can protect them when they leave. The last thing I want is to make them fodder for our leader's cannons. Cannons they will use to distract the riders when the brewing battle ensues.

"What do we have here?" My eyes shoot up to the face of the man standing over me. Not just any guy based on his size, clothes, and the massive ass sword strapped to his back. I'm going to go with he's one of the riders. Talk about out of the damn frying pan and into the fire. His hand surges out, grasping my throat in a painful grip I know I don't have any hope in hell of breaking out of. Something tells me I won't be fighting my way out of this situation. I'm so damn screwed right now. This prevailing thought races through my head while I desperately claw at the hand controlling me.

"It seems you have captured a spy." My head whips toward the voice. How did I miss not one but two men approaching me? One of them I understand since he's a rider, but not the other until my eyes land on the being I missed.

"Pestilence!"

"You know each other?" War asks as he looks from me to his brother, who has moved next to him.

"Not to my knowledge."

"Prick! You're fucking dead when I get loose." The words are out of my mouth before I can stop them. Real damn smart Ember, just announce your plan to the rider you intend to kill. Yeah, that will bode well for me. Because I'm sure he will be totally cool with letting me continue to draw breath now.

"So, you do know each other."

"Funny, brother."

"Well, she did call you by name."

"Pestilence, yes, I heard."

"No, I meant the prick part."

"You are not as humorous as you believe you are."

"Mouse would disagree with you."

"The lamb is easily amused."

"She has wit and can appreciate my charming personality." What the fuck? Is this happening right now? It's like these two are normal human siblings, playfully taunting each other, not the riders sent to wipe us from existence.

"Hey, assholes, if you plan on continuing this boring as fuck conversation, do you think you could do it without your hand wrapped around my throat?" I snap, having grown tired of listening to their inane exchange. Both riders turn their focus on me. What I expected to discover when they turned their attention to me was anger, hate, disgust, maybe even my own pending death. What I found was amusement.

"I like her. She has grit."

"She has something," the rider I plan on killing retorts as he adjusts the bow on his back. He moves his gaze from me to the woods around us.

"She comes with us."

What? What the fuck did he just say? These fuckers plan on taking me as one of their hostages. I am getting ready to tell them how wrong they are when the sound of someone moving through the brush has the one I assume is War slamming his hand over my mouth. His eyes move from me to his brother to give his silent directive. He lifts his chin in the direction of the noise, and the rider I plan on sinking a knife in pulls his bow from his back and nocks an arrow.

War twists me so my back is now against his chest as he holds me in a crushing embrace. Fuck, whoever is approaching has no idea of the shitstorm they are about to find themselves in, and I can't do a fucking thing to warn them.

Each snapping twig confirms the clueless wretch is indeed moving closer to where we are waiting. My attempt to warn them is useless with the big bastard's hand clamped over my mouth, so the best I can manage is a few muffled grunts and groans. The only other sound is the one making my heart race because it's the sound of bowstrings pulling taut.

"Em." My name may have been whispered, but it's all I need to know who is approaching us, which has me struggling to break the rider's hold.

"Ember, are you out here?"

Fuck-fuck-fuck! Sophie is walking into a damn trap. I have to do something. I can't let this prick take someone else from me. With every ounce of strength I can muster, I slam my head back and connect with War's face. It doesn't have the effect I had hoped for, which would have been for him to drop me, but the action dislodges his hand enough to warn her.

"Sophie. Run!" But it's too damn late when she steps out of the tree line, only to come face to face with an arrow pointed at her head. And with War back in full control of me, I am powerless to help her. They are going to force me to watch someone else I love die at the hands of this fucking rider.

"Oh... fuck balls!" Fuck-balls is right, but her standard snarky response isn't going to get her out of this shit... she needs to run.

"Fuck balls?" the deep baritone that rumbles from the rider holding me as he questions her reaction can be felt through my entire body.

"Fudge drops?" Sophie corrects, raising her eyebrows questioningly. And once again, the riders shock the shit out of me when War's roaring laugh echoes off the trees, and Pestilence chuckles as he lowers his bow. Soph, being Soph, decides using humor rather than running is the better option when she blurts, "Thanks, I'm here all week."

"This one is entertaining."

"As much as I hate agreeing with you, this time you're right." But this isn't enough to save her since Pestilence captures her before they spin to cart us away.

Chapter Twenty-Three: I Know You

I ADMIT TO being shocked when War and Pestilence returned from their scouting trip with two women who didn't appear like they wanted to be here. Are they going to start collecting humans like a hoarder collects trash?

"Let me fucking go!" the brunette yells. Okay, so definitely doesn't want to be here. The one who has no issues telling the riders to fuck off has been pretty banged up. The riders must have missed the damage while they dragged her ass back here, but now that she is on the ground looking up at them, they can't miss it.

"Who did this to you?" War asks her after inspecting the injuries some asshole inflicted on this woman. She doesn't answer, only glares at him, but when Pestilence attempts to look at her, she jerks away.

"Don't fucking touch me, asshole!"

"It seems our guest does not care for you, brother."

"Apparently," Pestilence declares, putting some distance between the newcomers and himself while I move closer. There is something awfully familiar about this chick. I think I've seen her somewhere before. I'm just having a hard time placing where it could have been.

Now that I'm standing next to her, the full extent of her damage is visible. Someone split her lip open. She also has a gash running the length of her cheek, and her eye is a swollen, ugly shade of purple. The prick who attacked her did one hell of a job beating the shit out of this girl, but if the injuries on her hands are anything to go by, I would have to say she gave as much as she received. Good for her.

It's not surprising she doesn't trust anyone here, including me, which becomes apparent when I attempt to hand her a towel, and she jerks away. The last thing I want to do is cause this girl any more issues, so I put my hands up. After a second, I lower the towel to her, which she yanks out of my hand before spitting in my direction. I won't give her any shit this time. She just got her ass handed to her. But she will only get away with it once.

"Mouse—"

"I told you not to call me that shit." War laughs while he continues backing away with Pessy.

"We could always return to Bella—"

"Mouse works," I snap as I attempt to place where I know this girl from. When I have had enough trying to figure it out, I ask her outright. "Do I know you?"

"I doubt it!"

"Yeah, and why is that?"

"Let's just say we run in different circles."

"I know you from some goddamn where," I snap, not caring that I just took their dad's name in vain, which means Pestilence is probably giving me the evil eye right now.

"And like I said, that's highly fuckin doubtful since my circle doesn't include the riders sent to kill us."

"Let me guess, you're with the assholes the riders are following."

"Like I'm going to tell you shit." The nagging feeling I know her from somewhere will not subside. In fact, it's developing into an absolute certainty, but it's not until she glares at Pestilence that it all clicks into place.

"I do remember you. You're the bitch who shot a damn arrow at my head."

"You'll have to remind me. I've shot a lot of arrows at the heads of plenty of terminally stupid idiots like yourself."

"Terminally stupid?" I snap. This bitch is calling me stupid when she's the one who is part of a group whose sole purpose is to rebel against riders who can't be killed.

"Well, if the insanity shoe fits. You know, I believe there are still some asylums around. I'm sure we could find you a nice padded room."

My fists clench, itching to lash out at someone for the first time since I found Jay raping Greer. "You know when you did it."

"Oh yeah, right. When you came to rescue the chick we were using as bait."

"Call Greer bait again. I dare you." Her eyes meet mine, and for the briefest second, I believe my hands may be granted their desire to throttle her, but rather than taking me up on my challenge, she makes the wise choice to shift back to the topic that started this whole interaction.

"Only because you shot an arrow at me."

"Because you were getting ready to shoot me!"

"Actually, I was getting ready to shoot someone else, but ya know, potato-patato."

"Don't say that shit."

"Why not?"

"Let's just say the last asshole who said this to me is dead. Now let's get back to this whole arrow at my fucking head conversation," I snarl. If this bitch is angling to get hit again, she's well on her way.

"Well, the way I see it, you should consider yourself lucky."

"Not sure I would classify it the same damn way."

"You should."

"Yeah, and why is that?" Suki snaps.

"Because normally I don't miss."

"Like ever," the girl who, until now, has kept her mouth shut interjects. This chick must have felt she needed to come to her friend's defense, much like Suki wanted to jump to mine.

"Lucky me," I retort.

"Glad we agree. But once again, I would like to point out you weren't my intended target. You merely inserted yourself into something you shouldn't have." The memory of our last interaction plays out. I wasn't the intended target. Someone else... someone I care for was.

And even though I already know the answer, this bitch will tell me who she wanted to shoot. That way, when I knock the piss out of her, everyone will understand why.

"Who was your target?" I growl as I move closer to her.

"He is." She jerks her head in Pestilence's direction.

"Is? Don't you mean was?!"

"You say it your way; I'll say it mine." I lose all control. Lashing out, I grab her by her throat and yank her to her feet.

"Try it, bitch, and I'll end you in the most painful way I can."

"Little lamb, what are you doing? This one has been through enough."

Tossing her back to the ground, I spin before calmly telling him, "She doesn't deserve your sympathy or your compassion." Glaring at her over my shoulder, I finish with the warning I feel in my gut is prudent. "Don't turn your back on that one, Pessy."

*****

Something about this girl didn't sit well with me. It's no secret that most mortals hate the riders, but she doesn't seem to focus on War as much as Pestilence.

I have grown accustomed to how most people are around the riders when they first encounter them. They're mindful, cautious, anxious... keenly tuned into the rider's movements. Then there are the assholes who try to appear unaffected. You know the kind, the ignorant defiant assholes. The ones who usually end up on their knees begging for their forgiveness. But regardless of whether it's cautious or defiant, one thing always remains the same... fear. It's the one thing none of them can hide because it is the only emotion you can find in their eyes.

But not this girl. I don't see fear in her eyes when she looks at Pestilence; it's hate. And this makes her unstable. An unstable person who holds no fear of the riders is dangerous. Which leaves me with an unsettled feeling. What if this was all a setup to get this girl inside our camp? A trojan horse the riders didn't just discover within their city walls. No, they willingly brought it in.

Her friend leans over to whisper something to her. Damn, I wish I was close enough to hear what they were saying. I bet they're discussing when and how they will spring their trap. This is the prevailing thought until the angry one laughs. Fucking laughs.

Okay, so she's one of the defiant assholes.

Or just ignorant.

Regardless, I think it's time for me to figure out what the hell this chick is up to. Marching over to where she's sitting, I yank a chair in front of her and plop down. She scowls at me, and I glare right back. The longer I remain silent, the more uncomfortable she becomes since she cannot sit still. When she huffs an exasperated sigh along with an over-the-top dramatic eye roll, I know it won't be much longer before....

"What the hell do you want?" She breaks. Bingo.

"Who said I want anything?"

"Then why the hell do you keep staring at me?" I'm sure you want to know the answer to your question, but I don't intend to tell you. At least not yet, because if I push a bit more, you'll be pissed enough—teetering on the edge just enough—to tell me everything I want to know. So the only answer she'll get from me is a smirk to accompany the glare I've been giving her since I figured out who she is.

"What the fuck is your problem?"

"That should be apparent."

"If you think I'm going to apologize for almost shooting—"

"While I'm not a fan of the whole arrow shot at my head shit. I found another reason to dislike you."

"Something worse than—"

"Pestilence. What's your issue with him?"

"None of your—"

"I don't like the way you keep glaring at him." Do I keep interrupting her on purpose? You bet your ass I do. Because one thing I am sure about this girl is that she doesn't like anyone trying to control her.

"Are you planning to let me answer at least one of your stupid fuckin questions? Or is your plan to continue—"

"Interrupting you? Yes." I figured she would have more to say, but her attention is pulled from me when Pestilence walks in our direction. Before anyone can react to what she is preparing to do, she leaps up and charges the rider.

At first, I didn't know why she was doing it or what she hoped to accomplish, but when I saw the glint of a blade in her hand, everything became clear.

She's here to murder my friend.

"Pestilence!" I yell his name, hoping he understands the intent I meant it to be. A warning.

"Ember." I imagine the chick, or should I say Ember's friend, is screeching her name, praying she can save her life.

Ember lunges forward and drives the hand holding the blade in his direction. Pestilence narrowly avoids her

249

attack. I realize she can't end him, but it doesn't matter because I also know any damage inflicted on the rider causes them pain. Maybe not like we experience, but it still fuckin hurts.

And, of course, Greer has to pick this exact moment to appear with Renny in tow. The food she was carrying for these bitches tumbles to the ground when she throws her hands over her mouth to stifle the scream. The bitch uses this to her advantage when Pestilence's focus moves from the one trying to kill him to the two people he will do anything to protect.

Ember shifts, sidesteps, and slashes at him again. This time the blade makes contact and slices through his shirt. The confirmation she damaged more than his clothes comes almost immediately when a red patch spreads across the fabric of the white material.

Pestilence pivots, placing himself between the woman and Wren, who is running over to greet his dad. Even though the rider doesn't need my help to handle one mortal woman, there's no way in hell I'm going to stand by and watch her attack him. Especially since Greer is frozen in place, her face twisted in a silent scream.

Her last attack throws her off balance, and I waste no time taking advantage of it. When Pestilence moves to scoop up Wren, I dive, knocking her to the ground and dislodging the knife in the process. One second, she is struggling under me to retrieve her weapon, and the next, she is screaming about Wren.

"Don't let that asshole hurt him!"

"Hurt him. That asshole, as you called him, is protecting his son from you." Shit. I shouldn't have said that. Lucky for me, I don't think Ember—and more important than this bitch, Greer—registered my slip up since I'm not sure if Pestilence has had this conversation with Greer yet. Nor do I want some psychotic bitch knowing Pessy's weakness.

"Save. These fuckers don't save. The only thing they know... the only thing they do is kill!" she shrieks. I heard more than enough from her, so right after I yank her off the ground, I push her ass back down on the chair, the one her ass should never have left to begin with. The ruckus has drawn others, and since Suk and Xander are among the crowd, I motion for him to grab something to tie her there. The glare I give her friend halts any retaliation from her.

"This isn't the first time Pestilence has been forced to protect Wren from assholes like you."

"What? I-I would never hurt that little boy, or any other kid for that matter."

"No, just the one soul who will protect him to his dying breath."

"I find that hard—"

"Hard to believe? I don't care what you believe because it was only after some assholes whose destination was to join up with your group tried to fucking kill Renny, '*that asshole,*' as you so carelessly called him, saved his life. Pestilence is a good man."

"He's not a man. That... thing is not even human!" Ember scoffs.

"He's a good *Man*!" I state the word man with extra emphasis and may be more growl than spoken. This is to ensure my stance on this subject is clear. "And if you ever try anything like that again, I'll stick the fucking knife through your heart myself."

"And then I'll kick it in there so far no one, not even your beloved leader—"

"Beloved? I can't stand those fuck wads —," but Suki doesn't let her finish before she interrupts to continue her warning.

"Will be able to pull it out."

"Wow, for such a tiny woman, you have a lot of hostility in you. You should really try yoga or meditation or some other shit like that. I heard it clears the chakra. And don't ask what chakra is 'cause I don't know. Regardless, I'm gonna go with you might need a tune-up on yours," Sophie says.

"I wouldn't need to meditate if assholes like your friend here didn't exist in this world."

"Yeah, I'm the asshole here."

"I would like to apologize for whatever I did to harm you." Pestilence's sudden arrival has all of us twisting to look at him. Why in the hell he feels he owes this bitch an apology is something he will have to explain in great detail to me, but not now. I will not give this chick the satisfaction of witnessing his heartache.

"You think I want an apology from the fucker who murdered my parents?" Pestilence's shoulders slump. Since saving Wren and declaring his love to Greer, he's changed. He deeply regrets having taken all those lives. The only reason he follows War is that the group we are tracking poses a danger to his family. Coming face to face with someone suffering because he followed his task when he first arrived here will affect him.

"Their names were Pete and Jane. They never hurt anyone. They only wanted to live in peace, but your arrows took all that away in the blink of an eye."

Pestilence drops his head. He knows nothing he can say will make this any easier on her. Hell, the rider probably thinks he deserves to die knowing he took her family away now that he understands what having a family means. "I know this does not erase my grievous error, but I truly am sorry."

"Fuck you!" Having heard enough from the newcomer, Greer attempts to interject, but she stops when Pestilence places his hand on her arm and shakes his head. Like the rider, she understands what it feels like to lose someone you love. She was just fortunate to have a rider who loved her and Wren enough to risk everything to bring him back. Ember didn't. And even though I still want to hate her, I can't. Because, like them, I also understand how losing someone you love changes you and causes you to do irrational shit like trying to slay a rider. Hell, I cracked a damn seal because of it.

It doesn't mean I'm okay with her continuing to torment him when he turns to leave with his family. It's not until she yells the location where this supposedly took place and the date that my sympathy shifts back to fury.

"You said he shot them?"

"Yeah, I watched him fucking shoot them. My dad's only weapon was the damn hoe he had been using that day to tend to the garden. My mom was unarmed and trying to run away from him. Even though you tried to conceal your face, there was no mistaking you or your white fuckin horse!" Yet another reason I don't believe her damn story. Because, for one, he has never concealed who he was from anyone. And two, Pestilence would never shoot someone in the back. If he wanted to kill a fleeing man or woman, he would have sent his tendrils to take care of them. His arrows were reserved only for the ones who fought back.

"And it was in Beaverton?"

"Did I fucking stutter?"

"In March 2025?"

"Are you just going to keep asking me to repeat what I already told you?"

"Nope, because you're lying."

"Why would I lie about something like that?" she screams, jerking in my direction. She doesn't make it far since she's secured in place with the bindings Xander returned with not long after this farce started.

"I don't have the first damn clue why you would make this shit up. What I do know is for Pestilence to have shot your parents, he would have had to be present—"

"Which he was."

"No, he wasn't."

"And you know this information how?"

"Because during the time you claim your parents were murdered, he was with my group a hundred miles away."

"Bullshit."

"I already told you I don't care if you damn well believe me about Pestilence just as long as you believe this...." I lean over, invading her personal space, wanting to make damn certain I have her undivided attention for the rest of what I have to say. Once her narrowed eyes meet mine, I calmly declare, "If you ever try that shit again, I'll fuckin kill you myself."

Chapter Twenty-Four: The Truth Can Hurt

*A*FTER STORMING AWAY from Ember and her friend Sophie, I went to check on Pessy. I need to tell him the truth; otherwise, he will continue to beat himself up over something he didn't do.

"I took that girl's life away from her, Greer. She has every right to hate me. To want me dead. I did—"

"Horrible things?" I ask from the tent flap.

"Yes."

"You did, Pestilence. There are innocent lives you took for no reason other than some stupid damn task. But that's not your fault either. Like us, you didn't ask for any of this.

And while you can't give back the lives you took, you can stop beating yourself up over these two."

"Avalon—"

"No, Pestilence, you didn't kill her parents."

"She saw me, little lamb."

"No, she didn't."

"How can you be so certain?"

"Because when she claims you did it, you were a hundred miles away with us. While I understand you're not human, I also know you don't have wings, meaning you would have had to ride there on Storm. Even though he's faster than normal horses, he couldn't have gotten you there and back without me knowing you were gone." Pestilence's pained expression doesn't change until Greer places her hand on his face and smiles up at him. When his eyes meet mine, I find hope filling them. A desperate wish for this to all be true. Right now, I want nothing else in this world more than to give him this absolution. Walking to place my hand on the arm cradling Greer against him, I hope he'll accept it.

"Pestilence, you didn't do it," I tell him softly. "I don't know why she believes you did, but it wasn't you."

I turn to leave only after he has acknowledged what I said with a simple head nod. Greer is the one who will help him process the rest because even if he knows this wasn't his fault, his thoughts remain on all the others who are. Her whispered words and healing kisses are not meant for me to witness, but he stops me just before I exit.

"If this wasn't me, then it means someone is out there pretending to be me, and I intend to find out who it is... and stop them. They will regret their actions."

"And I'll be right there next to you when you do, Pessy."

After ensuring Ember and Sophie are securely locked away with no hopes of carrying out her plans to remove the rider, I retire to my tent. I try to read, but the night's events keep playing on repeat in my damn head, making it impossible for me to enjoy the new book War gave me.

Ember may have lied, or I suppose it's entirely possible she may just be mistaken about who did it. Either way, Pestilence is right. Some asshole is out there massacring people and making it appear a rider did it. I will not stand for this, especially when Pessy isn't the same soul he was when he arrived here.

I don't know when I finally fell asleep, but I did at some point since I am now being jolted awake by someone screaming. No, not just one person, several people. Some shrieks are filled with terror, some fury, but one in particular stands out above the rest.

"Here, we're over here!" Fuckin Ember. I should have put a knife in this bitch when I had the chance. I sprint out of my tent and smack into War's massive chest.

"You're okay!" He pulls me into his arms, hugging me tight. I know this wasn't posed as a question. He was only confirming what his eyes and body had already told him, but I still felt he needed an answer.

"I'm fine. I've been in my tent all night. What the hell's going on?"

"Some fool has made a fatal mistake and attacked the wrong encampment."

"What are we waiting for? We have to—"

"No, mouse. You aren't going to do anything. Pestilence and I will handle this." When I open my mouth to argue, he ends it before the first word can trickle past my vocal cords. "Mouse, you will listen this one time. My brother and I can handle this, but not if we are worried about you the entire time. Stay here, please." It's the last word that halts any further dispute from me because it's a word he never uses.

He takes my soft exhale to validate that I will do what he has asked of me. He leans over to give the top of my head a quick kiss before he spins and stalks toward the invaders. Pestilence is protecting the women and children who travel with us while they flee from the men who came to destroy us.

Kids. Fuck, where the hell are Ellie and Duck?

I know I promised War that I would stay put, and while technically I'm not rushing into the fight, I don't think the rider will see a difference. But I don't care because I need to ensure they are safe. And by safe, I mean tucked in the one place I know Pestilence will do everything in his power to protect... his shelter.

Running around the tent still holding the bitch screaming for them to save her, I dash into theirs. My heart nearly stops when I find it empty until I hear a muffled sound coming from the corner. Not willing to take any chances, I pull my dagger out before I begin my cautious trek over toward their cots. When no one assaults me the second I'm within range, I sink to my knees to inspect the only space I can't see. Relief floods through my body when I find two sets of eyes staring back at me.

"Avalon?"

"Yes," I whisper before helping her pull Duck out from under it.

"What's—" I quickly cut her off when voices I don't recognize come from outside the tent.

With my finger pressed to my lips, I shush them. "Shhh."

258

"Remember what he said; no one walks away from this. We kill everyone who didn't come here with us tonight."

"What if—"

"Everyone. Are we clear?"

"I hope this doesn't blow up in his face."

By some stroke of luck, even with the little giggles from Duck, they didn't hear us and are currently moving further into our camp. I peek through the flaps to ensure no one is lingering before picking up Duck and grabbing Ellie's hand to lead them toward Greer.

With a clear path between us and her tent, I hand Duck to Ellie and instruct her to run to Pestilence's place, where Greer will watch over them. There is someone else who requires my attention right now. Unlike when I entered the kid's tent, fury has replaced fear when I storm into the one holding Ember.

"Fuck!"

"Not who you were hoping for?"

"No, not by a long shot. But you could still make my day by telling me the selfish prick rider with the bow you seem so enamored with was taken out by my friends."

"That rider you hate so damn much is busy putting himself between the Raiders and the people in this camp."

"Those Raiders only came to kill the horsemen. The people here have nothing to worry about."

"Those Raiders came to murder everyone here, and something tells me they wouldn't have spared you either."

"Bullshit! They wouldn't hurt the innocent men and women those riders forced into this place."

"Is that so? Well, Ember, you can call bullshit all you want. The simple fact is I heard the asshole leading them say to kill everyone. Everyone. Pretty damn sure you would be among that everyone group."

"They didn't know I was in here."

"Yeah, you keep telling yourself that shit, and while you're busy defending the assholes who wanted to kill everyone, I'm going to back the riders because what I saw was while War was busy fending them off, Pestilence was in the middle of rescuing the men and women stuck between this camp and your raider buddies."

"I will never believe one of those fuckers is capable of anything other than killing people." I plan on explaining where she went wrong when we are interrupted by some asshole who doesn't belong here. The problem is she seems to know him.

"Jon. Thank god."

"Well, what do we have here?" His eyes move from the bitch I want to throttle over to me. There is something about the way his eyes slide over my body that makes me uncomfortable. It could have something to do with how long he openly ogles my breasts. "Whose your friend?"

"We're not friends," she hisses through her gritted teeth. Something tells me these two are not on the best of terms, but I also don't think he's the one who did this to her face. "Get us out of here."

"Trevor's been looking for you," he may be talking to Ember, but his focus remains fixed on me. My lip twists in a scowl when he drops his gaze lower, and I decide to put more space between us when he sucks his teeth. The entire thing makes my skin crawl. But it seems this asshole isn't done talking yet. "To say Trev's pissed at you, Ember, doesn't begin to cover it. On a lighter note, what's your name, sweet thing?"

"It sure as shit isn't sweet thing."

"Jon, focus. Untie Soph and me."

"Nah, I think I would rather get to know your new friend."

"Like she already told you, we aren't friends."

"Doesn't matter." I guess it really doesn't since he's advancing toward me. I widen my stance in preparation to protect myself from the asshole, but his advance comes to an abrupt halt when Pestilence charges in.

"Little lamb, why does it not surprise me to find you preparing to fight one of these invaders?"

"Because you know me so well." The one Ember called Jon leaps behind Sophie to use her as a shield against the rider. Yeah, and this chick thinks these assholes are better than the horsemen.

Pestilence's focus shifts from me to the man about to discover that using humans against this rider is never a good idea. Even if the person hasn't shown the rider an ounce of respect.

"Um, Jo-Jon, what are you—"

"Shut up. You back away, or I'll slice this bitch's throat."

"Let her go, you asshole," Ember screams. Oh, so now these pricks are assholes. It's funny how quickly they changed from her friends or group to assholes. She can struggle to break the bindings holding her in place all she wants; she won't get out of them. If she hopes to save her friend, she better pray Pessy will do it.

I almost feel bad for her friend because I think she finally realizes how epically fucked she is right now. Sophie's face has gone ashen, and her eyes are twice the size of normal ones. The thing is, this Sophie isn't all that bad.

"Don't you dare hurt her, Jon!" When Pestilence moves, Jon presses the knife harder against her neck, causing the first faint line of blood to trickle past the blade.

"You should not have done that," Pestilence's booming voice fills the room. If he moves, nothing will stop the asshole from slicing this woman's throat, and unlike them, Pessy won't put her life at risk. So he does the only thing he can to ensure we all walk away from this in one piece. He releases his tendrils.

They streak across the room to claim their victim. Like every other person facing this death, he tries to swat them away but is no more successful than anyone else.

"NO!" Ember screams when the tendrils encircle not only the asshole but also Sophie. Pestilence wastes no time collecting the guy when they both collapse to the ground.

"Little lamb." Pessy nods toward Sophie, but I'm already on the move.

"He killed her. That bastard fucking killed her!" Ember shrieks.

"No, he didn't." I don't need her shit right now. Not while I'm busy checking to make sure the knife didn't cut her.

"You can't lie to me. I saw what he did. He gave her his disease and—"

"No, he didn't. He saved her, but your friend Jon… well, I can't say the same about him."

"If she's not dead, why isn't she moving?"

"Because she passed out."

"Bullshit."

"Like it or not, a rider just saved your friend."

"Oh damn, how could I forget the riders are merely misunderstood. Right? It's not like they're here to kill us at all." She dramatically rolls her eyes, her furious glare focused solely on me. "How could I be so stupid?"

"And exactly how many people have they killed since you've been here?" She remains silent because the only answer she can give is none. Well… apart from the asshole who just used her best friend like a human shield.

"Yeah, I thought so. On the flip side, how long do you honestly think I would have made it with the group you came from? Go ahead; I'll let you think about it for a minute." She continues to glare but remains silent. My guess is because she knows I would not have stood a chance with them.

"Don't want to answer because you would either have to admit I'm right or risk being a liar. So how about you stop looking at Pestilence and War like they're the monsters here because I'm pretty sure we mortals have this distinction sown up." I snarl before turning to leave but decide there is one more thing I need to say to this chick. "Oh, and so you know, neither one of those men has ever so much as laid a fucking finger on me to hurt me, something I can't say about the group you travel with!"

"I don't believe you. Let me out of this so I can help her."

"I don't give a shit what you believe. Just know a rider saved your friend from the assholes you travel with. And from now on, what you will do is give the men of this camp some fucking respect. All. Of. Them. RIDERS INCLUDED!"

*****

Pestilence and War both came back in to check on us. Ember was again forced to face how wrong she was about the riders when Pestilence gently carried Sophie to the bed after he brought us water and requested I remain with her until she recovered.

Xander also found his way into the tent to let me know Ellie and Duck were safe, and Greer insisted they remain in her and Pestilence's tent. I couldn't tell if the shocked expression covering Ember's face was because she found out Greer and Pestilence shared quarters or that they insisted on protecting these kids.

After her friend gradually showed signs of regaining consciousness, I think it was a wake-up call for Ember. One that has made her question everything. At least, this is my assumption since her face is twisted in a puzzled expression, and she seems lost in thought. I suppose she has a lot of things to consider.

"What will the riders do now?"

"What they planned to do all along. Put an end to your little uprising."

"There are good people with that group. People who don't want this." I want to ask her if this would have mattered to her or anyone in her group if the roles were reversed, but it would be pointless since they already proved what they would do. Her people would have swept through this entire camp tonight and slaughtered everyone they encountered if the riders weren't here to stop them.

"Then they should have chosen better."

"Chose better? How many fucking groups do you see out there willing to let new people in?"

"Don't know, can't say I care."

"How the hell can you be so cavalier about people? People like you, like the ones you protect. Suki, Greer, Wren, Ellie, Duck. I have people like them too."

"Suki, Greer, Wren, Ellie, and Duck aren't trying to kill you because of who you decided to align yourself with."

"You chose the beings who are here to eliminate us. All of us. You included."

"I chose the beings who showed me more compassion than people like the ones who did that shit to your face have ever shown me."

"Please, there are innocent people in there. If you see my friend Phil leading a group of people out, please just... just let them go. That's all I ask."

"We don't always get what we want in this life, Ember. It's something you should learn now. It might save you a lot of heartache later on." Sophie is still sleeping, and I won't risk her waking up only to release Ember, letting them either sneak away or start killing people in this camp. So she gets tied up until I can return.

"I should have known you wouldn't listen. Why the hell did I think you would care?"

"Don't know. Don't damn well care," I snarl, leaving the tent to ensure the riders receive this information. I know they will save anyone who doesn't fight back. No adult trying to escape with a child will be harmed by the riders, but I want to make sure they have this Phil's name. Because even though I would have never received the same courtesy, I want to save the people I can. And making her eat crow is just the icing on my 'don't you feel like an asshole' cake.

Chapter Twenty-Five:
Rebellion Who

*T*HE GROUP OF mortals and the ones directing them will soon regret every choice they have made since the first day the initiator of this faction formed this ridiculous rebellion. The error they made when coming into my camp to harm the people under my protection is something I plan to explain. Painfully.

"War, I need to tell you something," Avalon yells. I look up to watch her sprint across the camp. Whatever she is coming to say must be significant based on the hard-set line of her jaw.

"Are you going to their encampment?"

"I believe a visit from my brother and I is warranted. Don't you?"

"Yeah, but War, there are people there who may not necessarily agree with the leaders or what they did." When I do not acknowledge what she just told me, she forces an exhale and continues. "There could be innocent people in their camp."

"So are you asking me not to go, mouse, because I don't think I can do—"

"No. Absolutely not. These assholes need to be taught a lesson. But...." She closes her eyes, releasing a sigh before continuing. "Just promise me if you come across a group of people who look like they are trying to escape, maybe let them."

"And how would I discern the innocent mortals from the ones who will flee simply because we have arrived?"

"Phil. Most likely, a man named Phil will be the one leading them."

"And you ascertained this information how?"

"Ember," she mumbles, looking everywhere but at me. She forces another loud and dramatic exhale when I lean over to capture her attention. "I know we probably shouldn't listen to anything tumbling past her hateful lips, but what she said felt... genuine. Besides, she didn't do that damage to herself, which means someone in her previous group did. And dollars to donuts, whoever it was, is someone who isn't afraid of their current regime. Which means—"

"They are one of the leaders."

"Exactly." I know how difficult it must have been for the lamb to tell me. She does not like the woman who disclosed this information, and generally, when my mouse doesn't care for someone, she refuses to hear anything they might have to say. I believe this is from a long-forgotten life. One before my brothers arrived. The sense she has suffered hangs heavy on her. It formed her into someone who holds you accountable for every choice one makes, be it good or bad. It is part of the reason we are so… drawn to her. "So you will…."

"Provide them safe passage? Yes, they needn't fear Pestilence or my arrival."

"Thanks, War," she says with a smile—a smile I still find myself getting lost in. My brother is a fortunate soul to have discovered her first. Her smile morphs into a grin when I tilt my head and quirk up one eyebrow.

"What?" she asks me playfully.

"What's a donut."

"A sweet treat. Maybe if you're lucky enough, we'll find someone who's really good at making them. Only your dad knows how long I've been looking for one. Hell, donuts were my breakfast staple for quite a while."

"We shall see what we can do about such a grievous calamity."

"How 'bout you just worry about bringing you and Pessy home safe, sound, and in one piece. I'll take that over donuts any day."

"Pessy and I shall do our best."

"You can knock off the Pessy nonsense, brother," Pestilence says after draping his arm around Avalon's shoulders. "As for you, little lamb, promise us you will stay in camp with everyone else."

"Wait, you aren't taking anyone else with you?"

"No. This is something we will do alone."

"If you didn't plan on bringing your army into a battle with you, why did you collect the people in this camp?"

268

"Simple. To ensure all of your safety," I tell Avalon before raising her hand to my mouth and pressing a small kiss to her knuckles.

With her free hand, she lifts three fingers before declaring, "Scout's honor."

Afterward, she hugs Pestilence and me before spinning to return to her post. I may have believed her if I knew what a scout was and if she had said it without the devious grin tipping her lips.

*****

We arrive at the fort they have procured as their base. I'm sure they believed it would protect them, especially with all the additional fortifications they put in place. It's such a shame they are about to discover how wrong they are.

"Sto–stop right where you are."

"Perhaps you might like to try repeating this? Only without the stammer this time."

"We'll shoo–shoot you." I believe this attempt may have been worse yet.

"You will try," I yell back to the one doing all the talking. These simpletons believe the darkness gives them an advantage in this fight. It does not. We can see every son of Adam positioned on the wall. The moonlight provides more than enough light for my brother and me to see our targets.

"They still have not learned." Pestilence calmly states while withdrawing his bow from his back.

"They never do," I declare, pulling my sword. The blade hums in my grip, knowing we will soon enter battle. It is not magic nor sentient, but it is special. Made for only one task… removing humanity.

"Any who wish safe passage?" Pestilence asks as he nocks his first arrow.

"Receives it."

"Then shall we begin, brother?" In answer to his question, I click my tongue to signal to Sarge our time has come to begin this siege. As is our way when we fight together, our horses move as one.

The first of many arrows whiz through the sky. Their sounds inform us there are no less than fifty projectiles soaring in our direction. It doesn't matter since Pestilence has released his tendrils, and they have become a barrier while we move closer to the gate that will do little to hold us out. A house of sticks is what they believe will halt the ride of the horsemen.

Such a shame.

When we arrive at their barred gate, Storm and Sarge rear back to smash their front hooves into it. The first time, it groans. The second time, it cracks. The third time, it shatters, giving us access to the interior.

The screams and shrieks increase as several men and women scatter. Some grab their meager possessions while others move to protect their young. I lift my chin in the direction of those who appear to be defending other mortals. Pestilence nods his understanding before releasing the first of many arrows. This is the group we will pardon.

With us now on even ground, the tendrils switch from defense to ammunition, streaking away from us to begin their assault on the ones still on the wall firing down at us.

While Pestilence focuses on aiding his plague, I drop from my horse in a shattering descent. With my blade in hand, I block the first attack. Circling my sword, I disarm the untrained fool before I bring my boot up to slam it into his chest. He flies back, landing several feet from where we stand. His unmoving frame confirms that he will not rejoin this rebellion prior to its fall.

One after another, they charged in my direction only to meet the bite of my blade. The ones tasked with assailing us from the walls test their skill against the greatest archer ever to grace this realm. And the ones who fight from the shadows, the souls who believe this will save them, face the tendrils of the black death to end any further evasion.

What amazes me most is they continue to throw their soldiers in our path. Each man and woman make a valiant effort but ultimately fail in their assigned mission. Perhaps if their leaders were here to guide and direct them, the fate they now face could have been avoided. As I said, I would grant safe passage to any who requested it except the ones who formed, cultivated, and grew this into something they believed would spell our end.

Their leaders could have accepted the judgment Pestilence and I decreed. It could have been theirs to bear alone. It's what any decent leader would have done. It's what any of my brothers and I would do. It's a quality one should seek when determining who they want to place their faith in—a trait these individuals do not possess.

They were in this for the title and the power alone. Something I detest. Something they will regret they ever desired.

When we stop in front of the cluster of men and women, the air fills with apprehension and fear. The ones in charge left these sons of Adam and daughters of Eve to fend for themselves, deeming them unimportant since it appears by mortal standards they had seen far too many or too few summers to be of benefit. Only two men and one woman stand between us and the helpless behind them.

We wait to see what the three will do. Will they stand against my brother and me as the savior of the innocent? Essentially throwing away their own lives to spare the others. Will they turn and run? Leaving them to face us alone. Or will they present the weak to us as an offering to save their own life?

While we wait, they do too. Husbands are embracing their wives. Mothers are comforting their young. The sick hold their self since none remains to do it for them. In the end, the three guardians do not disappoint.

"Please, let these people go. The three of us will accept whatever you feel we deserve."

"And if we reject your offer?" With my question asked, the mothers clutch the young tighter, the wives look at their husbands, and the sick allow the first tears to roll down their cheeks.

"Then we'll hold you off as long as we can to give them the best head start possible," the young woman says, taking another step forward.

"You will die for the men and women behind you?"

"We will," the leader declares.

"Okay, Phil, we accept your offer."

"How-how do you know my name?"

"Ember. Now, if you would please wait outside the fort, we will take you to her after we complete what we came to do."

"Ember's alive?"

"Yes."

"And she's with your group?"

"She is at our camp."

"Why? Why would you do this for us?"

"Because we find you worthy," Pestilence replies over his shoulder. We still need to find the head of this snake. I slam my foot against the door, kicking it off the hinges.

"Have you never heard of a handle, brother?"

"Why enter like a lamb when we can appear as the lion."

"I believe a certain mouse might have something to say about your comparison."

"Only if you tell her brother," I confess, walking toward the man cringing in the corner. "You are not the one who I seek. Where is your leader?"

"I don't—don't know."

"But you were among their inner circle."

"Yes," he mumbles because apparently, if we believe he is meek, it equates to his innocence. It does not. This man trembling before us does not impress me half as much as the ones waiting for us outside the walls of this place. At least they chose to meet us on their feet. Not quivering on the floor like this elite member has chosen to do.

"One of the self-declared leaders, yet you hid in this room while they lost their lives defending this...." I look around, realizing how sad it is they believed this place could protect them. There is nothing else for us to do here since no one outside this irritant on his knees sobbing before us remains.

He is not worthy of my blade or my brother's arrow. Killing him in combat would mean nothing. Nevertheless, the sigh of relief escaping him when we turn to leave the room may be a bit premature. Right before we exit, I turn to ask him one last question.

"Are you the one who likes to beat on women within your ranks?"

"No—no."

"So you are not responsible for the damage done to the one named Ember?"

"Ember was hurt? Listen, if someone beat her, the bitch probably deserved it. She's nothing but trouble, trust me."

"I should trust a man who would rather cower on his knees than face us on his feet?"

"I don't think anyone would—"

"Ember would." I have nothing more to say to this coward, so when I nod at my brother, his tendrils race across the room to do what we have deemed beneath us. They claim the last victim of the night.

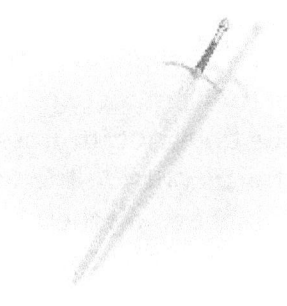

~Avalon~

These riders need to quit collecting people. When they left, they were alone, but upon their return, several individuals were trailing behind them. Looking at the new arrivals, I would say they were the ones Ember told me about. And the one in front is most likely Phil.

To say I'm shocked seeing an elderly couple perched upon Storm while Pestilence walks beside them would be the damn understatement of the year. Until I noticed Red carrying several kids. I don't think I could admire the riders or their companions any more than I do right now.

I greet every person coming into the camp and direct them toward the tents they can use until we can make other accommodations. And while I am playing the part of air traffic controller, Suki and Xander ensure they have food, blankets, and anything else they may need but could not bring with them.

If I liked Ember more, I might have awakened her to advise the ones she requested safe passage made it back here safe and sound. But I won't, and not for the reason anyone may think. She's been through a lot today. Between having her ass handed to her by someone in her own group to stumbling across the horseman, the one she's hated for the last year. Only to discover he isn't to blame for her greatest heartache, nor is he the asshole she wanted him to be. To her, fearing for the safety of the people she cares about, much like I do for my family. She finally fell asleep after hours of waiting to hear the outcome of her friends.

Even if she isn't my favorite person, if the riders can forgive these people who joined a group whose sole reason for existing was to remove them from this world, then I can do the same. At the very least, I can try.

"Welcome back, guys."

"Mouse." "Little lamb." The brothers greet me in unison.

"Storm. Red, glad to see you back, big guys."

"Red? Why are you calling him Red?"

"Because it's the name we chose for him. Isn't that right, Red?"

"You named him Sarge."

"No, you forced me to come up with a name. It was the only one I could come up with spur of the moment that you didn't shit all over. But after Red and I spent some quality time together, we decided this name fit him better."

"My horse decided this with you, did he?"

"He did. Didn't you, boy?" Red's snorts are the best I will get in the form of his friendly side.

"When?"

"A week ago."

"You didn't think to tell me about this change? I've been calling him Sarge this whole time."

"I told Pessy," I tell him, shrugging my shoulders while he glares at his brother, who is doing everything he can to ignore our conversation.

"And while we are on this topic, I want you to name me."

"Huh?"

"You have given my horse a name, my brother a name, and his horse one. I want you to name me as well."

"Umm, I didn't name Pestilence. Hope did."

"Then hope for my name as well. Perhaps it will come to you."

"Hope is a person, not an emotion."

"Since this Hope person is not traveling with us, you will have to assume her role as the namer of the riders."

"Seriously?" I ask him. With my arms crossed over my chest to the passing observer, one might think we're arguing again.

"Do I look like I'm joking?"

"You're supposed to be the fun one. Remember, War?"

"I am the fun one, just not the kind of fun you initially thought." I roll my eyes while doing my best not to laugh because, of course, he would find a way to make this conversation about his overly abundant sex drive. "Now, back to my name."

"Since you only have three letters in your name, there aren't many options for shortening it."

"Try, mouse."

"To what? Wa, or what about W? Something tells me these wouldn't work for you."

"Then choose something else," he demands before placing his fist against his hips, puffing out his chest, and lifting his chin. It's a damn superhero pose. The only thing he needs is a cape billowing in the breeze, and he's friggin Superman. Well, if he wants to give me this pose, then....

"Clark." Yeah, so I went with the Man of Steel's alter ego. He made it too damn easy!

"Clark? What does this mean?"

"It doesn't mean anything."

"Everything means something. Regardless, I'm not fond of it, so choose again." Damn, I kinda liked Clark.

"Okay, Ben."

"Ben?" He repeats, wrinkling his nose. If I want to return this conversation to more important business, I need to sell this shit.

"No, not Ben... Ben!" I say with extra emphasis, dragging out the word and dropping my voice to make the name sound masculine. I even give a little fist thrust while saying it.

"No, this word does not represent the being before you. I require something as powerful and dynamic as I am." I can't help the raised eyebrow quizzical look I give him. When he continues to stand there sporting his Superman pose, I let out an exasperated sigh while rolling my eyes.

"Thor," I say pointedly. I mean, who can argue with this name? He's like the most masculine god I can think of. Or maybe it's the memory of the man who played the Norse god of thunder in the movies I'm thinking of.

"Do I look like the son of Odin?"

"Wait, Odin's real?"

"He existed. And for some reason, the sons of Adam and daughters of Eve give him far more credit than he deserves, since he easily fell to me every time we sparred with one another."

"You sparred. With. A. God?"

"Well, I certainly could not train with a mortal."

"No shit."

"Are you planning to answer my question, or will you continue standing there gawking at me?"

"Gawking was my plan, especially since I can't remember anything prior to the whole sparring with a god thing."

"Do I look like the son of Odin to you?"

"Don't know, can't say I ever met him, but if you can introduce me." The sheepish look I give him while I try unsuccessfully not to laugh has him grinning. He taps his finger on my nose before returning to our conversation.

"I assure you I do not. My vessel is much more appealing. Now my brother Pestilence... he resembles Thor."

"I do not, šupak."

"Šupak?"

"It seems my brother's vocabulary has increased to include one of your favorite words, mouse. Asshole."

"Don't say I look like that arrogant šupak then." War throws his head back, laughing, while Pestilence

278

continues tending to Storm. The entire thing is so blissfully... normal.

"You do. He does. Now choose, mouse. And make it good."

"Your name has always been and should remain War. It's every bit as powerful and dynamic as the rider standing in front of me." I tell him with a tender squeeze of his arm.

"So it is, little mouse. So it is. Thank you for reminding me."

*****

After the riders fill me in on what transpired at the fort, I return to my task of watching over Ember. This wouldn't have been necessary if she never tried to kill my friend. Her companion Sophie is still sleeping. I can imagine fearing your life has come to an end by Pestilence's tendrils has to take a lot out of you. And watching a friend you believe is being killed by them can't be any easier. So when I arrive at the tent holding these two, I try to go in without waking them, but it's an epic fail because Ember jerks awake the second I enter.

"Have you heard anything?" Ember asks while pushing up from the cot.

"The riders are back."

"And?" She can't keep the fear from seeping out with her question. I guess I could have said they all made it back, not 'the riders' because the term depicts that only the riders returned.

"Your people arrived unharmed about an hour ago." She attempts to hide her sharp inhale. It's indicative of someone trying to hold their tears at bay. I understand the need to never cry, especially in front of others. Crying shows weakness. Weakness can be used against you.

"Can I see them?"

"I don't think—"

"Please. I just need to see them for myself."

"If you try anything."

"I won't." She must sense the disbelief rolling off me when I narrow my eyes at her since she is quick to elaborate. "You have my word as a woman who will do anything to keep the ones she cares for safe. Like I believe you do for your people. I just—I need to see them. People don't always...."

"Tell you the truth."

"Precisely."

After she promises me several more times she is not a threat to anyone in this camp and will not make any attempt to attack either of the riders, I relent. For the next fifteen minutes, I guided her from one tent to the next, allowing her all the time she needed to be sure they were here alive, well, and unharmed. She remains silent as we move from one tent to the next, trying hard not to disturb any of them until we reach a tent where a mother is curled protectively around her sleeping toddler.

"Did they kill Wayne and Trevor?"

"They weren't there."

"Of course, they wouldn't be there. They like to talk a big game and even knock around people they deem weaker than they are, but when a real fight shows up at their door, their true colors come out, and they run like the scared little bitches they are," she whispers.

"Which one of them did this to you?"

She remains perfectly still, apart from a single forced swallow, leaving me to believe she will refuse to answer my question, but she doesn't. "Trevor. Trevor did it." She gives an incredulous laugh before confirming. "But I give as well as I receive."

"Did Wayne condone this type of behavior?"

"He was worse than Trevor, so he would have been completely fine with Trev knocking me around."

"Assholes."

"That's an insult to assholes everywhere," she grins, and I can't hide the smile her witty comment evokes.

When she leans around me to confirm I found it funny, I give her a slight shove before nodding. "I suppose it is, and good for you. With any luck, you made the pansy ass cry like a baby."

After I return her to the tent Sophie is sleeping in and help her untie her friend, I turn to leave, but she stops me before I exit.

"Thank you, Avalon. For everything."

"Wow, I bet that hurt like hell to say," I tease.

"Worse than Trevor's pansy ass punches." We both look at one another for several seconds before we burst into a fit of laughter. When the laughs subside, I nod to show my appreciation for what she said.

I leave Ember to sleep without the ropes binding her because something tells me I no longer need to worry about her attacking my friend.

Chapter Twenty-Six: Horseless Rider

*I*T'S BEEN FOUR days since the riders found me in the woods. Ninety-six hours since they drug my ass back here. Five thousand seven hundred and sixty minutes since my entire world got turned upside down. But it only took one crazy-ass woman to make me question everything.

I may have despised the woman these riders hold in such high esteem when I first met her, but after what she did for me the night her camp was raided, I suppose even I have a newfound respect for her. Avalon didn't have to tell the riders about my people... my friends. She didn't have to welcome them in and help get them settled. She certainly didn't have to take me around their camp to put my mind at ease that they were here, they were safe, and no one could get to them without going through two horsemen. But she did.

Then there are the riders. You will never understand how much it can fuck with your head when you hate and blame someone for your every heartache, only to find out maybe it wasn't exactly what you remember. Talk about blowing your damn mind.

Avalon may have planted the seeds of doubt when she said he was a hundred miles away, but it wasn't until I watched him this morning when he was teaching a young girl how to use a bow it became clear. He didn't kill my parents. How could I be so confident? It was in the way he held his bow and positioned it. His spot-on accuracy. He is so deadly and precise with his weapon of choice he could easily shoot a fly out of the air mid-flight. He's that accurate with a bow. In other words, he doesn't miss.

Ever.

And the asshole who killed my parents... did.

A lot.

Pestilence's bow is a part of him, and even if all of this would not have been enough to convince me, the sound his bow makes when he releases an arrow is distinct. It's a sound that would have stuck with me. All of this combined led me to this... Pestilence may not be innocent, but he is not to blame for my parents, and admitting this is worse than thanking Avalon.

None of this means I want to linger in this place with these riders because the fact remains they are here to kill us. Generally, I don't hang around anyone who wants to watch me take my last breath, whether human or celestial. I don't want this for myself or the people counting on me.

After having lived with Wayne and Trevor all these months, I say it's high time to strike out on our own. Forge our own path and find a place where we can have a life. So, my plan is simple. I need to negotiate our release with the rider who runs this camp. War.

This is why I'm sitting here waiting for War to return to his tent like some damn stalker, because my offer isn't for the rest of the camp. I figure speaking to him alone might be the better option because if he is anything like the pricks from my old group, he won't want to appear weak, so he may flat-out refuse to let us leave if I make the request in front of others. Here's hoping he's reasonable and willing to lose potential members to his not-so-little army he has here. Perhaps it would be prudent to stay until Wayne and Trevor are located, but who knows when that might be, so I'll take my chances out on the road.

When he rounds the corner, I discover one slight hiccup with executing this plan. He's with Pestilence and another guy. If I remember correctly, his name is Xander, and he happens to be none other than Avalon's best friend's boyfriend. Yeah, try saying that five times fast. It's a bit of a tongue twister, I know. In any case, it doesn't look like I'll be talking to him about what I want right now. It's okay; I'm a patient woman.

This is an excellent trait to have when dealing with these riders because by the time everyone leaves his tent, we've lost the better part of the day, which means if he agrees with my request, we will either have to stay until morning or travel these roads in the dark. Something any sane person should avoid at all costs in this post-rider world, so let's hope he's feeling generous.

When I march inside, I quickly discover I should have knocked or yelled or cleared my throat, really just about anything other than what I did, because I find him without a stitch of clothing. After observing him for the last couple of days, I recognize it's not uncommon for him to be shirtless, but this... this is a whole lot of rider out on display.

And may I say his dad—the almighty creator did one hell of a job when he created him because his body looks like it has been carved from marble. And on behalf of all single women on the planet, I would like to personally thank him.

What the hell am I doing? Even though I enjoy looking at such a phenomenal body, I'm not here to gawk at the rider. I'm here to negotiate our freedom, so I tear my eyes away from him long enough to gather my wits before scolding, "Seriously? Do you know what clothes are?"

"I do."

"Then why are you fucking naked?"

"Because I was preparing a bath."

"Generally speaking, most people leave their clothes on until the bath is ready for them to enter it. What you don't do is walk around your room naked and glistening," he grins when he hears this part. Why the hell did I have to add the damn word glistening into the mix? Needing to remove the sight of the thick, lengthy, abundant, beautiful cock from view, I turn my back to him. To a rider, Jesus Christ, in what world do you ever turn your back on someone who wants to kill you? "Could you just put something on?"

He laughs but takes pity on me and does what I ask when I hear him tying something. "Is this more to your liking?"

When I face him, I want to blurt—'No, it most certainly isn't'—because this little sarong wrap thingy he has on doesn't cover enough for me not to continue picturing him the way he was when I walked in here. For shit's sake, Ember, I know you haven't had sex in a while, but how about reining in the damn hormones.

"I came in to thank you for saving my friends and let you know we'll be out of your hair today." He doesn't say anything, which can mean he's fine with us leaving, or it's a hell no. "If you're okay with us staying one more night, I would appreciate it because I prefer not to travel after sundown." Nothing. "Or we could go now if you want us to." Not one damn word. Not a head nod or a grimace. Nada. "So what do you say?"

"Leaving during the day would be prudent."

I take what I think is my first breath since finding him naked. "Okay, thanks. We'll be out of here first thing in the morning."

I don't think I could wipe the smile off my face if I tried. This was so much easier than I thought it was going to be. Taking one last look at the man leaning against his desk with his muscular arms crossed over a chiseled chest, looking sinful in all the best ways. It might be best to stop staring at him and take my ass back to the tent I can call mine for one more night. Clearing my throat, I nod my thanks and turn to leave until he stops me dead in my tracks.

"That is if I was going to allow you to leave."

My heart seizes in my chest. Is he fucking serious? War's going to keep us here against our will. Isn't that what his dad is known for, free will or some shit like it? Spinning to face him, I give myself a second to take a breath, hoping it will help me reel in my fury. It doesn't work. "What the hell do you fucking mean... if you were going to let us leave?"

"What I said. Why would I let men and women I can use in my army waltz out of here to some unknown future?"

"Because you don't own us. That's why!"

"No."

"NO? What the hell do you mean?"

"Commonly, this word is used when one denies—"

"I know what the fuck it means. What I want to know is why you think you have the right to deny us our freedom."

"Because I can."

"Fuck too."

"Well, it seems we are at an impasse. You want to leave, and I don't want you to. So if I willingly allow you to remove people I could use, what do you plan to give me in return?"

"Seriously, I have to give you something for our freedom?"

"Is this not how you do things? You want something, so you give something."

"Since I left my last group with only the clothes on my back, I don't have much to offer."

"I'm sure you'll think of something. You're a resourceful woman."

"Let's cut to the chase here, War. What the hell do you want?"

"Surprise me."

"You like to screw. So let's fuck!"

"You believe this is an even trade?"

"I'm fantastic at it."

"Are you?" he asks before pushing himself off the desk to stalk over to where I'm standing with my hands balled into fists. He looks me up and down. His proximity sends tingles rushing to my extremities. His lips tip up in a secretive grin, almost like he knows my deepest, darkest desires. Information that should never see the light of day or be shared with anyone. Least of all, this rider.

He moves in slow, deliberate steps, backing me across his tent until he has me pinned between the desk he was leaning against during most of this conversation and a wall of muscle that belongs to the mammoth man in front of me. My heart is racing so fast I'm afraid it might burst from my chest. And damn it, why is my body responding to his? Do I want him to do this? Shit, I think I do. He brings his mouth close to my ear, his warm breath skimming along my neck before he sensually murmurs his response.

"As much as I believe I would enjoy lying naked with you when we do, it will not be because you offered your body in exchange for something." With his rejection delivered, he steps away, taking all his luscious heat and manly smells with him.

He just let me off the hook. I should be relieved, but what I feel is something else altogether.

Disappointment.

There is no damn way in heaven or hell that I'm disappointed a rider doesn't want to have sex with me. Unfortunately... I am. But there is no friggin way I will let him know it. Nor can I let him think this wasn't a one-time offer.

"You think I'll ever willingly sleep with you?"

"Based on the inflection in your response, the accelerated pounding of your heart, and the rapid rise and fall of your chest with each breath, not only do I think you will, I'm willing to stake my horse on it."

"Well, I hope you like the idea of being the only horseless rider." He laughs, leaning back against the desk I just vacated. With his hands gripping the desk the way they are, every muscle ripples and bulges along his impressive arms.

"I believe Red would disagree."

"Red?"

"My horse. And currently, the shade coloring your face." I want to argue with him, but it would be pointless because I know he's right. The flush of color heating my cheeks is a mere drop in the bucket compared to the heat flooding my body. Tingling along my skin, causing my heart to race and my breathing to shudder. And, of course, this damn rider can sense it.

"So if you don't want to screw me..." Yep, still disappointed about this. Especially after seeing what I'm missing out on. Even more, since the only thing keeping his very impressive cock from my view is a wrap slung precariously low on his hips. Am I licking my lips? No. No-no-no, just no Ember. Stop thinking about it. "What do you want?"

"You agree to stay in my army, and they are free to do as they please."

"You'll let them go?"

"Yes. Your friends are welcome to stay or go. The choice will be theirs."

"Just like that?"

"Is this not what you were hoping for, Ember?"

"You know my name?" A grin I can only describe as sinful appears at the corners of his lips. And now the heat is flooding the parts of me I want him to touch. When he moves closer, it does nothing to halt the growing desire.

In fact, I have to force my fingers not to glide over the ridges of his well-defined stomach.

"I do. It's quite beautiful, like the woman who owns it. I look forward to moaning it while you writhe under me as I pleasure you in every way you have dreamed of." Fuck, now my clit is aching for him to fulfill this declaration. "Your people are free to stay under my protection, return to the fort the others have fled from, or go anywhere else they wish to go. They have no need to fear me. But you will stay."

"Why?" the breathy quality of my question informs him that he has me turned on and flustered just the way he intended me to be. But he doesn't answer me. He kisses the tip of my nose, drops the wrap, and saunters over to the bath he prepared. I almost rip my clothes off to join him, but one word repeating in my head stops me.

Rider.

Chapter Twenty-Seven: Paths Never Change

I HAVE NOT contacted my brothers since the night Ariel helped me. Even if War did not want to reject his growing feelings for Avalon, he will because I asked him to do it. My brothers would come to me if something significant happened, and even if War didn't feel I needed to be apprised of a situation, Pestilence would. I have to trust them. Besides, avoiding everyone makes it easier for me to fulfill my vow to let Apple have a mortal life, no matter how difficult. The simple truth is what I don't know about; I can't interfere with.

Thankfully, our father must have given Michael an assignment that took him far from here because he had not returned since the night he had Gabriel show me the vision of Avalon and my brother. In fact, aside from the occasional shuffling of feet as the guards stroll by, no one has come. And since Raphael has not visited, I have been unable to discuss Ariel with him. I hope she is not one of the guards I hear outside my cell. Not if what War said is true.

The passage of time here differs from Avalon's world. With the lack of visitors and windows, I have no way of knowing how long it's been. Part of my punishment, I suppose.

Until today, when the key clanging against my cell door confirms someone has come to call.

"Hello, Thanatos. I apologize. I have been unable to visit you as of late." Raphael.

"I understand, but I am glad you're here now because I wish to discuss something with you."

"Come, we can talk on our way."

"Way? We're going someplace?"

"Father has requested your presence."

"What, he didn't want to visit me in these deluxe accommodations he has relegated me to?"

Raphael chuckles before responding with a simple, "I suppose not."

When he moves to unlock my shackles, I snap my arms forward, yanking my restraints from the wall. Raphael's only response is to laugh while shaking his head. I have told him before I only allow this because it's our father's will. I have disobeyed him far too much as of late, and since Avalon appears to be in excellent hands, hands that are now at a respectable distance. At least they better still be if War knows what's best for him. I decided it was time for me to return to the role of his dutiful rider. One who does as he asks, even if what he requests is for me to stand shackled in a cell all day for the next century or two.

"You said you wanted to discuss something," Raphael said.

"Ariel."

"Is this regarding her visit to your cell all those months ago?"

"How long, Raphael? How long has it been?"

"Two months have passed on her plane since you last spoke to War. On ours, it has been a mere eight days."

"Two months? It's been two months since...." I didn't realize it had been this long. So much could have happened to my brothers and Avalon during this time. I need to make sure they are well. The only thing I can be confident about is War and Pestilence have somehow kept her from breaking another seal since I have not felt Famine wake.

But this is not the issue I wanted to discuss with him. Do I admit Ariel helped me reach my brother? That she knowingly broke the rules to give me a gift. How do I brooch this conversation without putting Ariel at risk? When he grins at me, I know I have answered his questions by saying nothing. So, rather than admitting or denying anything, I make a simple demand. "I want her removed from guarding me."

"I can arrange this; however, may I ask why?"

"Does it matter?"

"No, but I suspect this has something to do with why she makes her choices."

"What do you know about it?"

"My old friend, you think I am unaware she harbors feelings for you?"

"So it is true. I am the one...." How could I have missed this? How was I so oblivious to what everyone else around us saw?

"The one she is in love with? I'm sorry to confess you are."

"Your brethren will never again force her to hold the role of my jailer. This includes Michael. Am I clear regarding this?"

"You are. I will do my best."

"See that it gets done, and if Michael has an issue with it, he is free to bring his inconsequential concerns to me." We walk in silence for the rest of our trip. When Raphael escorts me into my father's inner chamber, he doesn't linger long.

"Father. Thanatos," he says while bowing his head before retreating through the door we just entered.

"Son."

"Father."

"Walk with me." I don't ask questions; I fall in line next to him. He has his hands clasped in front of him. Mine held at my back. When we enter his observatory, I find it impossible not to be awed by the beauty before me. The universe is a vast place full of wonders and grace, but none are more breathtaking than the view from my father's observatory.

"I would like to discuss something with you, but first, I wanted to thank you."

"You are most welcome, Father. However, I may be able to properly accept your gratitude if I knew what this was regarding." This is not something he often does.

"For leaving my veil intact."

"It will no longer be an issue."

"Because Avalon is safe with your brothers?"

"Yes." Even if I want to lie to my dad, I won't because it would be a pointless venture. He would know the truth.

"So if you felt her life was in danger, my veil would once again be in peril of falling?"

"Since this is no longer an issue, you need not be concerned."

"Nothing has changed, Son."

"What do you mean?" I turn my gaze away from the universe and give my father my full attention.

"Avalon's path has not changed."

"But if this is true...."

"She will wake your brother."

"How is that free will? She doesn't want this. Any of it."

"I'm afraid I have my answers. Raphael is waiting to return you to your cell."

"Father, don't do this. You can stop this if you want to." When he turns his attention away from me and back to his creation, frustration and anger replace my confusion. "What was the point of this? To inform me the one mortal I care for will forever be in danger?"

"Of all my children, Thanatos, you know that is not my way."

"Then why did you ask Raphael to bring me here?"

"I brought you here to see if you were ready to return to your previous task; however, based on your response, I know this is no longer an option. Because if I restore you to your role of ferrying souls, I would be placing everything I have created at risk of falling for one mortal woman who has somehow captured your love."

"Is this not what you wanted, Father, for us to love the ones you hold in such high esteem?"

"Yes, but not to the detriment of everyone else. I fear your love for her could end everything she and you are trying to save."

"It is about time you admitted your true feelings for this mortal," Michael snarls. Of all the souls who could have walked in on this conversation, it had to be the one being I knew would use her against me to overhear my confession. I can no longer sit back and hope my brothers will protect her because I know Michael will never leave her in peace. It seems my time in this realm is ending, and the instant they leave me alone... I am returning to her. And if any of my father's warriors come, it is their souls I will reap.

"Then return me to my cell."

"I'm afraid this is also no longer an option."

"What do you mean?"

"I'm sorry, son, but you have done this to yourself."

Chapter Twenty-Eight: Question

*O*VER THE LAST few months, I have developed a newfound respect for the woman who tried to kill one of my friends. After getting the entire story, Pestilence promised her he would do everything possible to locate the one who killed her parents. She only asked him once what he would do after he found the person, but when Pestilence did not respond, I think she understood what fate they would face.

The two idiot's—I'm speaking of Wayne and Trevor—whereabouts are still unknown. It's like they've disappeared. In fact, it might be more accurate to say they have fallen off the face of this world. Here's hoping it fucking hurt when they did. I don't know everything these two perpetrated against the men and women who followed them, but I know enough.

War and Pestilence go out looking for them every day, and each time they return without finishing the task they set out to do, War becomes more aggravated. They had better pray the riders never figure out where they're hiding because if they do, these two men are in for a world of hurt.

Just after dusk, Xander lit a bonfire and invited several people to join us. I think he did it for Ember, who is still trying to find her stride here. It would have been easier if her friends had stayed, but not long after the riders brought them into camp, they returned to the fort under War and Pestilence's protection, leaving her, Sophie, and Henry the only three who remained. I get the distinct feeling her decision was less choice and more sacrifice on her end.

On the flip side, Greer, Suk, and I have done everything possible to make the three who stayed feel welcome.

"I can't believe summer is only three weeks away," Greer said. Without delay, she takes her usual seat, which happens to be Pestilence's lap. I still think they are perfect for each other, and the loving looks they give one another confirm they believe so too.

With the fall of our technology, if it wasn't for Suki and her meticulous calendar-making skills, I wouldn't have the first clue what month we were in. For a long time, I thought she did it to hold on to something from our previous life, but when I said this to her, she responded with a laugh before informing me it was her no baby making calendar. She did it to keep track of her cycle so she would know when she and Xander had to avoid typical sex. Of course, me being the biggest idiot in the world, I had to ask. 'Typical sex?' to which she informed me rooster in the cathouse. Since you don't speak Suk, rooster as in cock and cathouse...well, I think you can figure out the rest. She also told me not to worry because she still satisfied her man during the no-fly zone days. I didn't ask her to elaborate on this.

"I have something for you, mouse," War says, holding out a new book for me, and when I see the cover, I leap from my seat next to the bonfire to retrieve it. It's from a new series I started after I found all the books except the last one, which is the one War is now holding just out of my reach.

"Are you going to give it to me, or are you going to keep teasing me?"

"Currently, teasing you is quite enjoyable, mouse. Especially since it has you pressing yourself against my body."

"Don't be an ass."

"So I bring you a gift, and you call me an ass as a thank you?"

"Well, if the ass fits...."

"Tell me why you like these so much?"

"I just do. Will you give it to me now?"

"That's not an answer, mouse."

"And you didn't answer me, War," I reply, jumping up to snatch it away from him, but the ass is too fast for me, and it remains just out of my reach.

"You give me my answer, and I'll give you yours."

"An answer for an answer then?"

"Okay."

"Uh, you might want to rethink this, brother. I've played this game with Avalon, and you tend to walk away with more questions than you began with."

"A game? How does this game work?"

"You get to ask one question, which I have to answer, but then I get to ask a question which you have to answer."

"This sounds like fun. Since I clearly have the larger body mass, I will begin."

"Never heard the saying ladies before assholes?"

"This is not the saying, mouse." I lift my hand, implying he should start. "Uh-uh, I insist ladies before gentlemen, or in our case, mouse before rider."

"Oh, I like what you did there. Are you going to give me the book?"

"Yes, right after we finish our game. My turn. Did my brother enjoy looking at you, and did you like looking at him?"

"That's two questions. You only get to ask one, so which one do you want me to answer?"

"Did my brother enjoy looking at you?"

"He never said he didn't. Where did you find the book?"

"I asked some locals where I might find one of those buildings you mortals used to visit for these. They sent me to a Lie berry—"

"Library," Sophie interrupts.

"Yes, thank you, little one."

"Anytime, proceed," Sophie tells us, leaning forward like we're the entertainment for them to enjoy this evening.

"A library is where I found it." He did all this for me. He asked people where a bookstore or library was located, then went however far it was without knowing if he would even find one there. I'm astounded he put so much effort into doing something he knew I would love.

"You did all that... for me?"

"Of course I did, mouse."

"Why does he call her mouse?" Sophie whispers, but Suki only shushes her.

"Did you enjoy looking at my brother?"

"Wait, are they talking about Pestilence?" Ember asks the others who are enjoying this show way more than they should.

"Thanatos," Greer tells her before shoving a handful of popcorn in her mouth.

"Who's Thanatos?" Sophie inquires.

"Death," Suk tells her as she leans across Xander to grab a handful of the popped goodness. Apparently, one of them was preparing to ask another question, which probably would have earned them a quick 'Shhh' from Greer, Suki, and Nehra, so Pestilence tells them prior to this happening.

"Thanatos, or Death, is our brother and the first rider who came."

"Wait, I thought your seal was the first one broken."

"It was. Thanatos's seal has not yet been broken—"

"And it isn't going to be," I quickly interject before returning my attention to War.

"Regardless, when he arrived, it was not to reap; it was to judge. Avalon is the one who convinced him humanity is worthy of our father's forgiveness."

"I'm still waiting, mouse."

"He is or was very handsome... so yes, I liked looking at him. Have you always been like this?"

"You will have to elaborate. Been like what?"

"This." I wave my hands around in front of him. "You."

"I don't know. Have I always been like this, brother?"

"You mean insufferable, bullheaded, infuriating? Yes."

"Yes," he repeats with a grin. It doesn't seem to bother him that his brother just insulted him. "Why are you like this?" he mimics my previous action only with one hand instead of my dramatic two. The question shocks me. I don't want to tell two more riders or the other people sitting around this fire how terrible my life was when I was growing up. About my horrible parents. About the man who raped me. About Ms. Deniker. I contemplate walking away without answering, but Death taught me I am stronger than my past, so I'll answer the only way I can right now and pray he doesn't ask me a follow-up question.

"Product of my upbringing." Okay, I managed to answer without it catching in my throat, which is a feat since I feel like I have a lump sitting there. When War's smile changes from cocky to understanding, I know he won't push. Clearing my voice to push down the damn blob of emotions so my response doesn't come out as strained as my last one, I ask. "Do you enjoy looking at women?"

Okay, I realize this was a stupid question. My hope was to redirect this conversation back to lighter topics, and the wink I get from War is his way of telling me he knows it.

"Some mortals I would delight in seeing without the barriers your clothes offer. You among them."

"Brother," Pessy's tone is clearly a warning to War.

"I know, Pestilence, don't get your knickers in a twist."

"I don't wear knickers," he hisses, making War and everyone else around the fire laugh.

"My turn. Did my brother ever touch you?"

"Every time I tried to escape, and he had to come after me."

"A rider hunted you?" Sophie probes. I would say she's more than a little shocked by my response because her eyes are wide, her jaw slack, her mouth is in the shape of an 'oh shit,' and don't even get me started about how high her eyebrows are right now.

"Yeah, it was loads of fun. Do you ask questions solely to embarrass others?"

"If the blush on your cheeks is any indication, I would say not only did I try, but I accomplished it. Did you enjoy my brother's touch?"

"Sometimes. When your brother wasn't tossing my ass over the side of Ghost."

"Wait, ghosts are real?" Sophie asks.

"Ghost is Death's horse."

"Death's horse is a ghost?" It seems it's Ember's turn to be astonished.

"Ghost is the name the lamb gave my brother's horse," Pestilence responds.

"Why do you riders call Avalon lamb?"

"Shhhhh!" Greer, Suk, and Nehra all shush Sophie so the entertainment can resume, but War answers anyway.

"The Lamb is what my mouse is. I believe it is your turn for a question, mouse." After seeing where War's eyes have settled most of the night, I ask him a question that will shock at least one person present tonight.

"Are there any mortals who you would like to touch? You know someone who you haven't touched already?"

"Besides you?" Okay, I take that back. Two people will be shocked tonight, although I don't know why I am since he always said stuff like this to me in the past.

"Brother!"

"Pestilence, you really need to relax. To answer your question, mouse, I find the female form beautiful. Ember here among them." Ha, I knew it.

Ember chokes on the glass of wine she is drinking before she sputters. "What?"

"Unlike you, I had no issues with my words," War teases.

"You do know I was planning on killing your brother, right?"

"While I will admit this would have been an obstacle, it does not make it impossible."

"You're an arrogant ass," Ember huffs.

"Thank you."

"I don't think Ember meant that as a compliment, War. And you are being an ass," I answer for Ember.

"Yes, but an ass who knows what he wants and is unafraid of obtaining it. Did you lie with my brother?"

"I'm not answering that."

"So, are you conceding this victory to me?"

Huffing my frustration, I grit my teeth and snarl. "During our travels, we had to share many things, including where we slept. Does your interest in the female form make you wish you didn't have to kill us?"

"If given my preference, there are many other things I would prefer doing with the daughters of Eve rather than removing you. When you lay with our brother, did you do this with… or without clothing?"

"War, you're taking this too far." Pestilence's comment was made hoping to defuse the tension building around us.

"Will you answer the question, mouse, or has our game concluded?"

"Both," I snap, extracting my prize from his grasp. With my book in hand, I walk back to my tent to the sound of the amazed gasps of my friends… apart from Suk, who murmurs, 'That's my girl,' a sighing Pessy, and a chuckling War.

*****

I imagined Ember and Sophie would approach me with inquiries about what they had heard last night, yet Ember was more interested in someone other than me.

"He's, um—"

"Confident?" War has evidently earned Ember's full attention after his comments.

"I was going to go with cocky."

"He can absolutely be cocky. A confident, cocky bastard." I confirm.

"Does he walk around like that all the time?"

"What? Half dressed?" I ask with a laugh as I follow her gaze, which leads to War, whose jeans sit low on his hips. As is typical for him, his upper body is out on full display because I think he may be allergic to shirts. The rider's boots - as I call them because Death and Pestilence each have an identical pair - resemble black biker boots and— par for the course—are unlaced. His jet-black silky hair has grown quite a lot since his arrival. Most of the time, he leaves it hanging loose and falls just past his shoulders with one small exception… the top half, which is pulled back in a ponytail to keep it out of his face. A necessity since he spends most of his time leaning over tables to study maps of the area with his brother and their council. "Yes… yes, he does."

"I mean, that's not distracting at all," she mumbles as she chews the tip of her thumbnail.

"Really?"

"Oh, come on, Avalon, even you have to admit he's hot as sin. Every woman in this camp damn near swoons when he walks by. Hell, I've actually witnessed some women end up on their asses if he so much as smiles in their direction. Not to mention, I see the way he flirts with you."

"He flirts with every woman because he knows you catch more flies with honey."

"He can have my honey anytime he wants," she mumbles before groaning when she realizes I wasn't the only one to hear it.

"Ohhhh, really?" Suki asks with a teasing tone.

"Hey, Greer. Hey, Suk, I think Ember has a little thing for a certain horseman," I tell them while bumping Ember's arm teasingly.

"I most certainly do not!"

"Well, the drool on your face would say otherwise," Suki laughs while wiping her chin, which has Ember flailing to knock her hands away.

"Okay, I dare you to deny how sexy he is." Ember's gaze moves from Suki to me. Her attempt at pretending she is irritated with her fist on her hips and frantic foot tapping is valiant but utter bullshit because she can't fool me. She wants War as much as Suki wanted Xander, Greer desired Pestilence, and I dreamed of another rider.

"I can't deny it because he is," Suki admits, and even Greer nods her agreement, which shocks me. "But I have my own sexy boy toy and one who knows how to handle me in the boudoir."

"Boudoir? Suk, we have freakin' tents here. There are no boudoirs in this little encampment," I tell her. I meant my statement to be serious. And it was until she started air-humping a whole lot of nothing while smacking a pretend ass in front of her, making all of us collapse in hysterics.

"And I happen to think his brother is every bit as sexy, especially because he's so sweet with Wren and me. Yet deadly to any a-hole who threatens the people he cares about." And this is why I love Greer. She's everything Pessy deserves.

I watch as each of these women takes in the sight of the men they go weak in the knees for, and I can't help but be jealous because these men tend to look at them the same way. Something I thought I had, but....

Nope, I won't let my self-pity poor me attitude ruin this day or this time with my friends. Even the crazy one who tried to kill me.

A roar of laughter comes from the men we have been staring at when Sophie walks over to where they are standing. She reminds me of a girl I knew from childhood, always joking around but never at someone else's expense. She doesn't linger like most women in the camp do, opting to join Suki, who has Duck's little hands in hers so she can spin him.

"Sophie's hilarious."

"Don't tell her that. She'll get a gigantic head."

"Alright, provided you never bring up sex when Suk is around because she could make a sailor blush when she gets going."

"Deal. You know Avalon, luck was on our side when we met those two."

"I don't know if it was luck, fate, or something else. The only thing I know is I'm damn glad for it."

"You have a Suk, I've got a Soph," Ember smiles.

"That we do." I grin as we watch our best friends play with Wren and Duck. And for the first time in quite a while, I remember my time with Death. His smile, the color of his eyes, his scent, the comfort I knew only in his arms, and how it felt when his fingers were gliding over my skin.

I remember him, and for the first time in a while, I let myself miss him.

Chapter Twenty-Nine: The Workout

*T*WO WEEKS AGO, I inadvertently announced to Avalon and her friends that I'm attracted to War. Since then, Suki and Sophie have joined forces in what they like to call the 'get Ember laid' consortium. Original, I know. I get why Suki would think I need help in this department since she doesn't know me yet, but Soph does. I had hoped it would have died down by now, letting them move on to their next big thing, but nope.

My way of dealing with my recent lack of fun physical activities is to work out. All the time. It helps relieve some of my pent-up frustrations. It usually works, but not today. I've been at it since the first rays of dawn crested the horizon, but the rider remains firmly rooted in my thoughts, so if need be, I'll continue until nightfall.

I spin, whipping my leg around, only to have my momentum stopped by War when he grabs it so I won't kick him.

"Shit, I'm sorry. I didn't know you were behind me."

"So it seems. What are you doing?"

"Practicing. It helps to keep me sharp."

"And who taught you these techniques?"

"My dad. He was in the military before...."

"Us?"

"Yeah. Before you riders came and sent our asses back to the stone ages."

"I can assure you this world has not fallen quite so far."

"I suppose if anyone would know this, you riders would." His wicked, hot as hell, makes me want to do all kinds of nasty things to him, grin appears. If he was any other man, I could play it off that he holds no effect on me, but the damn heat he brings with it has my face flushing. Negating every damn thing I have been trying to do out here this morning.

"Do you think I could have my leg back now?"

"If I must."

"What was that?" Did he just pull me closer before releasing me? Damn it, I hate how flustered I get around him.

"You drop your defenses right before you strike."

"Huh?" I mutter, still panting heavily from the workout. I am only doing it to get my mind off all the dirty things I want this rider to do to me. Did he have to show up when I almost had all the naughty thoughts purged?

"Allow me to show you." His hand snakes around my waist, pulling me back to his chest while his other hand glides down the arm holding the blunted blade they permit me to work out with.

"Each time you draw your arm or leg..." He winks. Fuckin winks, and it sends my heart rate from fast to racing. "back to prepare your strike, you pivot, leaving this side open to attack. Rather than swaying these hips," he guides my lower half to the correct position. I know they always twist in. Something my dad used to bitch about as well. War realigns me before drawing my arm back to demonstrate how I should stand. Maybe if he had been my teacher, I would have dropped this bad habit long ago. Or perhaps I would have kept it only to ensure he would have to continue training me like this. "Keep your hips directed at your enemies. Never give them your back, Ember."

"Why not?" I ask, a little too breathy. Maybe he'll think it's because of the workout, not his demanding presence.

"Because it allows your opponent to do this." Before I can react, he twists my body and has me pinned to the ground with his massive frame hovering inches above me. "And while I am certain most sons of Adam would enjoy this position, I am not so sure you would."

If only he knew how much my traitorous body is enjoying it. When he's near, I feel like my veins are filled with a million tiny sparks, a tiny flame that ignites every nerve and cell in my body. I can almost feel the energy radiating off of him, like a warmth that spreads over me. And damn it, if I don't want to live in the feelings he evokes.

No matter how often I tell myself it can never happen, the more I desire it, the more my treacherous body agrees with the desire part. Because the more time I spend around him, the more I want to explore every emotion he stirs within me. I suspect he is one of the few men who could satisfy me. Scratch an itch no one has ever reached.

When he strokes his fingers along my cheek, the last of my reserve sails away like an unmoored vessel caught in a squall and lost at sea. It's abrupt and devouring. For the first time, I allow myself to be consumed by it. Instinctively, I raise my head with the sole purpose of savoring his soft, full lips.

I've decided I'm done fighting this, whatever this is. I want to experience everything War has to offer, and then I plan to show him things he only dreams of. My eyes are fixed on his, his on me, and the entire time I move closer, the seductive grin never leaves his face. He is so close to me I can feel his breath tickling across my cheek and hear the sound he makes with each soft exhale. It's like a gentle whisper against my flushed skin. Mere millimeters separate us until I'll finally know my deepest desire, but he abruptly stands and pulls me to my feet. Putting an end to our moment.

His rejection leaves me feeling more than just disappointment this time; it also brings a sense of dejection washing over me. I want him, this much is clear, and I thought he also wanted me, but this is the second time I have offered myself to him and the second time he's turned me down. I suppose another miscalculation on my part.

"I'll let you get back to it then. Remember, never give them your back."

"Yeah, okay," I mumble, more out of frustration than to respond. The rider does the one thing he told me not to. He gives me his back while walking away.

Idiot. I am a damn idiot.

Over the next hour, I attempted to regain the same level of focused determination I had before he waltzed over here and erased all thoughts besides him. But it's pointless. I know it. My body knows it. Hell, the damn planet knows it since the sun has disappeared behind a wall of clouds. The gray dreariness matches my mood perfectly.

Giving up on the idea this will wipe all thoughts of him away, I head toward the tent I share with Sophie. Maybe she can do what the workout refuses to, but when I throw back the flap, I'm greeted with nothing but empty space. Damn, of all the times I need her to be here... she's not. I suppose I could try finding her. She has to be in the camp somewhere, or I could look for Avalon. If anyone can commiserate with what I'm going through, something tells me she can.

I almost have myself convinced his rejection has nothing to do with me per se and more to do with him trying to be a better leader. Yeah, that's totally plausible. It's not just me he doesn't want; he's turning everyone down. Of course, this is the reason.

And I almost have myself convinced of it until two random ass women have to go and ruin my fictionalized version of the events.

"No, I heard it was Samantha."

"No way would he let that skank anywhere around such a glorious cock."

"Damn, I'm so jealous you have firsthand knowledge."

"One of his first," she coos. "And it was fuckin amazing. Sex with War is life-altering." Ordinarily, I would ignore gossip because, let's face it, all too often, it's bullshit. But hearing his name piques my interest.

"Well, I hate to tell you this, but Samantha was with War last night, and the lucky bitch couldn't wipe the damn smile off her face all day." What the fuck. Is he still screwing the other women in this camp?

"Jenny plans on being first in line tonight."

"Wait, I thought Beth picked tonight?"

"We might need a signup sheet," the one who supposedly has already slept with him laughs. "Good thing he is damn near insatiable."

"I need to get on that list," the one who hasn't screwed him yet announces. The rest of their conversation I can't hear because they've moved too far away. Regardless, I have heard enough, and I plan on addressing it. Right. Fuckin. Now.

Marching across camp like a woman on a mission— since this is precisely what I am—I arrive at his tent in no time. I had planned on barging in there demanding to know what his problem with me was, but I hesitated because what if he's not alone in there? Could I handle seeing him in the arms of another chick? Or would I lose my shit? The last thing I need is the women in this camp hating me because I ripped some bitch off his dick before planting my foot up her ass.

In the end, I don't knock because, One: I'm too damn pissed. And two: announcing my arrival isn't really my style. When I enter, I find him leaning over a table, studying a map of the area. They have been searching for Wayne and Trevor by dividing the state into grids. War thought it would be pointless because he figured they would just come back to an area after the riders cleared it, but I assured him and his brother they would find a place to hunker down and stay put until they felt safe enough to slip by them unnoticed.

"You are not who I was expecting."

"Yeah, sorry, not Jenny. Or was it Beth tonight?"

"Actually, Pestilence," he advises before he leans back on the table, crossing his arms over his chest and his legs at his ankles. His head tilts and the same grin I've become accustomed to every time he looks at me is back.

"This won't take long, I promise." His left eyebrow rises, a clear sign he doesn't believe me. So I don't beat around the bush and choose to dive into the deep end, head first. "What the hell is it about me you don't like? Do I repulse you or something? I mean, you'll fuck every chick in this camp, but you won't give me the time of day. So what is it about me, War? Do you want me to leave? Do you hate me, or do you simply love tormenting me because of the group I used to travel with? Not that I want to be another notch on your belt, but I can't help myself. I need to know why."

He waits several seconds after my tirade is done before he pushes off the table to close the gap between us. "Are you finished?"

"You know what, never mind, this was a mistake," I snap, but he stops me before I can exit his tent.

"I do like you. I can assure you I do not find you repulsive, Ember. In fact, I think you are quite possibly one of the most beautiful women this world has to offer. I don't want you to leave. Nor could I ever hate you or torment such an exceptional woman. I'm fascinated by you. Everything about you captivates me. The reason I don't fuck you is that I would never want you to be 'another notch on my belt,' any more than I want you to be only someone to keep me company for the night." He takes his last step, ending right in front of me. "The reason I didn't kiss you today is simple… when I finally taste you,

315

I don't plan on stopping with these perfect lips, and I didn't think you would appreciate me dropping between these thighs..." he slides his hands up the back of my legs wrapping them to the inside until he gently grazes my pussy. Which is now dripping wet and throbbing with need. "in front of the entire camp."

"Oh." Real fucking brilliant, Ember. The being I've fantasized about for the last couple of months. The one I use for all my dirtiest fantasies when I masturbate just told me not only does he want to have sex with me, but he's also thought about it, and my totally enlightened response is Oh.

War pulls his hands from between my legs, making sure he drags them across my clit to completely drive me crazy before cupping my ass. He yanks me close, and the length of his hard cock pressed against me sends ripples of excitement radiating through my body, leaving me breathless. I push up on my tiptoes, preparing to claim the lips that have my full attention when Pestilence picks this exact second to come striding into his tent.

I want to scream. And throwing something is not out of the realm of possibilities. For fuck's sake, you have got to be kidding me. Every damn time we're close, something or someone ruins it. I swear to god, this better not be the case tonight.

"Oh, excuse me. I didn't realize you had company," Pestilence says, stopping dead in his tracks, and has the decency to avert his gaze.

War's eyes never leave mine. "We will not be meeting tonight, brother. I have made alternate plans for the evening."

"So I see."

"Perhaps Greer requires your attention." His wicked grin slips across his face, and I understand why after he finishes. "Again."

So it was Greer's screams of ecstasy distracting me during my workout and part of the reason why I couldn't get the rider currently kneading my ass out of my head today.

"Brother. Ember." Pestilence dips his chin, and then he's gone. It seems War isn't the only rider who is insatiable. The difference is this rider's brother only has eyes for Greer, whereas the rider pulling me against him couldn't care less which of the women in camp warms his bed. But I've known this for a while now. Maybe I just need to get him out of my system, and once I do, everything can return to normal. War's hand on my face guides my attention back to him.

"I plan to rectify all these mistakes tonight."

"And tomorrow?"

"And tomorrow and the next day," his fingers cradle my face. I am only vaguely aware he is backing us toward his bed. "And every day after until you order me away."

My hands run along the expansive muscles of his back. His earthy aroma fills the space around us, but what I like best is the underlying scent of leather. I've never smelled anything like it before, not like this. Not like him, and I can't help but inhale deep. I want to wrap this fragrance around me and live in it for the rest of my days.

His head dips, and I realize there is nothing left to stop us from this kiss. This very moment I've been waiting for. Until….

"War, are you in there?"

Chapter Thirty: Ride On

*Y*OU HAVE GOT to be fucking kidding me. I think someone up there might actually hate me. Or, in this case, the women of this camp.

"War." The sing-song voice can only belong to one person. Beth. "Oh, I didn't know you would be here."

"Leave. Now." War's demand affords no room for argument. The problem is his eyes are still focused on me, so I can't tell if he meant it for her or me. But when I attempt to step away, he shakes his head. The thumb he has been stroking my cheek with drops to run across my lips. My tongue comes out to taste him. The instant I make contact, his pupils blow wide, and this little taste is not enough, so I open my mouth to drag his thumb inside. I only get one caress before he yanks it out and smashes his mouth against mine. The sound of someone scoffing reminds me we were not alone when this began. But I don't care if Beth stands there the entire time because nothing will stop me from finally having what I have wanted for entirely too long.

His demanding tongue probes my lips, desperate to gain access, and I willingly grant it to him. I don't know what I expected he would taste like. I can tell you one thing... cinnamon wasn't it. But it's the only way to explain the taste when his tongue circles mine. Cinnamon and something just the tiniest bit sweet.

His fingers find the button on my pants, and before my brain can comprehend what he's doing, they are being lowered to the ground along with the rider. He kisses the space between my breasts, but I can't feel it how I want with my shirt still on. So rather than allowing such a grievous situation to continue, I rip it over my head, giving him free access to kiss them the way he wants. Or maybe it's the way I want.

He removes the bra, and thank god he did because the skin-on-skin contact is so much more satisfying.

"Beautiful." He lifts his gaze back to mine while his thumbs circle my nipples. He refuses to touch them. His focus seems to be keeping them hard, stiff, and begging for more. When I grow tired of the teasing, I knot my fist in his hair and pull his mouth toward one. My body jumps when his teeth latch down. The sting is instant, but so is the pleasure.

"Fuck," I hiss but pull him closer. The thumb still circling glides across the peak of the nipple that is currently not being assaulted by his tongue and teeth. But it's not what he's doing to my nipples that has me ready to beg. It's his fingers gliding along the top of my panties.

For a rider who has only been awake a few months, he sure as hell knows how to bring a woman to the verge of rapture. Each teasing touch, every flick of his tongue, has me ready to come, scream… or scream while coming.

"Lower," I demand, wanting him to fulfill his decree and taste me. Everywhere.

He kisses my breast one more time before his mouth moves down to my stomach. "Here?"

"Lower."

His tongue circles my navel while his finger dips inside my panties. "Here?"

"Lower," my breathy demand is more plea this time.

He slips the panties off my legs and runs his fingers along my slick folds. The heat pooling in my core makes me wetter with each passing second he refuses to give in. His lips brush along my right thigh. "So, this is where you want me?"

"Left." This time I grab his hair to place him where I want him. He clicks his tongue before he chuckles as he kisses my other thigh. God damn him. I don't plan on waiting for him to ask this time. I jerk his head back to capture his eyes before I give my directive as a growl. "Front and center, soldier."

"Yes, ma'am. Anything else?"

"I want you to kiss my pussy."

"Kiss? No. Devour? Yes." With his promise made, his tongue flattens against me, running from back to front, and when he reaches my clit, the punishment truly begins. And it is bliss. Utter fucking earth-shattering euphoria. With every demanding flick, my legs quiver more, threatening to give out any second. If not for his firm hands holding my ass so I could not move away from his divine ministrations, I would be on the ground already.

"Is this what you wanted?"

"Yes—fucking hell—yes!" I scream as my legs finally buckle, and I tumble back onto his bed. He wastes no time wrapping his muscular arms around my legs before he returns to devouring my soaking-wet core. Wet from his tongue and dripping from my excitement.

"Come for me. I want you to scream my name." My hips no longer refuse to stay still. The harder I grind against him, the louder he groans, and I feel the rumble everywhere.

"Fuck-yes. Do that again." Two fingers push inside me seconds before he attacks my clit, and this time when he growls, I explode. White lights fill my vision. The world spins, time stops, and I fall. I want to push him off me. To beg him to stop his assault. But my arms are like rubber, which means they refuse to comply. After such an intense orgasm, the only thing they are capable of doing at this second is raking through his silky hair. But rather than letting the waves subside, he keeps them coming until another orgasm crashes around me. Something no one else has ever given me, back-to-back climaxes, and he deserves to hear how much I approve when I don't just moan this. I scream it. "Oh. My. God. WAR!"

It seems he is not done yet since he lifts me off the bed, backs us to a chair, wraps my legs around his waist so I'm straddling him, then impales me with his massive, beautiful cock. The cock only seconds ago, I was salivating to taste. His mouth finds my nipples rock hard and waiting for the warmth of his tongue to encircle them.

My hips grind, rock, pivot, and swirl. Each grunt and groan I pull from War informs me he approves of my skills. When I abruptly stand, he grabs my hips, hoping to return me where I was, but I have other plans. Grasping his cock I stroke him. It's for his pleasure yet also for mine because when I slide my mouth around him, I want to taste the rider, not myself. The glistening pre-cum is a start. Before it can slide too far down his shaft, I drop to my knees, collecting it with my tongue. There's a salty sweetness to it, making me want more.

My hand grasps the base of his shaft while my mouth encases the top. His hips jerk up as his hand begins to direct my head. Oh no, this will not do.

"Trust me, handsome, I know how to do this." To drive home my point, I swirl my tongue around the tip, taking a couple of extra seconds to lick away the evidence of the come trickling down to meet my hand working him. This time when I suck him in, I take him down to the base. His length makes me gag, but I force my throat to relax as his hips rock in swift, hard thrusts.

With one hand still fisting my hair so he can ensure my mouth remains wrapped around his cock, the other drops to tease my nipple. He needn't worry because I have no intention of stopping until I get what I want. This includes him screaming while I swallow his release because, unlike women who say they like giving head. I fucking love it, especially when the cock looks like his.

"Ember," his second hand joins the first to guide me how he wants, and unlike last time I don't stop him because him doing it is different. It's hot as hell. It makes my pussy ache to feel him inside me again, so I let him command me. I know he's close when his thrusting quickens. However, it's not until he pulls my head against him roughly, pushing himself down my throat as far as I can take him, that he explodes.

His release is like a wave of salty, sugary bliss flooding my mouth and coating my tongue with the sweetest come

I have ever tasted. His roar was deep and powerful, reverberating through the air and making everything around me shake. It's primal and wild and makes my core clench with need. If I weren't still so busy licking his cock, he would see my triumphant, beaming fuck yeah grin.

I'm used to most men rolling over to let sleep pull them under, but not this rider. He's still hard and eager to continue pleasuring me. Something I have no objection to even when he yanks me to my feet, bends me over the desk littered with the maps he was studying when I came in, and takes me from behind. He ravishes me in the most deliciously sinful ways he can think of. For a fleeting second, I wonder if I'm forfeiting my place in heaven by corrupting a rider, but the utter ecstasy he provides me outweighs any risk.

"This time, I want to feel your pussy clamp my cock when you come, minha beleza." His fingers press against my clit to ensure he can achieve it. He circles around the tight nub while he slides in and out, slowly drawing out the pleasure. I can feel my core clenching, and I want to beg him to pick up his pace, but I don't because it feels so fucking good. I want him to keep screwing me until I shatter into a million pieces, and he has no choice but to stitch me back together.

"You're close. I can feel it." His fingers stop circling, but they don't leave my clit. Oh hell no, he pinches it, and the extra pressure causes my orgasm to rip through me as the third of many satisfied screams fill his tent. The wave I am riding hasn't fully diminished when War hits the peak and roars his release.

Afterward, while lying in his arms, I realize a rider of the apocalypse... a being sent to eradicate us is the best fucking lay I've ever had and the only one I want anymore.

Chapter Thirty - One: Closing In

*W*HEN *EMBER FINALLY* came to me willingly, I did what I had wanted to do since the second my eyes landed on hers. I claimed this beautiful daughter of Eve. And it was everything I imagined it would be. I enjoyed it so much that I did it over and over until she fell next to me in my bed, exhausted but unimaginably satisfied. If she had allowed it, I would have slept with my cock inside her. This way, when I am ready to fuck her, I am already sheathed within her velvety delicious pussy that I plan to feast on several times before she leaves this bed today.

Usually, the women I screw wait for me to tell them what I like, but not Ember. She demands what will satisfy her every need. I like it. More than I will admit to anyone other than the woman I want grinding against my face soon. And the magical thing she does with her tongue makes my cock ache for her to do it again.

In fact, she has remained in my tent every night since she stormed in and demanded I tell her why I didn't want to fuck her, and Ember can stay as long as she likes. The simple truth is I like waking to her in my arms.

For the first time since I gave up on the idea of Avalon, I believe I understand what my brothers have discovered because lying next to her, with her bare ass pressed against my rock-hard cock, I know I would do anything to keep her safe.

Could it be possible? Is it possible to be so enthralled by a daughter of Eve that I would forgo my mission? Turn away from my path and happily live beside her until time cruelly takes her from my embrace. I would have said no when I first arrived, but I have learned much since entering their world. Taught by the best of them… Avalon and now Ember.

Other women have laid with me. They have satiated an immediate need, yet none has ever fulfilled me as she does. Damn it, Pestilence will never let me live this one down.

Speaking of my soon-to-be gloating brother, I promised him last night as I carried a wiggling Ember slung over my shoulder to our tent that I would meet him this morning. And morning has nearly slipped away to noon.

When I pull my body away from hers, she murmurs, "Where are you going?"

"I promised Pestilence I would meet with him this morning. I have kept him waiting long enough."

"Are you sure you have to leave right now?" She presses her ass against my thick cock, making me groan. And, of course, as has become my way, rather than leaving this bed, I cave to the woman next to me, pushing back between her legs. I bask in the warm wet velvet of the most amazing pussy I have known.

Her hand slides between her legs to massage my balls. Something she has discovered I enjoy immensely. With my thumb circling her clit, my teeth latch down with gentle pressure on her ear to tell her what I know she wants to hear. "Delicious."

"Oh, fuck, War." She moans, arching back into me further.

"You should never give your opponent your back."

"When my opponent impales me with such a glorious cock as you are now, giving you my back is the only thing I want to do."

"You do not fight fair, love."

"And I never will when it comes to you." Flipping her onto her back, I tease the entrance of her pussy with the tip of my cock. It takes every ounce of my reserve not to slam inside her, but I must prove to her she does not possess all the power in this relationship.

"What are you waiting for?" Her breathy tone is filled with the same unbridled need coursing through me.

"Tell me how much you want me."

"I want you," she moans when my thumb slides along her wet folds.

"I believe you can do better," I tell her. It is hard to deny my desire when my response is delivered in the husky timbre she loves.

"WAR!" Her hand slides between her legs, grasping my engorged cock to glide it inside her. She does not bother to stifle the moan I create when I grant her what she wants. Ember won't because she knows if she does, I will withdraw and refuse to fill her until she agrees never to do it again. She will scream for me, and I don't care who hears her.

*****

An hour later, I have thoroughly licked, sucked, and fucked my woman, leaving her to cover her glorious body from my view. Pestilence and I met to discuss the intel one of my spies returned with, and we have a solid plan in place. Now I am going to prepare my horse. It does not surprise me to discover Avalon there, tending to Storm and Red.

"Mouse."

"Big guy." The moniker she began calling me after I again insisted on her giving me a name. "Heading out?"

"Yes. Pestilence and I need to check on something. The sooner we leave, the faster I can return." Avalon does not miss my eyes following Ember across the yard while she runs after Duck, nor the smile crossing my face, seeing the unrestrained joy filling them.

"I'm glad you and Ember found the same happiness Pestilence and Greer have." When I tilt my head and soften my expression, she continues with what I imagine she felt I needed her to say. I'm just not sure if she did it to convince me or herself. "It makes me realize everything I have gone through is worth it. I'm happy for you. Really, War."

When I look at Avalon, what I discover is loneliness staring back. I don't think anyone, Pestilence included, thought about this when they warned me to stay away from her. Because as I found myself growing closer to her, this emotion slowly began fading away. However, it returned when I abided by their request and distanced myself from my beautiful lamb. Thanatos has never told her how he feels, believing it would only hurt her more if she knew, but seeing her like this, I can't help but think he's mistaken. I believe she deserves the truth.

"You should know that Thanatos—"

"Before you say whatever it is you want to tell me about Death, can I ask you something?"

"Of course."

"If your father called you home, would you go? You know now that you've found Ember. Would you stay, or would you go?"

"I would like to believe I would heed my father's call, but...."

"You wouldn't. Because of Ember. Because you would rather face his disappointment than never be with her again."

"I suppose so."

"Suppose?"

"I know I would no longer go, not if she wanted me to stay."

"You would choose to remain with her... not leave?"

"Yes."

"She's fortunate. Just like Suki is with Xander and Greer is with Pestilence. Do you know in my entire life, no one... not one damn person, has ever chosen to stay for me? Just once, I would like someone to choose me."

"My brother—"

"Didn't. Death left. He made a choice to leave me like everyone I have ever cared about has done. I have to stop excusing people or riders who do this. It's time I quit hoping for shit that will never happen. Stop waiting for someone to put me first. I learned that lesson long ago, and damn it if I didn't let Death make me believe I was incorrect, only for the reality of how right I actually was to smack me in the face when he *decided* to leave me too. So if what you want to tell me about your brother is how much he cares for me... don't, because it's a lie. And I won't continue living in that world."

Her heartache is written across her face, but I don't think it's entirely Thanatos who has put this here. I know many times I have felt an overwhelming sadness surrounding her. It fills her eyes when she watches Greer with Wren and Suki with Xander. Even while she watches Pestilence and me together. It is the kind of grief you only know from a lifetime of heartache and loss. Something I plan to inform my brother about after I take care of another pressing issue.

We have located the whereabouts of the two who lead the rebellion, and I cannot risk them slipping from our grasp. It is past time for us to deal with them.

*****

The two soon-to-be-dead men thought an hour was enough separation to stop us from finding them. They were mistaken, and I plan to prove it. Painfully. Especially to the one named Trevor. The one responsible for the shape we found Ember in that day in the woods.

It seems this so-called man felt he was entitled. He believed she should and would submit. He never understood that she was incapable of bowing to anyone, be it mortal or rider. And I would not want it any other way. It is what makes her perfect for me. I see the same strength and fortitude in her I find in Avalon. But where Mouse's resolve comes from a hard life, Ember's comes from a caring father.

The place they selected is a large building the mortals called a school. It has several rooms in which they can hide. While I can trail most creatures with ease, the interior of a building does not leave much in the way of tracks to follow. This means we must meticulously search every room without alerting them of our presence.

With simple hand signals used in place of words, we hope to find them quick. Neither of us wants to tip them off that we have arrived. Especially since we already know they will throw others in our path to slow our approach, allowing them time to escape. Had this been two years ago, I would have leveled the building while my brother released his tendrils to chase them from their holes, but everything has changed. We will not risk killing innocent people if we can help it.

We clear the building room after room until we both stand facing the last door they can hide behind. My apprehension that they somehow slipped away again dissipates when we hear subtle movement from the other side. I lift my foot, prepared to smash the damnable thing to the ground, when Pestilence gives me his patented—don't be an ass—glare. When I lower my leg and cross my arms, he twists the knob to grant us access. What we find is not what we wanted or hoped to see.

One man is bound, restrained in a chair in the center of the room we entered. His grunts and mumbles are impossible to understand with the gag shoved in his mouth. His wide eyes dart between Pestilence and me.

Recognizing this may yet be a trap we are slow to enter. Once we are confident the room holds no one other than the man frantically trying to garner our attention, we remove the object keeping him from explaining what happened.

"You have to get back," he yells, making us both take a step away from him. "No, not from me. Back to your camp."

"Why?"

"They're in danger. Wayne and Trevor, they're out for blood. They want to make you and the people at your camp suffer."

"When did they leave?" I ask as the first bit of trepidation sinks in.

"Two, maybe three hours ago," he confesses while Pestilence pulls away the last of the ropes holding him.

"Why are you telling us this?"

"Because I never wanted to hurt anyone. I just didn't want to choke on your plague or end up impaled at the end of your blade. But Wayne and Trevor, they—they don't care who they hurt. Listen, you need to return to your camp right away. They plan on burning the entire thing down with your people trapped inside it." When we turn to leave, his next confession sends waves of dread crashing over us.

"Trevor said you took someone who belongs to him, so he plans to take someone who belongs to you.... And make them pay."

Chapter Thirty-Two: Who's It To Be

*A*FTER *PESSY AND* the big guy left, Xander and I began assigning job duties for the day. Everyone has something to do, and we rotate the responsibilities so no one gets stuck doing the shit work twice in the same week. Even Pestilence and War help when they are here. I think it's good for the people to see them willing to pitch in and work. It proves no one is above the tasks needed to keep this camp thriving.

We have almost everything completed, which means I can spend the rest of the day reading the book War got for me. I'm almost done with the series, and it's a bit disheartening since it serves as a distraction for me from everything trying to drag me under. Sometimes my demons are hard to keep at bay. Lately, they have been almost impossible to block out.

When I turn the corner, I see Ellie running out of camp towards the woods. Since Pestilence and War chased away the other group, we don't worry as much as we used to. This group is far too large for roaming raiders to tangle with, but it doesn't mean I'm okay with Ellie out in the woods alone, so I chase after her. I catch her seconds before she could slip into the thicker brush.

"Ellie, what are you doing out here?"

"Duck," she tells me, sucking in a deep breath.

"What about Duck?" I ask, even though my eyes are already scanning the woods for the little guy.

"He left his truck out here yesterday when Pestilence and Greer took us for a walk. I told him we could get it later, but he didn't listen. I saw him entering the woods right before I ran to stop him."

"Do you know where he lost it?"

"Yeah, he left it on the stump in the clearing." She has to be talking about the clearing two hundred yards through the thick tree line and heavy underbrush. I strain my ears, hoping to pick up on any noise from Duck to point us in the right direction.

I don't think Ellie is lying, but on the off chance she is mistaken, I would prefer not to let him get any further head start than he already has. When I hear his song coming from the same direction the field is located, I grab Ellie's hand to pull her through an area not thick with brier and sticker bushes.

I use the song to keep me moving in his direction. "What is he singing?"

Ellie tilts her head to better hear him before she laughs, "The finger song."

"You mean 'Mommy finger, where are you,' right?"

"Yep, the very same." I suppose it's fitting since at this moment we are searching for his little butt.

Thankfully, we find him heading back in our direction, truck in hand, still singing his song. I scoop him up when he gets close enough, and I delight in the sounds of his giggles.

"What do you think you're doing out here, little Ducky-do? You know you're not allowed out here by yourself." He answers me with gibberish. Something I'm still trying to learn, so I can't understand most of what he says.

"Aunt A, what is that over there?" I look in the direction Ellie is pointing. Something shiny is glistening on the tree stump.

"I don't know. Did Duck have anything with him when he came out here? Something he might have left behind in favor of his truck?"

"I don't think so. At least I don't remember seeing anything in his hands, but this is my little brother we're talking about."

"Right, so anything is possible. Here," I pass Duck to a giggling Ellie, and I can feel the love between these two when she hugs him tight. "You and Duck head back to camp. I'll check it out and be right behind you. Okay?"

"Are you sure you don't want us to wait?"

"Do you know how to get back to camp without me?"

"Yeah."

"Then no. I'll grab whatever this little squirt left behind and probably catch up with you before you can step one foot into camp." I rumple Duck's hair before pointing her in the direction she needs to go in.

"Is this a challenge I hear, Aunt A?"

"Could be," I laugh.

"Game on. Come on, Duck, we have an Avalon to beat." Do I enjoy playing with the kids? I do, but this was said to remove them from the area since I clearly have no damn idea what I'll find.

Once I'm confident they are heading in the right direction, I walk over to see what it is. I suppose it comes as no surprise what I find isn't a toy.

It's a hand mirror that, by the looks of it, hasn't been left out here for long. I wonder if my original assumption Duck brought it with him is correct. But the closer I get, I realize it's the same mirror I once held in Death's tent before I ran from his horde after he killed the three assholes who beat me. How the hell did this get here? I know I didn't take it. And I damn well know he didn't bring it when he came to reclaim me, which means someone put it here for me to find. My head jerks up, allowing me to inspect the area while my apprehension morphs into gnawing panic. I swallow hard, hoping to push down the dread threatening to overtake me.

Movement catches my attention, and I don't hesitate to whip my head in the direction I believe it came from. Scanning the woods, I'm looking for anything out of place. I squint my eyes and strain my ears in search of something, but all I feel is an eerie stillness. Blowing out a deep breath, I turn, hoping to catch the kids; however, the next sound stops me mid-step.

It's the caw of a crow, or more accurately... a fuckin raven.

I turn in a slow circle, and this time I focus my search on the branches rather than the forest floor. And that is when I see it... a massive black raven staring back at me.

335

Fuck-fuck-fuck. What the hell am I supposed to do?

I can't turn tail and run back to camp because if this is Raum, he will just follow me, putting everyone back there in danger. There is no place else around here I can hide. And the horsemen are hours away from here.

When it soars down from the branch it was sitting on, my heart doesn't merely speed up... it pounds wildly. I wait, holding my breath to see what this bird will do. The bird hops across the ground, tilting its little black head almost like he's listening without ever removing those inky black eyes from me.

If this freaking bird is Raum, he sure is taking his sweet time revealing himself to me. When the raven slams its beak on the ground, I almost jump out of my skin, believing this is it. But when he bobs his head toward the ground in rhythmic repeat motions, my hope shifts to thoughts of the damn demon somehow stuck in his bird form. When he yanks his head up, I know if he plans to reveal himself, this is when it will happen. Fingers crossed, I can hold this bastard off long enough for the riders to return.

Wait, is that... a damn worm dangling out of its mouth? The raven gives me a cursory look before taking to the skies with its prized supper in tow.

Not a demon, just a bird. A hungry bird that was looking for something to eat. For Christ's sake, Avalon, get your shit together. I release the breath I've held since spotting it in the trees, shake my head at how silly I acted, spin, and run straight into the damn demon I thought the last bird was.

The impact sends me slamming hard against the ground. It's jarring, and had I not been staring up at the demon I stole a rider from, I might have taken a second to collect my thoughts but did the prudent thing and scrambled away from him.

"Not every raven is yours truly."

"Thank fucking god," I snarl, quickly finding my footing and pushing to full height, which is nothing compared to the bastard in front of me.

"I see Ember found her way to your camp."

"How do you know Ember?"

"Let us say I may have given her a slight nudge to continue moving when her group lingered too long for my liking. I couldn't have the riders catching up to them."

"Nudge? What do you mean nudge, and did you talk to Ember?"

"Yes, ma'am, I reckon I did. Only she didn't know it was me she was gabbing at," He says in a ridiculous Southern dialect while he flicks the brim of what I can only imagine is a fake hat.

"It would have been more believable with the cowboy hat."

"Of course it would have. Why were you so worried about getting Ember's group moving?"

"Couldn't have them missing the opportunity to meet up with the other band of idiots. I wanted them to keep moving so their group would converge with another heading the same way. Essentially, this ensured that the riders took out both camps. Better collateral damage." When I scoff, he grins. "No? Don't like it? How about more bang for the buck? Is this term more to your liking?"

"You're a prick."

"No, I'm a being who is sick of toiling in the shithole my creator tossed my ass into while you humans get all this." He lifts his arms to demonstrate the world around us. "I thought I had what I needed in War until the idiot went and fell for the bitch who wanted to kill his brother. Bit self-serving if you ask me. I mean, if I were his brother, I would have been pissed. Do you not agree?"

"I'm glad War found Ember because she showed him what it's like to be loved. I suppose I have you to thank for that. So thanks, asshole." His nostrils flare, and his upper lip twists into a snarl.

"You really are quite pathetic. I see why the riders take pity on you."

"Fuck you. They don't pity me. They respect me."

"Poor pitiful broken little lamb—"

"Shut up!"

"So hopeful that you're mistaken. That this time will be different, only to have the world kick you back down. This is what makes you pathetic, little lamb, because every time humanity has shown you that you cannot trust them, deep down, you don't want to believe everyone is like your parents and Calvin."

"What do you know of Calvin?"

"I know it all, little lamb. Each time he stroked your soft skin. Every desire and jealous rage he felt looking at you. Every pleasure he experienced when he came inside you—"

"Shut up!" He doesn't know. He can't know he's fucking with my head and nothing more.

"You did ask. Tell me, Avalon, you enjoyed shoving that knife into his chest. It made you wet, didn't it?"

"Fuck. You. Bird!"

"That might have more Bite," he pops his lips when he says this word. "If you weren't so pathetic."

"Who are you really?"

"You know the answer to this already."

"I know the bullshit you keep telling me, but not who or what you really are or why you are so hellbent on ending humanity."

"Would you believe I was once an angel?"

"No. No, definitely not."

"Well, little—"

"Let's knock off the little lamb shit, okay?"

"Then whatever shall I call you?"

"My name. Which you already fuckin know," I snap while rolling my eyes. I did this to give myself a second to look for any means of escape. Since the only weapon I have is a damn mirror. What the hell can I do against a demon with a damn hand mirror? Scare him to death with his own reflection? Would he even be able to see himself, or is he like a vampire and won't see how hideous he is?

"Very well, Avalon," he clicks his tongue after saying it. His way of telling me how insignificant I am before he continues. "As much as you do not want to believe this, I was indeed an angel until the creator cast me aside for my beliefs that you mortals held too much of his favor."

"Why?" The tilt of his head, eyes filled with wicked glee, along with the smirk he gives me, results in my skin crawling.

"Because humanity has been given respite long enough. The time of you mortals ruling this world is at an end. It is time we take our rightful role. He believed casting us from the heavens would stop the inevitable, but it has only fueled the flames of the fire stoked long before you ever existed, Avalon." Again with the cockiness when saying my name.

"War and Pestilence would disagree with your assessment."

"Only for the love of their brother. The one they both look up to. You should have done nothing more than release them from their long slumber. But instead, you dared to meddle with the head of his fiercest warrior. By doing this, you have given him pause and made a rider of the FUCKING apocalypse question every damn thing he was created for. You would think the dumb prick mistook himself for the chubby cherub who shoots arrows at your loving fucking hearts." This is the first time I have witnessed this being before me lose much of his calm, cool demeanor. Hmm, I wonder if I can do it again.

"And if the opportunity presents itself, I'll do it every damn time I can."

"I eagerly await the day you recognize the unimportant part you play in this conflict."

"You can't end the world without me breaking the last two seals. Something I have no intention of doing."

"It is admirable you believe you have a choice."

"You can't be so damn dumb to believe Death will be happy with you if he returns."

"If?"

"That's what I said, asshole."

"Thanatos will return, and when he does, I hope he remembers his true purpose."

"And if he doesn't?"

"A calculated risk, but one I am willing to take."

"I could end this all right now by taking my life," I snap, slamming the mirror against the stump. When the mirror shatters, I grab the largest shard to bring it up to my throat, fully prepared to end their extermination. No Avalon means no lamb. No lamb means the final two seals remain intact. If there was ever a time for selflessness, now would be that time. One life for millions seems like a fair trade to me. His hand flicks, sending the glass flying toward the tree, impaling it with enough force to shock me. I'm not sure how it stuck rather than shattered.

"I will not allow harm to befall you, little lamb. Not when I have such a wonderful surprise for you."

"There is nothing you have that I want."

"You shouldn't be so sure of this. Specifically, since you yet know what gift I have lined up."

"So where is it?"

"In due time, little—pardon me—Avalon. In due time. For now, let us return to a much more interesting conversation."

"Which is?"

"Your mission, of course. Since you have not yet completed it."

"Thanatos deemed humanity—"

"The pale rider was weak. So easily swayed by a pretty face, ample breast, raven hair—although I must admit I admire this about you too—and magical pussy."

"Shut up!" I snap for the third time during this inane conversation. The sound of something racing from both the right and left side of me in our direction momentarily distracts our discussion. But the damn bird pulls it right back when Raum blows something in my face. "What the hell was that?"

"Camouflage. I'm afraid our time is coming to an end."

"AVALON!" War's deep voice echoes through the trees, making Raum's eyes snap up to scan the area around us. His composed demeanor has slipped away, revealing his weakness. He's afraid of the riders.

"What do you really want with me?"

"Soon, Apple."

341

"Don't ever fuckin call me that." His smirk is annoying. To think I ever helped this asshole. In a moment of blind weakness, I say something I never intended to admit. Not to the riders, certainly not to him, not even to myself. "I thought of you as a friend."

"A mistake I imagine you will not make again."

"Message received loud and fucking clear," I say to the empty space he once stood in. A second later, a hand clamps over my mouth and pulls me into the tree line seconds before Pestilence, War, and Xander burst into view.

Chapter Thirty-Three: Visitor From The Past

I DON'T KNOW what the hell that shit Raum blew in my face was. I suppose it doesn't matter aside from one issue. Whatever it was kept the riders from sensing me, even though I was only fifty yards away from where they were standing. And as an added bonus, it knocked my ass out for lord only knows how long.

Then there was the asshole restraining me. Some big, burly bastard who probably left bruises on my face from where his hand covered my mouth and across my chest from where he had me pinned against him.

When I woke up, I found myself slung over the rump of a horse half the size of Storm or Red. When I turn to look at the rider, I realize the shit is also somewhat screwing with my vision because everything is a blur of hazy shapes but little else.

"Ay, air r ewe aching ee," I mumble around the gag, cutting painfully against my mouth at the expansive back of the guy who took me because, of course, I want to know where he's taking me. But he must not be the talkative type since he doesn't even glance over his shoulder at me, let alone respond.

How the hell do I keep putting myself in situations like this? For fuck's sake, this is the second damn time someone has taken me against my will since Death showed up. I'm generally not this... girly. I've always been able to handle my shit. It's because I let the riders get into my head. They made me feel safe, so I dropped my damn guard and look where it got me. Tied up and tossed over the ass of a scrawny, dirty, one-foot-in-the-grave horse. Dumbass.

I try to flip myself forward, but something has me restrained. Since I can't move, it leaves me to endure this ride with the blood rushing to my head. When I fist my hand, attempting to break loose of the bindings, a surge of pain followed by a burning sting has me inspecting it. Two long cuts run across my palm and fingers. Damn, I must have sliced it open on the damn glass shard. Well, that sucks.

The first thing I see to inform me we are getting close is archers lining the roadway. By the time we arrive at their camp, I'm going to guess I don't look much better than one of the rider's victims. Thankfully, when we got there, the leader, who wasn't the same one who had taken my dumb ass, decided he wanted to chat with little old me. They ripped the gag off my mouth with one violent tug, but the rope around my wrists remained, digging painfully into my skin from the knots. The bindings are so tight I can barely move my hands, and it doesn't take long before I feel warm blood dripping down my arms from the large gashes the ropes caused on my wrist.

The room they drag me to is enormous, with a massive table occupying most of it. I don't suspect they invited me here to have dinner. I suppose it's a good thing I ate the handful of nuts this morning. If I had known it was going to be my last meal, I would have splurged, maybe thrown in a grape for good measure. Since it appears these assholes don't like me. Especially the crewcut prick glaring down his nose at me. It would have been nice to have something substantial in my stomach.

"This is her?" his booming voice fills the room before he shoves another mouthful of meat into his pie hole. His massive arms flex and bulge with every movement. He must be their leader, making the dipshit sitting next to him his second. Great, Tweedledee and Tweedledum plan on judging me. This ought to work out in my favor.

"Yeah, she's the whore traveling with those fuckers."

"Definitely not a whore," I interject, only to have the one holding my ropes backhand me.

"Damn, that hurt," I snap, which wasn't the best idea since he hits me again. I guess I am only supposed to speak when spoken to. This may be an issue since I have the whole 'tell an asshole they're an asshole' thing.

"When you fuck someone solely to escape punishment, it makes you a whore."

I look around from the one talking to the one who keeps hitting me. I may have an issue with keeping my mouth shut, but I'm not stupid. And given my preference, I would rather not continue having the back of the asshole's hand meeting my face. Here's hoping I can keep my mouth shut long enough to avoid it. When the leader appears to be waiting for me, I take a chance to answer his ridiculous assessment.

"I disagree."

"Most whores would."

"Still not a whore, and I disagree with your assumption that someone who sleeps with another to survive is a whore."

"What do you call them then?"

"Smart. A fighter. Take your damn pick," the sting from his hit this time has my entire face on fire. "Fuck."

He doesn't bother with the backhand. Nope, he doubles me over this time when he delivers a blow to my abdomen. He's lucky I didn't eat anything today; otherwise, he would be wearing it all over his boots.

"If you were half as smart as you believe yourself to be, you would have figured out we do not permit women, even ones like you, to speak in this manner."

"I have never had sex with Pestilence or War, which I believe is the defining action that makes a whore, as you like to call women, a whore."

"Then why are you traveling with them?"

I know I can't tell them the truth, leaving me with only one option. Lying. I hope Pestilence will forgive me and War doesn't get a fathead. "I'm their hostage."

"Why?"

"You think I know their minds or what they have planned?"

"If you're going to fib, you should make it believable at the very least."

346

"I don't care if you believe me or not." Before the one holding my ropes can hit me again, the leader stops him. His massive, muscled frame lumbers across the room only so he can deliver one himself.

"I know all about you, Avalon. I know you traveled first with Death, who you did fuck. Then with Pestilence, who you probably fucked, and now with Pestilence and War, who has made it clear you two are fucking. So tell me, horsemen whore, do you let them fuck you at the same time, or do they take turns?"

I smirk the second before I slam my head forward, shattering his stupid fucking nose. I know I'll pay the price for it, but it felt damn good in the moment. And he does not disappoint.

*****

When consciousness brings me out of the haze from my beating, my eye is swollen shut, they split my lip open, and my cheek feels like I ran headfirst into a brick wall. More than once. But on the upside, the assholes who did this shit to me are nothing more than a blurry blob now. I can also feel the warmth of the blood pouring out of my split lip and taste its metallic tang in my mouth. But it was still worth it.

"Wayne, you know what they said."

"I don't give a shit. No goddamn woman is going to talk to me like she did and get away with it, Trevor."

"Wait, you're Wayne and Trevor?"

"I see our reputation proceeds us."

"Sure does. As pansy ass women beaters who run like scared little bitches when facing someone you can't beat."

"Worth every damn penny they paid us." Wayne's laugh is the last thing I hear because his next punch knocks me out cold.

*****

When I come to this time, it doesn't take me long to realize I'm not in some damn dining hall with the two pricks who would keep running if they knew what's best. Honestly, something tells me I'm no longer in their camp.

This place feels like... like some damn underground bunker. My face is pounding, my head feels like I have a jackhammer going at it, and I'm short of breath, leading me to believe I might have a broken rib or two.

With all the damage done to me, you would think whoever my newest jailor is would at least give me a damn bed, but no. I'm chained to a pole in the center of some musty damn basement, cellar, underground bunker. Whatever it is, I know it can't mean anything good is in store for me. I could use a little divine intervention here. Pestilence and War would be fantastic, but either one showing up right about now would be fine with me. Hell, I'd be happy with Storm or Red.

I can feel a presence in the room with me making my eyes dart from one dark corner to the next, but with the only light directly above me illuminating me like some damn piece of art out on display, it does little to chase away the shadows.

"Hello?" Nothing other than the distant dripping of water, which further cements that I'm underground. Well, that and the lack of any other sounds. The metal door is reinforced with massive rivets and more locks than needed. The skeletal metal beams crisscross on the ceiling and run down the walls to form what I suppose is the support for this place.

The first clue I'm not alone is the crunching of stones under heavy booted feet. Followed by a sickly sweet smell. This is something I have experienced before, but I am having issues placing where I've smelled this before right now. When I attempt to turn toward the sound, a firm hand clamps around my throat, locking me in place and preventing me from seeing who is in the room with me. They place something in my hand, and I can barely move my arm enough to see what it is.

A fucking seal.

Whoever has me wants me to break another seal, something I have already said I have no damn intention of doing. I figure whoever it is will get the hint when I let the paper tumble past my fingers and out of my grasp. But the delicate fingers of a woman's hand snatch it off the floor before cramming it back into my palm.

"No!" I choke. It's the only word I can get past the hand tightening painfully around my neck, further closing off my ability to breathe. This time when I try to drop it, the hand of the man choking me clamps around it, squeezing until bones splinter, but it is not the bones I'm worried about.

It's the seal, and I feel it snap the instant before he releases me.

Fuck no, it can't be.

I didn't break the seal. Someone else forced me to do it. Regardless, my hand is what snapped it, so does this mean the rider will still come?

I lift the paper to inspect it. I know it's pointless because the name I am desperate to see will not be the name I find.

The only sound filling my ears is my erratic heart's frantic thumping while my eyes land on a solitary word.

Famis.

Famine's seal has been broken, and it's all my fault. Yet again, I am to blame for waking a rider. Although this should be my priority, it isn't when the individual who made me shatter it steps into view. His dominant presence destroys the illusion I may still make it out of this in one piece.

"Miss me?"

No goddamn way can it be him! It's fuckin impossible. He's dead. Right? No, I won't believe any of this. I can't because there is no way he could have survived. This is my last thought before I address the asshole standing before me....

"Nevil?"

Coming Soon....

Famine's Punishment

Also by Marcelle Valentine

Scarred by Fate Series

Start Reading

Ritual Nightmare
Breaking Purgatory
Fate's Ritual
Opposing Tartarus
Sacrificial Endings

The Ash Rock Series

Shadow's Moon Season One
Shadow's Moon Season Two
Shadow's Moon Season Three
Shadow's Moon Season Four

Arrival of the Four Horsemen Series

Death's Inquest
Pestilence's Judgment
War's Verdict
Coming soon Famine's Punishment

Vella

Shadow's Moon Season One through Four
Seized by Sin
Silverwood Throne

Teaser

Betrayal brought me to this world. Henley keeps me here.

When my father fell ill, I soon discovered this betrayal would cost me more than my father. I am forced to leave the fae realm I love behind to track the one responsible for this and protect my best friend. Navigating through this new realm, I am intrigued by Henley, the mortal woman I recruited to aid me in my search for Ayaan. She is everything I shouldn't want but can't resist.

Our attraction grows stronger the longer we work together to save my father and the fae realm from a looming threat. But the closer we become, the more I realize Henley has secrets of her own. Secrets that could destroy her and shatter everything I once thought I wanted.

Our attraction is like a flame burning brighter every day, but will it be enough to conquer the obstacles we face? Or will the weight of our past keep us from what we both desire?

Join Atlas and Henley on this steamy adventure as he battles to save the Silverwood Throne and his growing attraction for Henley. Return of the Fae Prince is a fantasy romance novel for adult readers.

Acknowledgment

Three seals have been broken, with only one more left intact. I hope you enjoyed reading War and Ember's story. Up next is Famine, and next to Death, he's the rider they should fear. While we will meet new characters in his book, the ones you have already grown to love will have cameos. With the return of Nevil and Raum interfering, things are about to become heated.

As always, my deepest heartfelt thanks go out to every reader who took a chance on my books. If you love one series, I hope you might try the others, and if you like them, perhaps you'll let other readers know.

I could not have completed this series without those who supported me, including my beta readers, my niece Ashley, my mom, and my daughter Melanie. This time around, I based my youngest characters on my granddaughter and another grandson, who is also autistic, and the younger brother for my character, which is why he sings but doesn't talk, something my little guy does all the time. While my granddaughter has never had to take care of a child herself, Ellie is a good representation of the lengths she would go to in order to keep the boys safe.

I have several projects in progress. Book four in the Horsemen series is in the final stages of publishing. I also have a Vella underway about a certain fae prince, which readers of my Ash Rock series may recognize. My standalone serial killer novella will be available in select markets soon. Readers of my other series may find an Easter egg about the next series I have planned within the pages of this book.

Thank you to my husband and family, who have been my biggest cheerleaders. I love every one of you.

And finally, to every author who has ever put pen to paper, fingers to keyboard, whose work only inspired me more to follow this dream, I hope I do not disappoint.

Thank you Marcelle

Newsletter

Consider visiting my website and signing up for my newsletter to receive updates on this series and all my future projects.

https://www. marcellevalentine. com

Please consider leaving a review if you enjoyed the book. Any thoughts are appreciated and will only help me improve the story. Reviews also provide new readers with a way to find my books.

You can also follow me on social media:

Facebook
Goodreads
Instagram
TikTok

About the Author

Marcelle Valentine has long been an admirer of creating worlds where people can get lost. From a young age, her active imagination took her on epic journeys to faraway places where troubles and friendships abound. After discovering the intriguing world of Paranormal/Fantasy Romance, which stirred up memories of all those distant places and friends, her desire to write returned. She invites you to travel with her during these journeys and get lost in a world with friends, enemies, and lovers, all firmly rooted in the supernatural realm. Marcelle is the author of the Scarred by Fate Series and the episodic series Shadow's Moon. She lives in Ohio with her husband. She has two children, three grandchildren, and one lovable, lazy Great Dane.

www.ingramcontent.com/pod-product-compliance
Lightning Source LLC
Chambersburg PA
CBHW072025020726
47501CB00006B/1965